MORE LORE FROM THE MYTHOS

EDWARD MORRIS   VALERIE LIOUDIS   AARON WHITE

JON TOBEY   OLIVER LODGE   RYAN COLLEY

L.E. HARRISON   KARI LEIGH SANDERS   DALE DRAKE

CHARLES REIS   STEVE VAN SAMSON   PATRICK RAHALL

MICHAEL CLARK   EV KNIGHT

Edited by

LILY LUCHESI

Copyright © 2019 Fractured Mind Publishing. All rights reserved. This book or parts thereof may not be reproduced in any form, stored in any retrieval system, or transmitted in any form by any means—electronic, mechanical, photocopy, recording, or otherwise—without prior written permission of the publisher, except as provided by United States of America copyright law. Each contributing author retains full copyrights to his or her respective story contribution to this anthology.

This novel is entirely a work of fiction. The names, characters and incidents portrayed in it are the work of the author's imagination. Any resemblance to actual persons, living or dead, events or localities is entirely coincidental.

Designations used by companies to distinguish their products are often claimed as trademarks. All brand names and product names used in this book are trade names, service marks, trademarks and registered trademarks of their respective owners. The publishers and the book are not associated with any product or vendor mentioned in this book. None of the companies referenced within the book have endorsed the book.

CONTENTS

Foreword — vii

Everything That Was Before — 1
Little One — 19
The Call — 31
The Damned of Eldritch Creek — 57
The Flood — 95
Sweet Oblivion — 103
The Mines of Innswich — 113
The Time Guardian — 131
The Wyrd Voyage — 147
Last Orders — 173
The Maze — 193
Growing Just Beneath — 221
The Shed — 237
The Gate Keeper — 249

Acknowledgments — 263
About The Authors — 265
Also by Fractured Mind Publishing — 271

FOREWORD

H.P. Lovecraft. Maybe you've heard the name, or seen a cool movie based on one of his stories, or heard Cthulhu mentioned in the lyrics of your favorite band. I'm not surprised... for a pulp author from the 1920s and 30s, with a fairly niche following, he travels in lots of circles. It's a bit ominous actually... is it a conspiracy of secret knowledge? He definitely has a cult-like following that permeates all walks of life, all over the world.

Lovecraft himself was extremely generous with his own works and actively encouraged others to borrow ideas from his stories, particularly with regard to his Cthulhu mythos. By "wide citation" he hoped to give his works an "air of verisimilitude", and actively encouraged other writers to reference his creations, such as the Necronomicon, Cthulhu and Yog-Sothoth. After his death, many writers have contributed stories and enriched the shared mythology of the Cthulhu Mythos, as well as making numerous references to his work.

His vision has been captured by innumerable artists, including Mike Mignola (Hellboy), Lee Moyers, Michael Whelan, H.R. Giger, Gahan Wilson, Raymond Bayless, Ian Miller, Virgil Finlay, Lee Brown Coye, Rowena Morrill, Bob Eggleton, Allen Koszowski, and many more. Filmmakers like Stuart Gordon, Brian Yuzna, Roger Corman, Aaron Vanek, and Guillermo Del Toro have adapted his words to the big screen. There are even dozens, if not hundreds, of bands directly influenced by Lovecraft's unique fiction, like Fields of The Nephilim, The Unquiet Void, Yog-Sothoth, Cradle of Filth; he's big with black metal and even surf punk (check out The Darkest of The Hillside Thickets). Oh, and then there are the writers: Stephen King, Ramsey Campbell, Clive Barker, Robert Bloch, Cody Goodfellow, Stanley Sargent, and many many more have all written tales inspired directly by Lovecraft, and most have acknowledged his mastery of a special brand of genre fiction.

But instead of boring you with a bunch of dry facts, I'll just share with you how an author's mother describes Lovecraft and his body of work to her friends and family.

"So basically there's a dead guy that made up some stories and since he died there have been people keeping his characters going."

The authors of this anthology are here to keep the characters going and add to the mythos. We hope you enjoy them all.

MORE LORE FROM THE MYTHOS

BY EDWARD MORRIS

Every city's overrated. The whole counterculture's overrated. Counterfactual. The same sad, dirty, hard-scrabble roach motel songs we all sing while we wash dishes in the bathtub and wring blood from our hearts over a sink where only the cold water works. For some, that'd be infinitely preferable.

In Northeast Portland, close to the river, everything smells like freshly baking bread. Now that smell just makes me ill every time I have to go back, on every bus trip or crosstown snag or whim.

Even when This All Started, Portland was morphing from hip squalor into million-dollar condos virally replicating in shapes no one would miss after a hurricane knocked them all flat. But sometimes, the old ways are worse.

Even writing this down, I see the page sag through in parts like half-rotten lath; shattered, shattering, shot through: showing an upstairs room in an old eyesore property that no longer exists anywhere. And the filth that -

No. I'm cool.

I'm cool.

It all happened just off the MAX line, a little south of I-99 in between Broadway and the Steel Bridge, under thawing cold skies at the border of so many nights, where all the old divey neon of Broadway and Sandy Boulevard drizzles its wet rain of light on the Portland That Just Was, as that tiredly gives way to the Portland That Wants To Be.

That smell of baking bread from the Franz Bakery can never mean what it meant to me again. Under it now for me will always be that other river, underground, and many worse things.

Even in memory, the angles of that other house, that other upstairs room mirroring mine, where a person could see into our bedroom, across the street, dear God... don't add up to anything but a whole bubble off-plumb, as my contractor Dad used to say when we were out on a site.

Exactly like one of Dad's spirit-levels, too, the light inside and out was green and cold in that other room. Around both houses, both properties. They had their own bubble there, and their own geometric measure that never added up to anywhere near Plumb.

It All Happened behind the Irving Park Post Office, in a little boat of a house, peeling a bit but well-kept against the rainy days of six-month night. In the beginning, the sun at Eighth and Hancock did that thing. That Portland-sunset, bottle-green, croaker-marble thing. The color of Vivien Lutka's endless eyes.

I remember the first night Viv and I held each other until

the birds got loud and the sun came up and we told each other Everything. On subsequent nights, our souls flew like kites above the clouds, entwined. There were a lot of those...Which made our ending that much worse.

In the beginning, when it was warm, Vivien and I drank pitchers of beer at the Goodfoot and wrote Everything together, then stumbled to the Lone Fir Cemetery with the first smell of Halloween creeping from the trees and from Viv's skin.

That night, she let me push her in some rando-ass shopping cart the whole way to the graveyard where I took her in my arms, leaned her against an old crooked tombstone and...began, until Vivien came under that bloated full moon, gasping and trembling and it was the best time ever until we woke, entwined beneath the cracked-open sill, tasting an amphibious tongue of chilly wind down every open place.

For a little while, we did everything together, helped each other and played together, grew together and usually ended up battered and beaming a day and a half later with a class or a job missed or something. For a little while, that didn't matter.

After a while, though, Everything started to matter. Now the tracks are all gone from the house across the street from our old place. The one whose faded sign named it Marsh Printing. All the windows are covered with plywood.

When the sun sets on that block, the light's not honey-gold-green any more. It's yellow. maggoty. Tattered and distorted, spread thin to the far reaches of the streetlights' wan crescents, where blind crack-pipers fear to tread.

The streetlights aren't all shot-out. They might as well be. Vivien's old place is horrifying to look at: There are marigolds growing in the flowerbeds. An SUV. A soccer ball kicked to some random place on the lawn. Of either of us... not a trace remains.

The first time, I didn't look long. I couldn't. Part of me wanted to walk up those spavined steps, back through that living-room, and into the kitchen. Where the other basement door finally turned out to be.

Waiting to turn, and see some unthinkable Last Supper table prepared before me, and a flippered neonate at my place, eyes burnt white by devolution as it crawls back into the water-table to die.

I'm at the top of my game now, and it's all dust and ashes in my mouth. The corners of the mouth that trembles. The eyes that can't stop looking behind me. The hands.

The hands that can still type. The Man Booker Prize nomination. The string of lucky breaks. The MFA I flipped to an MA in mid-stream because all I want to do is teach.

The poetry I still write, and read out at the mics to maintain my own craft, my own sleep cycle---such as it ever gets without every means necessary to achieve something like four nightmare-free hours at a go. Sometimes that works. Just enough. My students will never see this. Nor the Portland Police Bureau.

I crashed at Viv's house many a night. But I never really saw that block, until the day I came to stay, like some troublesome, snappy stray that Viv decided in her infinite self-righteousness to feed.

She'd rented the little gray frame house for a song, for a little over a year when we met, due to its uncomfortable proximity to the looming bulk of the shuttered print-shop across the street.

That leaning, ramshackle old logging-era, opium-den-and-hobo-jungle-era thing, gone green and gray, but a worse green than the sunset. The green of old things left to gather moss, stagnation, and mold that will pull anything down eventually.

802 Northeast Hancock Street, in its gravel lot, looked like a patch of melanoma. There was no graffiti. The clapboard siding of the graying, mossy edifice looked like fishscales. There was a plate glass window on the front; which had no porch, merely a swinging door at street level with once-bright Visa/Mastercard/Amex stickers coruscating above the big lock-bar.

On the north side, there was a tiny, sloping driveway that led down to what must once have been a basement garage. The bottom of that driveway, hidden in shadows, would have been a prime, proper, easy-to-tarp-up campsite for homeless folks. But there were no beer cans. No cardboard. No shattered crack pipes.

Only a few odd footprints in the cement. None of them looked very old. The door at the bottom appeared to be painted shut.

One more abandoned eyesore left vacant for the tax write-off. Some of the windows were boarded up with random signs. LETTERPRESS. OFFSET. BULK RATE NEG-- (obscured). MARSH PRINTING. RARE BOOKS. ANTIQUITIES. MARITIME LITERATURE.

Along the inside of the plate glass were stacks and boxes of moldering books turned sideways or upended. Many of those had water-damage, and most of the spines were illegible or facing away. HERMAN WOUK THE WINDS OF WAR. LEBOR GABçLA ƒRENN. THE

SUPREMACIST MISSION. STEPHENI (obscured). DAEMONOLATRIA.

I turned my head, at the first view of those moldering, scaly spines. Feeling Viv's insistent, irresistible animal sexuality, her smell and heat and presence like something more than human. Something wet and slithery and just us, I thought.

"We're in the sunset," Vivien murmured, locking the front door, locking us out into that timeless light as it fell over the tops of the houses and all the windows for miles turned to gold. I leaned on the rotten rail, standing near the bottom riser of the slightly-less-rotten front steps, and turned around.

The two of us were thus eye-to-eye by position. Viv's nose was the most kissable thing I ever saw. The soap she used on her dreadlocks smelled like an herbalist's attic. But it was Viv's eyes that drove me wild, lit nearly solid-green with that light.

Her eyes. Green, and gold, the light that now filled up even the few unboarded windows of the shunned print-shop to the exclusion of all else. This strange, deliberate, trembling creature was leaning in and kissing me.

Viv tasted like snow and ozone and bitter cherry-blossoms, and her small hands were warm and careful at the back of my neck, on my shoulder blades, like there was no one else in the world she ever wanted to kiss or touch again.

Every part of me responded before my brain had much to do with comprehension. I took her warm, pale face in the cold palms of my hands (she shuddered, but didn't pull away) and kissed her all the way slowly back into the house for another half an hour before we left....

"...OK. Really Leaving Now. Anyway, that print-shop," Viv murmured up at me when we finally made it back out on the porch. "The old couple who lived next door until last year would cross the street to avoid it. Kids won't play around it. It looks like they're still doing some kind of business. Sometimes."

"Meth is big this year," I joked, and got swatted on the ass. Viv's mouth pursed, the way it did around juicy bits of gossip, and her nose twitched as she pondered the way to say what she had to say.

"There's a tunnel that goes between the houses, the land-lord says. Mine and That. I don't want to stay here that long. Creepy. Don't think ab—Awp. I can see you thinking about it."

Viv was leading me by the hand down the block, looking up into my eyes. Those were so utterly only for her at the time that I could barely cross the street right.

"Seriously, though. One night I was up late studying, and I saw two or three guys in a panel-truck roll in and out of there with a few boxes full of books. Plain-looking trade paperbacks. Big shapeless coats, and hoodies with baseball hats underneath. They dragged their feet weird. I wasn't even on anything. And I.."

She swallowed. "I... kept waiting for them to come up the... wrong set of cellar stairs."

Then Vivien turned me around, pointing. "LIBER IVONIS. THERE WAS A CROOKED MAN... Those are stacks of titles. All mostly the same. See? Like they print them there. Just stand still and look at it all for a minute. The more you do, the more out-of-place Everything looks..."

Viv's bright eyes scanned me all over. It was going to be

dark soon, and the walk was nearly done. We'd taken to pausing in front of 802 on the way back.

"I've lived around here for two years. I know all the landmarks. That print-shop is the weirdest. Because of the caves under it. According to the geo-survey maps I got up at the library. I'm pretty sure they go all the way to the East bank of the river. Near to where we're going."

This was getting good. Viv continued, "I've been around the back of the print-shop. Before they built onto it, the original house was brick, and some of it goes up under the ground. You can see in a few of the cracks in the walls. I found a stairway. Carved in the dirt."

I tried not to scoff. "Where does it go?"

Viv shrugged, wiggling closer. "I dunno. I got the creepin' willies, Mr. Bouncer. Come with me."

I smiled, patting the work-flashlight still shoved in my back pocket, as it usually was. "Sure, baby. I'd follow you anywhere...." God, we must have been enough to make everyone sick. I remember. I do---

I'm cool. We walked all the way to the Burnside Bridge that night from the Steel Bridge, then part of the way back. It was Cinco de Mayo, and at dusk the fireworks happened.

Viv showed me this place up on the bank where she always went to watch fireworks, on May Fifth and July Fourth and during the Rose Festival. Her private beach, she called it.

There's a mermaid-face carved into the rocks up there. Viv could tell it was a mermaid because the form continues into the rock, and I saw it the way she did when she showed me.

I'm remembering more. Her eyes glowed every time she

kept looking up further up and in, toward the whistling caves along that bank. Some of those caves looked built. Not recently, either.

We came out there more than once. I always wanted to leave. I remember that now. I'd forgotten that. We just hiked or hung out and rested on those walks, but I always wanted to leave.

I've never been able to find that beach. Or the trail she took. Not ever since.

All I ever wanted to do was watch Viv paint. Listen to her talk. I believed the best of her. I did. With all my heart, I believed. And that made me blind.

But the sunset was basic, and I still recall what that light did to her eyes---

———

"You're not tracking me." Viv was walking behind me. Lurching a little. She did that when she walked fast. It was the shape of her feet. The webs between her great and second toes that were as much a part of her as her freckled cheekbones or the curve at the small of her back.

Viv kept telling me I walked too fast. I kept forgetting. And then remembering. This was one of those times.

I fell into step with her, choked down a few choice things, and then said Something Else: "Okay. Yeah. It doesn't sound like I am. Could you back up a bit?"

Viv's eyebrows furrowed. She chuckled slowly. "Fair enough. Wow, I usually ask you that, when we're mucking around out here." That time, we both actually laughed. It felt good. She took my arm and looked in my eyes.

"See, it's like this. If we can't find out who actually owns the print-shop, I want to talk to the City about acquiring the property. Would you... would you help me figure out how to do that? Look stuff up online and stuff, you're always so fast... I... Thoughts?"

That took me aback. This was different than the long day of bickering about Nothing which had preceded it. "What all exactly were you thinking of doing with the shithole?" I heard myself ask back.

Viv beamed. "A....storefront art gallery. We could hang all our friends. Assuming I finish Grad School sometime ever. I could set up a private Counseling practice from there as well. Totally write off a home office for two careers instead of one."

Her eyes lit like sunsets. I couldn't look anywhere else when they did that thing. That croaker-marble thing. "Plenty of room for a writing studio, too." Viv made the statement sound offhand. "For workshops..."

Then Vivien showed me at the other end of that trail, a gray sand beach just wide enough to be called one. Pebbles in the sand, every color, every size, worn down smooth by what might have been a million years of few other people knowing that cove was there.

And when Vivien did, she had my whole heart.

Famous Last Words.

———

Our...well, our...Reasoning, our chain of choices, from there crawls away now, in my brain. Something to do with some back-ass interpretation of the phrase 'squatters' rights' that I learned from some street kid in Sellwood and have since researched to find untrue. Sigh.

"As long as it doesn't come back to my name," was Viv's oft-repeated refrain. "I'm about to be licensed as a Mental Health Counselor. I could lose that forever."

"It won't get that far." I shrugged. My own inner street-kid was never far from the surface. "All we're doing for now is looking. The paperwork will be harder. It'll come later."

Viv stopped us where we were, and squeezed both my hands. "Yes, Edward. It'll be an adventure…"

HOOM. I kicked the stout door in with a steel-toed Doc Marten work boot when Vivien stepped back from unscrewing everything her Leatherman could reach. A ball of dust blew down a second set of stairs, not cut into the dirt…but fitted stone, worn into a shape that was very identifiably steps.

(rustle…)

I had my work light. Viv had a baby Maglite. Both of them had seen some use. I kept having to flick mine on my hip. "Fucking rats," I said resignedly.

(rustle)

Flicking it again perfunctorily, I reached for the flat pry-bar in my belt. Dad's old flat-bar was the most basic weapon to hand besides my flashlight, which was too little to be much of a club.

Those steps cut into the rock where we were walking couldn't really be for steps. Not for feet. Not feet-shaped feet. I could hear a whole lot of water, not that far away.

I couldn't focus. My light wouldn't focus. Or...come back...on...Damn it... The air tasted terrible...but not. Like something I almost remembered---

Cedar. Salamanders. The algae that turns a centimeter of standing water green, green, green in the Pacific Northwest. Dry rot. Wet rot. Transitional aftertaste. Slithery mud. The mineral milk of hard groundwater.

I was tracking Vivien. After perhaps twenty yards, Viv wasn't lurching any more. Like something in her knew the terrain and was...leading. So I just let her.

At the other end of the corridor, we emerged in a section that felt and looked and smelled like water-worn limestone. Light was coming from all around, showing no real source but the walls. The rock.

"Ooooh..." Even in the near-dark, Vivien was already trying to take a picture. Then:

(rustle)

My light went out. A frantic round of slapping led me to look around. Viv's had gone out again. I heard her breathing hard, in the wrong place from where I knew her to be.

"Damn it, Edward, my light---"

"Mine too, babe, trying to---"

"Oh, for fuck's sake. Wait, I think I... Damn it. Wait---"

Things were moving. There was motion somewhere close, everywhere I turned. The phosphorescence from the strange stone of the walls and floors began, incredibly, to fade.

There were too many shadows that didn't fit. Whether or not they moved. Too many directions I turned, beginning to lose my own. To pant. To panic. To let down the side. Then:

(rustlerustlerustle) (rustle)

Under the house across the street, near a basement door with 807 HANCOCK on it on - a door that I didn't want to kick down, one that might or might not have led back to Viv's own cellar, which the landlord kept locked and of which she claimed no knowledge and I had no reason to---

(rustle)

Shit suddenly Got Real. There was no way back up to the surface. No way where there wasn't something moving. The cool air was blocked by squishy warmth.

Blocked. Waiting. Trading ground for time.

(slap)

"Dammit ---"

(slap)

(rustle)

"Hey, Nature Boy, quit touching my ---"

"Vivien. I'm the whole way over here."

Then I sparked my lighter.

Some of the shadows were making the wrong kind of Sense.

Four or five of them, oh my God, blocking various parts of the path. Just there.

Just there. And there.

And there.

And...there. At first, I thought they were just the world's largest newts, some kind of evolutionary transitional, just really huge. But then... the light. When it worked, it was pretty bright.

Too bright.

"Run like fuck. If you don't mind..."

And we did.

I ran one step forward. Viv ducked-and-dodged two

steps backward, put up her light...and just kept running away from me. Not even thinking.

Into the dark. Into the mineral milk of the dark up under the bank, where those...things danced in glabrous light up on the shore, and lurched through the scant ground fog near the water.

———

I WOKE up screaming four hours later, with Vivien's side of the bed empty and cold. And my side covered with weird clay and black stuff and No No No I Am Awake Now. No. Gonna Do Laundry. Until Dawn...

I've lost wallets. Bags of weed. Backpacks. School textbooks that were worth mad cash. But in that one night, I lost everything I never really had, and that part twisted my mind in half like a beer can.

One night. Gone. Gonegonegone. Vivien was sleepwalking. Repeatedly.

I had to bring her back, but I couldn't always. It didn't always wake me up when Viv did that. Only sometimes. Either way was scary. They're working with me about that now. I'm doing the work. I am. So I can sleep.

I don't talk about this to people much. I just show what it did. All that's left. Left.

———

THE LAST NIGHT. The slow erosion. Grotty, gibbering layers of limestone. The glowing jade-stuff within it. The sunless underground creek. The turning away. The loss of all sense of stairs.

The last night, I went over there in my old ski-mask. With my homie's sawed-off shotgun I was going to get in a lot of trouble for 'borrowing.' Maybe. Maybe I didn't care, and just wanted to take a few along. Instinctively.

Even then.

"It's a place of power. A bad place. I have to do something to stop dreaming about it. About them singing, across the street. The people in that house. Except they're some kind of common ancestor. Mossy backs and webbed feet, just like most Oregonians, except...Well, I'm sure that they're probably just making meth or some awful thing... Still. Wouldn't you rather be a fish?"

"Um, no. What're you going to do, burn sage at it? We could move. The lease is month-by-month. Why do you insist on doing everything the hardest way possib---"

And on. And down. And back. Backward. I remember it backward. Sideways.

Slowly, with deep breaths and the vow to not come apart. Any more. There's almost nothing left to puke up. But maybe, under the memory is more of me.

Because, you see, the last night that happened, I went downstairs and found the front door wide open. A trail of green whose direction was entirely unclear. Things I didn't need to look at.

Broken things never mine. Vivien's things I didn't break. Broken. Our home. Gray clay on them, and green... Green. Broken.

The next two nights, Vivien stayed gone. And I let the side down. Way down. And I came jocking. Packing. Jacking.

Looking for my dear one. And I saw. Not just what was going on, either.

I saw the supreme horror of that print-shop, for me, the one seared into my brain to this day when I close my eyes, when I open them. When I drink. When I use. When I am clean and go to Meetings. Meetings are easier. I can cry.

I saw the view through those rotten curtains, out the tall, ornate Pulp-Baron-Victorian windows of that unspeakable upstairs room in the old Marsh Print Shop. The view... of a tie-dyed knotwork tapestry hanging in an oddly-shaped bedroom window with a pane that swung out on a hinge and knob.

A bedroom where the light was still on, and the tapestry hanging like a skirt that showed just an inch or two of leg. Our skirt. Our legs. Our room. Our home.

One by one, the true occupants of 802 NE Hancock St. slithered, some of them groaning at the effort it took for them to walk on two legs for that long, up from the basement garage and the back stairs.

Some of the fellers from the cellar left shiny trails on the carpet-remnants still affixed here and there to the floor, like the liquid-crystal trails of the banana-slugs Viv and I saw when we went camping. But this wasn't camping. And the only slugs pertinent here would have been lead ones.

As if. One by one. BUMP. BUMP. Most of them made it up the stairs. A few of them took several tries.

In the master's chambers at the top of the topmost staircase in the house across the street, in the mold-feedlot-eel-blind-robin-stinking emptiness of the old print-shop across the street, I couldn't put two parts of what I saw together.

I had to process. And couldn't. Bemused. Sobbing. Trying to string thoughts.

Vivien liked to be tied up, sometimes. But not like that. In that room full of green light that wasn't green light. Not bound to a post in the middle of an empty upstairs room in a print-shop where I realized I couldn't charge in and remove her, if...

If she didn't like it. "GO HOME, SAM!" was the last thing I heard Vivien shriek, from that upstairs room with the unbelievable view of our own. "I DON'T NEED YOU!"

I saw: Viv's white-girl dreadlocks misted wet-red-black, clinging to her pulsant shoulder blades, her skin, the gray scale. Scales. Forming. Not appearing to need much help.

Forming. On. All. That. Exposed. Skin. Changing. Wanting more Change. Change came. And came. Like waves on an underground river. There were more. Sweating black stuff worse than blood.

I took off the stupid ski-mask, and the black exam-gloves to match. Then I shucked open the sawed-off, removed the shells, and just stood there. Because none of the fellers from the cellar paid me any mind the whole time.

It Was Complicated, all right. It Was Pretty Complicated to watch what was going on up in that room. One at a time. One at a.

Time. Time crawled away, and the germ of all things drew frightfully near its termination. One at a time, the white-white newt things crawled up the stairs, then down, and away, through the blood and the muck and the--

Eggs. Say it, alcoholic. All their eggs. I could see. Inside. Some of the eggs. And inside that. Inside--

The last one in the long, long train did notice me. He

stopped dead, looking me in the eyes. His didn't have lids. Mine couldn't blink. Made us even. Except not really at all, ever.

He? Yes. Very identifiably a He. He cocked his angular head, laying a webbed, prehensile paw upside lips not quite lips.

"SSSSH."

After that, I'm afraid I really can't remember anything. Not in a row. The meds are helping now.

BUT I REALLY, really came all the way back here. This street's deserted. No one saw me sitting here in my VW finishing this joint and just ...saying this, into the Sound Recorder app on my phone. Remembering. For the shrinks.

The Marsh print-shop's all boarded-up now, with giant sheets of flooring across the windows, tagged with Russian gang sign and hilarious anarchist epithets. My swollen terror thunders in my throat. Now there's no world, and ghouls squabble among the scraps.

802 Hancock is stripped. There's nothing and no one there. Not anymore. The green light in the window hasn't come on.

So I'm just sitting here in my car, trying to laugh or cry or do something. We could move, I said back then.

Maybe I can move again.

BY VALERIE LIOUDIS

Morgan hated Mondays. She spent most of her Sunday night growing more aggravated as the clock ticked forward and brought her closer to the morning alarm. "I wish I never had to deal with another Monday with Karen and her superior attitude." Morgan seethed in her bed. Nothing was worse than Karen and her stories of her new boyfriend who was sure to be her fiancé before Christmas. God, she hated Karen. "I would give anything to not have to do it one more time."

"Anything?" a squeaky yet raspy voice asked inside her head.

"Great, now I'm hearing voices. This just keeps getting worse."

"I'm not a voice inside your head. God, humans can be so ridiculous."

Across the room, from inside the shadows, Baell, stepped

forward giving Morgan a chance to take in all that was Baell, The Deal Maker, Destroyer of Dreams. The little red head with the wiry curls seemed less than impressed, and unlike her fellow humans who had fainted or screamed, she seemed almost bored. Baell was intrigued for the first time in centuries.

"I hope your feet are clean. I can't imagine where a beast like you likes to hang out. Surely, it would be somewhere filled with dirt and cobwebs. I better not need to pull out the rug machine when you leave," she grumbled from her bed.

"You are a pessimistic little thing, aren't you?"

"Stop calling me little. I'm normal sized for my kind. It isn't my fault that you're an oversized freak. But I won't be talked down to in my own home. Karen does enough of that at work all week."

"Ah, Morgan, let's talk about Karen. I can take care of her for you."

"Sure, you can, but what is it going to cost me? I know how these deals with the Devil work. You give me what I ask for in the most literal and detrimental way possible, and all you need is my soul. I grew up watching paranormal shows and reading horror. You aren't going to get one over on me," she challenged him.

"I like you," he said, and instantly regretted the words.

He had never liked a human in all the years he had been dealing with them. Mostly, he was indifferent to their existence. They were a way to a means. The more souls you collected and darkness you were able to spread across the Earth pushed you higher up in the demon hierarchy. Baell was finally in one of the top tiers. You didn't rise in the ranks by befriending the prey.

"Let me hear your pitch. Then we will see if I like you, too," she said, finally giving him the opening he needed.

"I'm here to help you, Morgan. That is all we want, to make your life easier and better. If you want Karen to be out of your life forever, I can make that happen. You want to win the lottery and be rich and famous, I can arrange that, too. You are right that nothing is free, but before we talk about payment, why don't we see what it is that you really want? Tell me what would make you happy. Let me do that for you." He was laying it on thick, but for the first time ever, he meant it.

He really did want to make her happy. As he stared down at her, he was impressed by how she seemed unfazed by the towering monster in her presence. Baell tried to pry his eyes away from hers, but she had him locked in with a determined stare. A twinge of fear snuck in his head. He was being entranced by a human. Something was terribly wrong. Morgan smirked as she recognized his apprehension.

"Don't bullshit me, demon. I know you have no power until I agree to something. Right now, you're a cat without its claws. The way I see it, I have the upper hand here. You must need me for something. It isn't like people, or demons, go around giving away free stuff without an ulterior motive. So, what's the gain for you, my friend?" she challenged him instead of caving to his salesmanship.

Baell backed away from the small redheaded monster. Every bit of his eight-foot-tall body was screaming at him to run. His nerves could sense the trap, but his master would knock him down if he didn't get the prize. Demons didn't just sit around waiting for people to utter words that allowed them to bargain away their soul. The master carefully selected the ones that he wanted. Each served a purpose to add to his strength for the final battle. The minions on both sides were busy collecting as much of humanity as possible, just in different ways.

"I asked you a question." She was growing bolder and had stood on the bed, so she could look Baell right in the eyes.

His skin crawled, and the fur that lined his body stood on end as her voice grew louder and more determined. His affection for this human was being replaced by a mixture of fear and respect. "This isn't how this normally works," he stuttered. "You are making this more difficult than it is intended to be. Let me help you, Morgan. Channel that hate into your wish. You could rule this world if you wanted to. Burn it to the ground. We have no need for the mortals to be comfortable, actually we encourage that they aren't."

"What if I don't want to rule over the Earth? What if I want to take your home? Can you give it to me? Is every wish something that you have to grant? Are you bound by my imagination?"

She was pushing him, but he had no answer for her. No one had ever asked for the keys to Hell. Most humans spent a lifetime running from it. Now this small, yet bold woman was demanding that he crown her queen. He pushed himself further back against the wall hoping to disappear back into the blackness that he had emerged from. His master would punish him, but somehow the Devil himself seemed less scary than the creature that was crushing his confidence with just a look.

"What is your name, demon?"

He knew not to answer. Names held power, and he had been taught never to share his, but her voice held a compulsion. He wanted to disobey but couldn't. His fear turned into terror. "How are you doing this?"

"Doing what, demon? Tell me your name."

"Baell, The Deal Maker, Destroyer of Dreams." His wings folded down around himself, forming a protective shield.

"Well, Baell, I know what I want. Now, I need you to get it for me." She sat back down and waited for him to work his magic.

"That isn't how it works. I'm not a mind reader. This magic is as old as time itself and needs your words to spin it into a binding agreement." He was emboldened by the rules. They might be able to save him.

"Talk me through it, Baell. Tell me the catch."

Her movements became snakelike as she bridged the space between them. He was mesmerized by her. Demons were a giant race, but near her every inch of his frame tried to pull itself down into the ground. She reached up and grabbed his lower jaw, completely unafraid of his fangs, and tilted his face towards hers.

"Do I make you nervous, demon? Imagine what I could do with all that power. Look deep inside my eyes and see the fire in my soul. You say I can make the world burn. Look now and tell me you can see it. I'm going to take more than just the world."

Flames danced where the whites should be. His head filled with the screams of all things living and dead. Baell saw himself torn to pieces by her will alone. There was nowhere to run, the portal he arrived in wasn't opening. She squeezed his face harder, "Look at me, demon! You will obey. You will all obey, or I'll destroy every single one of you."

He had to try something, anything to get out of this

room. The master may want her soul, but it was far too dangerous for either side to wield. At the very least, it was far too dangerous for him to try to collect it. She sensed he was working on an escape plan and wrapped herself around him as he screamed to Hades. The wall began to melt away to fire and brimstone. Morgan pulled her arm back and smashed her fist into the plaster. The portal closed in a flash and took the tip of Baell's tail with it.

His roar shook the walls and roof of her bungalow, but not the owner of it. "Where do you think you're going?" She ran her nail down his face cutting his thick skin along the way. "You get to leave when I'm done with you, and not a minute before that. If you try something like that again, I'll make sure you lose more than a little bit of tail."

"You are but a small human. A child in my eyes. How are you doing this?"

"You keep asking that, Baell. I was born this way. Maybe I should let you meet my friend. That may answer your question, or it may just give you more to ask." She turned away from him and walked to the closet. As she opened the door, she whistled. "Come. Time to meet our new friend. If he doesn't do what I ask, he may be staying with us a long time."

"Aryal!" he cried out as he saw a figure emerge.

Thirty years earlier a demon had gone missing. The master brought a council of demons in to search for their lost comrade. Demons could be exterminated, but that was the first time one had just disappeared. All demons could be pinpointed through their energy tie to the Devil. Aryal's power was still around, but it was being shielded from everyone, including the Devil himself. He was a boogeyman. The kind of demon that fed off the fears of children.

No one had thought to look in the closet of a mortal. It had always been assumed that one of the light ones had turned him or trapped him in the land in between. Apparently, it had been a small human child who had bested the beast.

"Aryal, Terror Maker, Thief of Screams, are you okay?" He pulled himself out of the corner towards Aryal. He stopped short as the lesser demon recoiled in fear. His eyes screamed of torture that had lasted for decades.

"He doesn't talk much anymore. Not since my teenage years. I think I was a little harder on him than I needed to be. Did you know that you demons can grow back bits if given enough time? It is a pretty handy trick when dealing with an overly emotional and sadistic teenager." Her words alone made Aryal flee for the closet.

"Oh, Aryal, don't run. We don't want to have another lesson, do we?" He froze in place, and his eyes glassed over to a dead emptiness.

"How are you doing this?" Baell cried out. "You are just a human."

"Am I?" she hissed. "Or am I better than that? Look at me again, demon. You will see it. You will learn just like your friend did. I'm not human, and I'm not one of you. I'm something new. And since the day I emerged from the womb, I knew I would be at this moment. My whole life has played out to me. You will give in. You will take me to the Devil, and I'll claim his throne, but not because I beg for it like some common piece of trash. I'll take that throne because it is mine."

"I'll never do what you ask," he protested.

That outburst was met with a scream from Morgan as

she flung herself at him. Her hands landed on his chest, and as they met his skin they burned their way through. He screamed and tried to claw her off, but she was impossibly strong. With one last shove, she threw him through the wall into the living room.

"Stay down, Baell. Take a minute to think through your next moves." Her voice was calm and sturdy, a sharp contrast to the unhinged maniac that had just attacked him.

He took her advice and played possum for a moment, so he could think of what to do next. Aryal stepped through the demon shaped hole in the wall, repairing it with his dark magic as he made his way next to his new housemate. Without a word, or even a look, he kicked Baell in the sores on his chest sending him reeling across the floor.

"Oh, Baell, what hope do you have? Aryal was built to strike fear in the hearts of children and I was able to break him into a tool that does my bidding. You're just a trickster, a shyster, a con man. You have no tools to keep you safe from me. You will break. All you have to decide is how long and painful you want this to be. It could all be over tonight. You can save yourself from the years of torment that I have planned for you. This is the last time I'll offer you a way out for a long time. After tonight, I'll want you to be as obedient as my pet here before we march through those fiery gates."

He turned her words around in his mind trying to find a flaw in them, but she was not wrong. He wasn't a soldier. His weapon was his slick sales pitch. Humans may stumble in fear around him, but he was never there to hurt them, at least not in the immediate sense. His was a long game. Their wishes would always backfire causing destruction in their lives and when the time came, the Devil got their soul for the privilege.

He couldn't betray his master. The pain he felt now would be nothing compared to the fate that would befall him if he brought this menace to the underworld. Or in an even scarier thought, what if she was right and would take the throne? That look deep in her soul had shown him a fate worse than death. No one would be safe from this monster, not demons, humans, or even the light ones. And as much as he wanted to destroy his enemy, he didn't want it to come at the destruction of his own kind.

"Time's up, my friend," she said as she unsheathed a sword adorned in runes and old magic. The glyphs were from the time of Azaroth, the Elder God and ancient ruler of all that came before his master.

"Where did you get that?" The Demonslayer was said to be lost in the Dark Ages.

"You have to earn the right to knowledge from now on, little one." She laughed at her own joke. It was a rich, earthy cackle, and both demons grabbed their ears in pain. "Remember this moment, demon, for it will be the last time you have free will." She raised the sword up and brought it down, removing both of his feet.

He screamed but no sound came from his mouth. His dark blood pooled on the floor around him, and as he looked up at Aryal for help his gaze was met with pity. Now he knew why Aryal didn't answer him. She was being literal when she said he didn't speak much anymore. Whatever magic that had kept him from returning home was now holding Baell in the same prison.

She straddled his chest and brought her hands down once

again onto his exposed chest, burning their way into the wounds that had begun to crust over. Fire burned in her eyes, and a smile engulfed her face. "Once we're settled in for the night, I'm going to prep my bag for tomorrow. There is no need to waste a good wish. It would've been so much easier if you had just answered my questions and taken me on my way. But that is neither here nor there. Now, we take this path, Baell. You, me, and Aryal will be busy once you break. So, for now, I get to play."

He longed for the gift of unconsciousness, but it wouldn't come. Demons had notoriously high pain thresholds, but this was something else. Whatever held him to her home, kept him awake and aware. Hour after hour ticked by with her inflicting some new kind of Hell. Each physical wound pushed his psyche further away from the sanity it once held. He was doomed to turn into a shell like Aryal before him. It seems that in thirty years she had perfected torture to an art.

By the time the sun broke above the horizon, Baell was changed forever. He was hanging on by a thread, but his new master would give him no relief. She showed no mercy and cared little for the deals he was now willing to make. A beam of light poured in from outside landing on Morgan's face. Lit up, he could see she was beautiful by human standards. A deadly surprise wrapped in a pretty package.

"Get ready, Baell. I know you can shapeshift. We have a busy morning ahead of us. I may hate Mondays, but this Monday the whole world is going to hate them as much as I do. Especially, Karen, that rotten bitch. There's no need to make a deal with me, I have more than enough power to make this happen. But it would be a good idea to make your-self useful. "

She opened the door for the last time on a world unaware of her intentions. By the end of the night, the city would be burning, and Morgan would be collecting souls to add to her strength. A storm was coming for the dark and light. One they had never considered while fighting with each other all these eons. One that if not stopped would swallow everything in existence whole and grin while doing it.

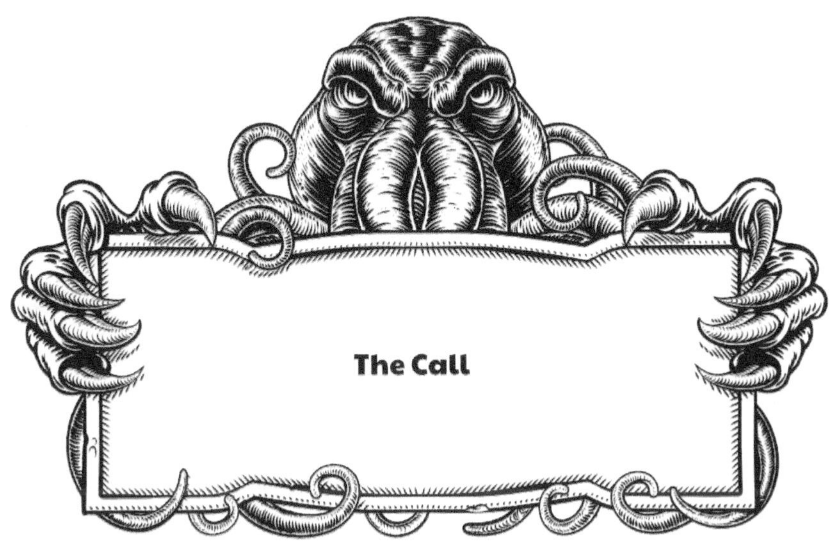

BY AARON WHITE

6:41 AM, November 12, 2021

"Can someone explain this to me? What the hell I'm looking at?" Police Chief Roger Steadman asks after about a minute of looking into the water. There is only fear and confusion in the question. The officers around him make no reply, for they are stunned into silence.

They stand on a small cliff overlooking the Atlantic Ocean. Below them, over two dozen dead bodies float in the briny waters. Some of the bloated corpses are almost casually tossed by the restless ocean into the jagged rocks cluttered around the base of the cliff. Others are slowly pulled out to sea by the hands of the tide. It's hard to see exactly what they are wearing, but Steadman can make out corpses dressed in nightgowns and bathrobes, while others appear fully dressed. Only a few are naked, and their pale flesh makes Steadman wince. It's an unusually cold November, and regardless of their varying stages of undress, the sight makes him feel sick and apprehensive. But that's not the worst.

Christ, there's children down there, Steadman thinks to himself. His head spins. This is so much bigger than anything he's had to deal with, but already the proper calls have been made. Soon, state troopers will arrive to help, followed by the feds if this gets ugly enough. It's 6:47AM. A chilly mist hangs in the air like a shroud. It's going to be a long and miserable morning.

DETECTIVE DAVID CARTER arrives on the scene in a beat-up Oldsmobile Sedan – once black, now a mottled and dusty matte grey. He parks his car away from the clutter of emergency response vehicles, partially out of respect but more for the anonymity. He is a study in monochrome, with his equally dark grey trench coat and unkempt hair. Lean and handsome, his lined face makes him appear to be older than thirty-eight, and he carries a quiet confidence that makes it difficult for others to talk to him freely. His walk is brisk and soon he finds himself amidst the officers. There's little talk amongst them, and the few conversations heard are hushed and nervous. He spots the Police Chief, but waits for him to make contact first. The scene is visibly tense.

"Detective Carter?" the older gentleman in uniform asks as he approaches. "I'm Police Chief Steadman."

David shakes his outstretched hand. "Anyone know what happened?" The question is little more than formality, as David's been filled in with as many details as possible.

"I've never seen such a thing," Steadman responds, and

for a moment there seems like he has more to say, but the words trail off.

"May I take a look?" Carter asks, but doesn't wait for a response. He strolls to the edge of the cliff and peers down at the dead. A harsh wind whips at his coat. His eyes only linger for a moment, and then he looks to either side of the cliff. He is not sure what he's looking for, but he knows instinctively that there will be no clues in the wreckage below. Something propelled them into the water, and that thing came from land.

He walks back to the group of officers, beyond which a small crowd has formed. Word has already gotten out.

———

11:42PM, November 12, 2021

The incident is scarcely mentioned in the evening news, and when it is the details are vague at best. Reports refer to it as a "tragic accident at sea off the coast of Marblehead Neck, Massachusetts". Roger Steadman is glad that many details are spared, considering the mysterious cause behind the misfortune. He doesn't want this to become a spectacle. The thought disgusts him.

He is up late with worry and confusion. There will be many hours until the results from the lab come back – specific causes and time of death, toxicology reports, the identities of the victims. He feels helpless and impatient without the results. Beyond that, however, lurks a fear that the exact reason behind the deaths will remain an utter anomaly.

· · ·

David Carter returned to his new house on the other side of Marblehead, having recently transferred from Ipswich after a bitter divorce. He pacesd the floor of his almost empty bedroom, troubled by the bizarre deaths. His fear, however, is not the mystery being unsolvable, but that he alone will gain insight to the nature of the occurrence. Only the bedside lamp provides illumination, and it is meager at best. Stacks of cardboard boxes stand like sentinels in the corners of the room. By the feeble light, David allows himself to dwell on his past. His father, his father's father, and so on into centuries past, were all plagued with a unique madness and an obsession with the strange and unknowable. His great-grandfather, Randolph Carter, had been the worst, and there had been wild gossip about his abrupt disappearance and his mental condition before he vanished. And while the incessant fixation on the arcane diluted after him, it didn't die out. David's father was a morbidly superstitious and troubled man who seemed to be afraid of his own shadow. And even David had suffered from bouts of vivid nightmares for most of his childhood. He sought order to conquer this, and studied law and criminal psychology when he came of age. The mind fascinated him, and he strove to reveal the fallacy behind the dark delusions of his ancestors. The lunatics in his lineage were mere products of an unfortunate chemical imbalance combined with an improper upbringing, not the result of anything supernatural.

And yet... he sits on the edge of the bed and wonders about the paranormal for the first time in years. He can't quite ignore the ominous undertone of the event, as if some greater force orchestrated everything. But to what end?

For the first time since childhood, David finds himself afraid of the dark.

———

8:07AM, November 13, 2021

The grey light of dawn brings with it more horrors, both seen and heard. The reports have come in. The bodies belong to the families who lived in the houses surrounding the shore. Now the houses are empty and the bodies are in the morgue. There are no foreign chemicals found in their blood, nor does there seem to be any tampering of any kind. Upon death their adrenaline levels were perfect and there are no bruises or abrasions anywhere on the bodies. It seems that entire families simply walked over the cliff and into the ocean, drowning roughly at the same time, given the varying distances of the houses. What could've convinced dozens of family members to abandon their lives and throw themselves into the frigid waters is an absolute mystery.

More bodies float in the ocean this morning, including a few officers brought in to patrol the coast for anything or anyone suspicious. Their cruisers are found a few blocks away, the driver doors still open. There had been no radio contact the night before.

The mist has turned into a light snow that falls from the sky like ashes.

By noon the coast swarms with emergency response vehicles and personnel. The ones closest to the shore wear hazmat suits, and while there were no toxins detected in the victims' blood, they test for abnormalities in the environment nonetheless. An air of futility weighs upon everyone at the scene. Steadman and Carter are both there, but have said little more to each other than awkward greetings. Steadman responds to his radio frequently, for his officers, aided by the Coast Guard, again search the empty houses as well as the homes that neighbor them, which are now devoid of life. Once more there are no signs of struggle.

By early evening concrete barricades have been put into place, roads blocked and detours mapped out. Entire neighborhoods are off-limits. Officers are stationed in patrol cars around the perimeter in the vain hope of spotting something... anything. An unnatural silence permeates the world around them, and many officers resort to turning their stereos on as a distraction, the volume low but a small comfort in the quiet dark nonetheless.

The rest of the town is silent as well. Many have gone to bed early in hopes of putting the night behind them, while others remain awake, pretending to watch talk shows while their minds churn with fear and worry. Eventually they too retire, and the town settles into a fitful slumber.

Officer Jason McGann is awake in his patrol car. From the stereo light jazz plays quietly. Beyond the windows there is only darkness. Not a single star is visible, and he imagines that the town and the world around it has vanished. At 11:50PM a loud and sudden burst of static emanates from the speakers... only it's not just static. A low throbbing noise undulates beneath a high-pitched frenzy of noise, and for a moment the static itself is a vast choir of screaming. Jason quickly reaches for the radio dial to change the station, but the cacophony remains, no matter the call numbers. The deep pulse is like a heartbeat. He fumbles for the power button, and before he can get a firm grasp around it there is a voice in the chaos – a singular female voice that he knows very well.

"Jaaaasoooon..." the voice says, a drawn-out whisper barely audible over the din of tortured shrieking. It's his wife, Cynthia, who was visiting a nearby friend when people first disappeared. He hasn't seen her since.

A nonsensical bit of shrill music plays for a moment, almost lost in the din. The rhythmic beat becomes more pronounced. It sounds like a celebration fit for Hell, and it sends a chill down the middle of Jason's back.

"Cynthia!" he cries as his hand finds the volume and turns it up, hoping to hear more of her voice. It doesn't make any sense, hearing her voice on the radio with these odd sounds, but he doesn't care. The only thing that matters is hearing more of it. Within seconds her voice is lost in the flux of odd noise, which reaches a blood-curdling frenzy before it stops abruptly. He waits a moment, and part of him wants to hear the hellish discordance again if only to hear scraps of her voice. It never comes. The following silence is almost more disconcerting. Feeling sick to his stomach, he exits the car for some fresh air.

———

11:50PM, November 13, 2021

Anthony Gaines dreams that he's standing in his kitchen. The light above the stove is the only one turned on in the room, and the majority of the space is dim and crawling with shadows. By the feeble glow he notices that someone sits at the small table against the wall on the other side of the room, next to a window. He knows immediately that it's Jennifer – or Jenny, as he's fond to call her – an attractive woman in her late thirties that lives a few blocks down from his house.

No, that's not right. That section of town is now mysteriously empty and lifeless, its residents dead or missing. And yet Jenny smiles at him. She wears a white nightgown that clings to her shapely body, and he notices that she is soaked for some reason, and that the garment clings to her as if she's just stepped out of a body of water. Her dripping wet skin is unnaturally pale, almost matching the gown. He finds himself moving closer to her, and he can see that her flesh is corrupted and discolored in places. Here and there a layer of silvery scales reflect the faint light. A sickening scent comes off her. It smells of the briny ocean and of things dragged onto the shore and left to wither in the summer heat. Beneath that stench is something else, something much more putrid and ancient.

As if on cue, flickering green lights erupt from her eyes like twin chemical fires. He can see that she is in much worse condition than he'd thought, and that her amphibious, sagging dead skin looks ruined. Where there are not the smattering of scales, the flesh is withered and discolored, like a fish left out in the sun for too long. The soaked nightgown is transparent and only reveals more putrefaction.

"Hello Tony," she says in dead monotone. The same eerie light flickers between her teeth. "I know this is strange, but I need you to listen to me for a second." There's a strange inflection to her voice. It almost sounds like she's talking underwater. She pauses to look down at her hands, which are now webbed and vaguely aquatic.

"There's a change coming, and I know that it might be scary, but it doesn't have to be," she says, looking at him again. "I didn't really have a choice, but given the chance to go back, I wouldn't. Not in a million years. It's amazing here. You'll see. But we need more of us to make things really happen." And then she smiles, and it's the worst thing Anthony has ever seen. He wants to scream, to vent his confusion and end this maddening assault on his psyche, but he can't. His voice is stuck somewhere in his throat.

"Here, let me show you something," the thing that was Jenny says as she presses a webbed hand against the window. A moment ago there was just an uncanny and opaque darkness, but now a sickly green radiance – the very same color that flickers inside Jennifer's skull – blooms from far away. He is instantly drawn to it regardless of Jenny's rotting body and the pungent odor that envelops it. He sees that his house now somehow resides on the ocean floor. Seaweed brushes against the windowsill. Within the sea's incalculable depths lies something of immaculate and alien beauty in the far distance. It seems to be at once a mountain range and a vast city of gargantuan proportions. Dazzling green light spills from a countless amount of irregularly shaped openings that could be either windows or doors. The radiance illuminates the incredible space between, and within the murky depths swarms of giant things that defy scientific explanation drift about the bewildering structure. The architecture is both nightmarish and astonishing, the workings of a thousand lunatics, and at once he is compelled to journey to this place of terrifying wonder. It's a pull that defies logic itself, but he knows deep within his heart of hearts that he absolutely must make the pilgrimage, or die trying.

· · ·

Lisa Caulway dreams that she is in her bed, as if she's woken from another dream. In fact, she's almost certain that she's awake, except for two weird things. First, an old nightlight she had when she was younger has been placed on top of her dresser. It's the type of nightlight that has a cover with holes shaped like stars. The light inside shines through the holes as it gently rotates, and the stars drift around the room. But these stars don't look like the stars she remembers. No. These stars are bent and misshapen. They remind her of starfish, only their crooked arms are too long and spindly. The other weird thing is that Meme and Pepe are there. They're not her real grandparents, but friends of her mom's parents who happen to live a few streets away. She met them when she was really young, and those nicknames just stuck over the years. They are standing beyond the foot of the bed near the wall with the window. The lights of the scary stars float across their bodies, and Lisa can tell that something's wrong with them.

Suddenly their eyes and mouths glow like jack-o'-lanterns, only the light is a bright green. Lisa tries to scream but nothing comes out. She tries to pull the covers over her head but she can't move her body. She can't even close her eyes.

"It's okay, honey," Meme says. Her voice sounds different, and she looks really sick. "It's just us, Meme and Pepe."

Pepe nods his bald head and grins. Green light spills out of his mouth. On the walls the stars are whirling around faster and faster, and now they look different. The points are longer, and the shapes seem to be of creatures made of five tentacles, all of which appear to be moving.

"We want to take you with us to a wonderful and magical place," Meme continues. "You won't believe your eyes! Now, don't be nervous, dear. Once you get there, you won't be afraid. You'll never be afraid again. Ever."

Meme and Pepe move away from the window and gesture at it. Beyond the glass the world is pitch black, but after a moment a brilliant green glow erupts from far away, bright enough to illuminate the huge distance between it and the house. Lisa notices with strange curiosity that the house is somehow underwater, and that there are things swimming outside the window. A weight is lifted from her and she is able to move. She crawls out of bed and approaches the window, ignoring the rotting fish smell coming from Meme and Pepe. She presses her small hands to the window and peers out. She sees what looks like a strange city made of spiky grey rocks, and all of the million windows and doors are open, and the bright green light shines out of every one. She also sees the things swimming around the city, and she knows that she should be scared, but the city reminds her of the Emerald City from the *Wizard of Oz*. It would be a lovely adventure to take, she thinks.

"How do we get there?" Lisa asks in a small, innocent voice.

"We'll show you," says Pepe.

ACROSS TOWN DAVID CARTER dreams he is standing on the shore of an ocean at low tide. He has seen this ocean over a hundred times, but now it is different in ways he cannot explain. The entire scene is a dull and timeless grey, neither dawn nor dusk. Between him and the water there are more than a dozen figures dressed in wet, dripping rags. The figures all stare at him. Something has put a strange fire into their heads, for a sickly pale green light spills from their eye sockets and mouths. Their ruined skin is light grey, and the garish light from their faces reflects off what looks to be patches of small silvery scales. In unison the figures raise an arm and point at David, and in unison they say a word or a sentence. David can't make out what they are saying because the words are gibberish nonsense, but the syllables... the syllables fill David with an almost unendurable dread. Behind them the ocean swells as a wave approaches, and the wave climbs higher and higher, and higher still, until it becomes an impossible wall of water. Before the wave breaks, David can see the silhouettes of things undulating in the waters of the surf. Their forms are half-hidden, but the shapes suggest giant bulbous entities with a series of fins circling their amorphous bodies. The wave finally curls and crashes into the figures, but they remain upright like statues, somehow immune to the tremendous force of the water. The deluge comes at David in the blink of an eye, and he tries to scream, but he is already submerged and tossed to the sand like a ragdoll.

———

12:06AM, November 14, 2021

Officer McGann is standing outside the cruiser, smoking a cigarette. The neighborhood is dimly lit by the scant street-lights that dot the rural landscape here and there. Deep shadows pool in between. He is supposed to be surveying his surroundings, but his mind is haunted by his missing wife's voice. The way she whispered his name replays in his head over and over again, as well as the shrieking chaos behind it. He wonders if it's possible for Cynthia to still be alive, and where those sounds could have possibly come from.

There's a sudden movement in his peripheral vision to his left and across the street. A shambling form is coming in his direction. The figure is a mere silhouette until it reaches the edges of a streetlight, and Jason sees that it's a man wearing light blue flannel pajamas. His gait is all wrong, and while McGann would like to blame the jittery stumbling on drunkenness, there's an inhuman aspect in the way the man is shambling. A strange jerking quality permeates his movements, and it looks like some invisible force tugs him forward. His arms droop at his side. Jason moves to his left so that he is parallel to the figure.

"Okay, I need you to stop right there," he says with authority, extending his left hand forward while his right hovers around the holster of his gun. The man continues to stumble towards him, and picks up speed.

"Sir, I need you to desist." A moment later, the gun is drawn and gripped in both hands. The way the guy moves is strange enough, but it's his expression that almost sends McGann running back to his car. The muscles in the man's face are slack and lifeless, his eyes are wide and his mouth gapes open as if his jaw has been detached. It is the face of someone who has died of terror but somehow still lives.

"Sir, stand down," McGann says with more authority, and is still ignored. The figure is almost upon him.

"I repeat, stand down!"

Left with no choice, Jason quickly fires off two rounds, center mass. The body twitches but still presses on, not even raising an arm in defense. Jason is forced to take two steps back before firing a final shot into the man's forehead. Now lifeless, the body crashes to the asphalt. Jason is about to inspect the body when the glare of the cruiser's headlights catches another person scampering over the barricade far to his right.

"Stop right there!" he says as he aims the pistol in the general direction, but it's too late. The figure is up and over, loping into the darkness beyond.

11:27AM, November 14. 2021

The coast is chaos. Inexplicably there are more bodies floating face-down in the ocean. Many of the officers that were on duty overnight guarding the barricades tell of their experiences with people who were driven to the ocean in ways that are startling and vaguely inhuman. Some were attacked, others were forced to put down their would-be assailants. Eleven civilians are reported dead, while the body of an officer will be discovered later with a broken neck and a bite wound to the face. Such events would've been accounted for had the radios not malfunctioned, resulting in static that seemed to disguise other noises. Electronics have stopped working the way they should. Cell phones can't pick up a signal, and the screens are garbled, pixelated nonsense that seem to change at random. Television screens are a mess of white noise with the suggestions of certain shapes within the static.

Bent pieces of black metal are strewn about the corpses, remnants of a helicopter that crash-landed somewhere nearby. The tang of smoke and gasoline still hangs in the air. There are also curious bits of wood and fiberglass that litter the waters and can be traced all the way to the horizon, which has become a churning wall of fog and storm clouds.

Police Chief Steadman is standing near the edge of a cliff, looking at the wreckage below. His hands are in his coat pockets, and a deep chill seeps into him that is colder than the icy wind that whips at his face. He feels small and hopeless, like a little boy lost in a nightmare.

Detective David Carter stands nearby, peering at the same dismal scene. His mind can barely process the details, however. Instead, he is trying to turn over a few details that may connect to form a bigger picture. Nocturnal suicides and families disappearing overnight. People vanishing neighborhood by neighborhood, stretching out from the ocean, systematically. The houses nearest the shore being affected first, and then the ones beyond that, and beyond that still. The dream of undead things and the wave that came to submerge them all. He turns to look inland as a thought occurs. As he mulls the idea over, he approaches Steadman.

"We need to evacuate everyone who's left in Marblehead Neck and bring them to the mainland," Carter says to Steadman without any introduction. Roger's attention has shifted to the horizon and the swirling wall of grey that engulfs it, and he stares at it for a moment before replying.

"I'd be lying if I said I hadn't thought of that myself," he responds. "But how do I justify that? What do I tell them?"

"Tell them anything," says Carter, and then, a moment later, "Tell them their lives are in danger."

"From what? We've ruled out anything viral or biochemical. We can't pinpoint any kind of signal. There's no evidence of any groups of people responsible. We've got nothing," he pauses and finally looks at Carter. "What do you think is going on here?"

It is Carter's turn to pause. "Something's screwing with the electronics. If it's not a signal, what if it's something… what if it's a suggestion that's more psychological or subconscious? Thoughts are a form of electricity, right? Maybe the electrical interference is a side effect of something else."

"I don't follow."

"It's almost like it's… organic. Think of the ocean at high tide. Each time the waves come in they break further inland in steady cycles. Whatever is happening is acting like that."

"But what the hell is causing it?"

"Whatever it is, it's out there in the ocean."

4:52PM, November 14, 2021

State Police officers from across Essex County are aiding in evacuating the population of Marblehead Neck and the eastern coast of Marblehead itself, relocating them in schools further mainland. The process hasn't been smooth, as most people are not willing to vacate their homes under vague conditions. Members of the National Guard are also present and responsible for detaining the more unruly citizens. Numerous arrests are made, and the holding cells at the Marblehead Police Department are crowded with those who have become belligerent with panic.

Police Chief Steadman is overseeing the activities, making sure nothing devolves into chaos. It's a daunting task, but as the sun slips towards the horizon Marblehead Neck is emptied and silent, as Ocean Ave itself is blocked off with heavy barricades.

AMIDST THE DISORDER, Detective Carter has taken the time to return to his house. He begins to empty the boxes of their contents, dumping the items on the floor, searching for a small wooden box. When he was a young child, his father had given him the box and the thing within with only the vaguest of explanations. It was for protection, against what, he'd never learned.

An eccentric alcoholic, his father believed in odd things and eventually descended into the same esoteric madness that claimed Randolph Carter. Over time he began to strongly believe that the same insidious forces would claim the rest of his family. Tired of the man's ramblings, David had left him after graduation, left him to waste away in the make-believe world he so desperately clung to, a world of phantoms more real than his family.

Over the years he's kept the box hidden from view. Perhaps it was a stubborn and lingering superstition that prevented him from throwing it out altogether, but now there's a peculiar and crucial need to find it. Ignoring the contradictory thoughts in his head, he rifles through more boxes. The floor is littered with knick-knacks and debris, flotsam and jetsam of a former life. His room in shambles, he finally finds the box, and he holds it up to the meager light filtered through the blinds that cover the windows. The sides of the small wooden cube are burnished with centuries of handling. A simple hinge allows the box to open. Inside there is a leather cord to which a thin rectangle of worn iron has been affixed. A symbol has been stamped into the metal, something that looks like a branch with three twigs on one side and two on the other. For a moment he holds it by the end of the cord, and it spins in lazy half-circles. He can see his father's wild, bearded face in his mind's eye, and there's a sadness at the center of David's heart despite the pain of the past. With a heavy sigh, he slips the necklace over his head and tucks it under his shirt. The metal is cool against his skin. He doesn't know why he's putting the amulet on or what even brought him here. The sudden change of heart seems impossible. A part of him thinks he's being foolish, chasing his father's ghost and the ghosts that he chased, succumbing to some ridiculous fairytale. Perhaps he's been driven here, like the countless others driven to the ocean's depths, an unseen and sinister hand moving pieces into place. He lets his thoughts drift, and they only return to the dream he had the night before. Without notice or instruction, his hand has wanders beneath his shirt and he fiddles with the necklace.

It is well past sunset when he finally decides to return to Marblehead. It's an almost empty gesture on his part, as he feels the mystery behind the occurrences are far too great for his presence to have any real meaning. A strange and unknowable force has descended upon the shores of Massachusetts. Investigations into the matter will remain futile. He believes this, and yet he finds himself climbing into his car to make the journey back to the place where people are drawn from their beds and into a watery grave.

. . .

As the world is plunged into darkness, a thick wall of fog that extends far into the sky rolls across the shores of Marblehead Neck. The mist seems to bend the walls of the houses, distorting their lines and angles, and the resulting geometry is a mockery of natural law. Paint withers and plants shrivel as if the very air is caustic. The once serene landscape becomes ancient and alien. Green lights flicker between clouds and deep in the ocean.

9:47PM, November 14, 2021

Emergency generator lights dimly illuminate the gymnasium of Marblehead High School, which has been transformed into a make-shift shelter for some of the survivors. The people inside are tense but mostly tired, worn down by constant anxiety. Officers act as guards, and a small medical staff has been assembled just in case. Steadman and other high ranking officers have taken over some of the faculty offices to be closer to their friends and families.

A young boy wakes up screaming and his mother comes to his aid.

"Everyone's dead and under water!" he screams. "There's a monster that wants the whole world dead! I don't wanna die, mommy!"

The mother is holding her shaking child in her arms. "Shhhh, everything's okay," she says quietly, stroking his hair.

"I don't wanna die," he says again, in between sobs.

"You're going to be fine, sweetie. Everyone is– "

The child begins to pull away from his mother's embrace. "That place hurt my eyes!" His voice continues to rise. "I don't wanna go back there! I don't wanna change when I die!"

"Lady, you shut your kid up," says a belligerent middle-aged man, rising from his cot.

"Oh stop it, he's just scared," the mother retorts.

"We're all scared here. That doesn't mean he has to–"

"It's the Lord's judgment," a nearby elderly woman cuts in. She sits on a makeshift cot, her small wrinkled hands folded neatly on her lap. "We have to atone for our sins."

"That's a bunch of horseshit," replies the man.

"Will you guys knock it off?" says another man in a neighboring cot. He's younger than the other stranger. His eyes look tired and haunted.

"Look, my son just had a nightmare," the mother responds.

"We're all having nightmares," the man says, stepping closer now. He's in his upper 30's, unshaven and disheveled. "I see my wife and daughter every time I close my eyes, and they're..." His face crumples as he trails off. He clamps a hand over his eyes to stem the tears. "Christ, I was on a business trip, and they just... they..." Pure anguish erupts from him. "They drowned themselves! They just walked into the water to die, and now I... I..."

At this point the young boy is wailing.

"Okay, okay, enough," the mother says, trying to calm her son. Meanwhile the man continues.

"What on Earth would make them do that? Does anyone know why they would just–"

The older man rushes forward and grabs him by the collars. "Will you just shut the hell up already? Shut up!"

Without warning, the other man begins to beat upon the

older man's face and head. A skirmish erupts, and the two topple to the ground after one trips over a cot leg. There they squirm while biting and hitting each other. A few people rush in, some to help, others to join the fray.

Four officers run in to pull people off each other. They are followed by two doctors who sedate the more aggressive, as well as the boy who is still sobbing. After a few moments, an uneasy silence returns to the gymnasium. Whispers drift across the room like wind over the ocean.

DETECTIVE DAVID CARTER has been parked outside Marblehead High School for a while now. He is supposed to meet with Steadman and the other officers to discuss potential plans for the future. Instead he is fixated on another idea, one born of madness. The thought has wormed its way into his brain and will not let go. The ocean. As the minutes tick by, the urge grows stronger. Abandoning all reason, he puts the car in gear and heads towards Ocean Avenue.

The headlights pierce the gloom as he nears the sea. There's a barricade set up just as Ocean Avenue begins to stretch across the water. Portable metal gates run the width of the road, behind which two cruisers are parked. As Carter nears, a spotlight turns on, flooding the street with a bright white glare. The two officers on patrol are already moving to the car. Carter brakes and the car comes to a stop. The first officer turns on a flashlight and aims it at the car while the other hangs back, his hand poised by the holster at his waist. Carter rolls down the window.

"Sir, you are in a restricted area," says the cop, leaning in and shining the flashlight into Carter's face. "Oh. It's you.

Look, no one is supposed to be out here. No one. I can't allow you to pass."

"I'm not going inland. I just need to get about halfway across the bridge, maybe a little more."

The officer stands and looks towards Marblehead Neck. He seems to be searching for details within the darkness. An uncomfortable amount of time passes by.

"There's something I need to see for myself," Carter says. That's the extent of his honesty, he realizes, both to himself and the officer. He doesn't want to focus on the details. To do so would invite madness. "Look, I can pull rank if it comes down to it, but I know we both don't want that."

The officer continues to stare at the horizon before slightly shaking his head. The movement is almost imperceptible, but it's there, and it's born of anger and resignation.

"It's your funeral, buddy," he says without looking in David's direction. "Okay, let him through!" he calls to the other cop, who begins to move the gates aside. Carter is in the process of releasing the brakes when the officer leans in again.

"You listen to me," he says, shining the light into Carter's face again. "If anything weird happens out there, you're on your own. I have a wife and kids to look after. Are we clear?"

"We're clear," David says, and proceeds down Ocean Avenue.

SOMETHING INSIDE DAVID forces him to slow the car down to a stop. He is almost at the end of the bridge. Ahead of him, Marblehead Neck is little more than an inky smudge that takes up most of the dark grey horizon. He puts the car in park and, against his better judgment, opens the door to get out. The air is cold and clammy. Though there is no wind, there's a strange agitation like a static charge that ripples against Carter's skin. He is amazed and a little unsettled by the silence that envelops him. It's as if the ocean itself is holding its breath, waiting for some dark force to disturb its waters. David himself waits in turn, backlit by the car's headlights.

———

11:50PM, November 14, 2021

A sudden violent and steady wind comes at David from the ocean, bringing with it the stench of rotting marine life and something worse. It's a pungent odor that smells of old dirt and blood.

The road darkens as the car's headlights go out behind him. The engine dies as well. The only sound now is the howling of the fetid wind.

The gale blows apart the wall of fog like a vast curtain. The moon is full and too large in the sky, gleaming like the vast singular eye of a maniacal god. The cold light illuminates buildings that are no longer familiar houses. In their place, crooked and broken black towers pierce the sky, surrounded by dead and twisted trees.

With a sudden flash dozens and dozens of windows come ablaze with a garish green light. The entire town shines with an evil radiance. Carter recognizes the color. It's the same glow that came from those things in the dream. In fact, he can see them now, dotting the shoreline, carrying in their heads lights of their own.

The amulet underneath his shirt begins to burn his skin. It tingles at first, but soon feels like a hot iron pressed against his breastbone. He quickly digs beneath his shirt to remove the necklace and cries out in pain as he makes contact with the metal. An intense electrical shock passes through his arm and leaves it numb. Startled, he looks down at his twitching fingers. Soon, however, panic engulfs him and he looks to the horizon.

Further out at sea, a giant column of whirling wind and water stretches from sea to sky. Pale green lightning, the very same green, flickers in the churning clouds. The lights pulse and partially reveal shapes that drift within the cyclone. He can make out several ragged wings that flap against the wind, and the writhing of massive tentacles. There seems to be a cluster of things that look like giant winged amoebas caught in the middle of the vortex. The mass of shapes continues to rise from the depths of the ocean, an army of monstrosities. For a moment it looks like the bulk belongs to one entity, but surely such varied anatomy couldn't be part of a singular creature.

At first he is stunned speechless, and then the other-worldly terror hits him, and he staggers backwards, finally understanding the sight before him.

The confusion of forms does belong to one unspeakable thing, still rising from the ocean. It rights itself and reveals a disproportionately large head in between a pair of wings like the tattered sails of ships, huge and ragged. A thick profusion of tangled growths the width of trees hangs from the bulbous head, and in the middle of the ropey mass six eyes like green spotlights glare at Carter, pierce through him and gaze at the mortal world beyond.

"JESUS! JESUS GOD!" he hears himself blurt out. He backpedals and trips over his own feet, landing hard on the asphalt. His mind doesn't register the pain. It's only trying to make sense of the confusion of shapes behind the monstrosity. He sees clouds that are also mountains that are also cities. He closes his eyes but the images are burned into his retinas. A wind whips at him and carries voices – the same syllables he heard in his dream. The nonsense words loop over and over again. It's too much. As he feels his sanity tearing apart, he scrambles to his feet and lunges for the car. Once he manages to get the door open, he throws himself inside. He knows that the car is dead, but he turns the key and tries over and over again to start the car. Nothing happens. He risks a look out the windshield and sees the amphibious undead horde coming across the bridge. Behind them, the mammoth creature slowly crosses the body of water, its wings unfurled to blot out the sky.

Wrought with fear, David staggers out of the car and into the street. He sprints down Ocean Avenue, trying to put distance between himself and the horrors behind him. There will be safety in numbers back on Marblehead. It was foolish to come out here on his own, and he is lucky to have his sanity still intact.

He slows to a jog and then stumbles as his legs almost give out. On the other shore, dozens of Marblehead's citizens calmly walk into the water, their faces expressionless. The sinister influence has reached farther than Carter or the others had anticipated. One by one they calmly submerge themselves. Bubbles rise to the water's surface as each of the enthralled exhale their last breaths, trading air for cold, briny water. There is no struggling, and soon the bodies are lost to the depths of the sea.

———

4:05AM, November 15 2021

The town of Marblehead is mostly empty. The few survivors on the western side are as of yet unaware of what happened the night before. They are huddled in their bedrooms or in the basements of their homes. Grim news will soon reach their ears, and a grimmer fate will follow.

Detective David Carter's abandoned car will eventually be found, but of his body, there is no trace. Nor is there a trace of the giant thing that surfaced. A lone helicopter flies a slow circle around Marblehead Neck and the waters that surround it, and the pilot can just make out the suggestions of buildings poking up from the depths of the ocean. The towers are all but lost in a fog that never seems to leave. The pilot brings the chopper closer and the blades momentarily shred the heavy mist so that the ruins of the impossible city below are exposed. He sees the blackened iron frames like the bones of alien skyscrapers, and a cold shudder runs up his spine. He jerks on the cyclic stick and the helicopter jerks up and through the curtain of fog. The pilot, who will not make it back home, whose body will never be found, refuses to look back at the city that is inexplicably rising from the ocean.

BY JON TOBEY

Once, not so very long ago, explorers had to pore over endless maps and scrolls just to find the unmapped regions in between, those regions that have always called to men to fill in, as if once our knowledge was entire, so would be our dominion. Today, when you can peruse the globe on a computer, the illusion that the world is entirely mapped in infinite scale is complete. Yet, you might be surprised to find that there are places on those maps that were incorrectly filled in specifically to keep you out. Places that are closer and more numerous than you might imagine, each with some dark and buried history where exploration would be detrimental to the progeny of man. What did Melville say? "It is not down in any map; true places never are." Herein lies the last of those tales.

In the hubris of youth, I too was not aware of such places. As intended by the secret cartographers, because the map was seamless, it did not call to me; I did not feel the need to explore. I assumed implicitly that if other men knew it, had mapped it, had frozen their knowledge in dusty tomes in dusky rooms, that the call was heeded, the work was done. There was no fame left to be had in these maps wrung pale of mystery. So, I searched for other places where men were yet lost amid incomplete maps. The atom intrigued me, but the math was a mountain range whose heady peaks I could not conquer. Art, for a while, drew me, but I could not draw it back. So, I was cast adrift between the hard sciences and the scienceless into the soft sciences of archaeology, anthropology, and natural history to find and make my mark.

Like many young men of moderate means and copious time, the sources of my family fortunes seemed like ancient history. I knew my grandfather had made some small profit on natural resources here in the Northwest before these territories were fully settled. My father had managed these assets with the intent I should be freed by them and not burdened by them, and so I traveled and went to school, dabbling in my various pursuits as I have previously listed. But even as I had settled myself into a potentially mediocre career in natural history, it was unnatural history which pursued me. We think we can always control our fate, right up until the moment it comes up from behind us, takes us down by the hamstring, and then goes for the femoral artery like a honey badger. All the while leaving our brain intact so that we may witness and reflect on our exsanguination, perhaps to carry the lessons forth into another life, or in this case, perhaps just as a cruel joke.

It began when I was in New Brunswick, ostensibly counting the ear bones of char, looking for a certain lost subspecies of which to append my family name, but in practicality, fly fishing the late season for brook trout and Atlantic salmon by day and quaffing brandy and cigars with likewise indolent youth by night. Had there been fewer insects and more brandy, I might've stayed longer, but when I got a telegram from my father asking me to come home immediately, I packed up my scant samples with promises to return on the next season. Dawn found me flying home to Seattle, chasing the sun across the Canadian Great Plains. I looked at the vast geography and wondered if perhaps my Great Adventure still lay somewhere before and below me. Would that the prodigal son had refused the call.

My father had a car for me at the airport that took me to the house, high and lonely on a Magnolia bluff, our family fortunes sufficient to hold off ravenous developers for over a century. My mother having died back in her native Bali when I was young, and there being no female presence gracing my father's side in all this time, the house always had the air of a seasonal home, just opened for the occasion of my arrival. It was never warm, and the huge rooms, though stuffed with busts, trophies, artifacts, and mounted heads, were empty of the slightest human warmth and emotion that women have been bringing to abodes since the days not so long ago when we lived in caves. That somethingness that turns a house into a home was sorely lacking here.

I was surprised father did not meet me, but rather the help ushered me up to his rooms. I began to feel a cold dread as I trudged up the southward side of the symmetrical center stairway that wraps the main hall like a winter scarf wraps a throat. With each step, my feet got heavier and I began to sum and weigh my life in laborious breaths. At the top of the stairs I paused and Maubry, the valet, as old and straight and wrinkled as the velvet bell pull next to my father's bed, also paused to wait for me. As far as I knew, Maubry came with the house, for he had been there since my first memories. I could not tell if he was breathing hard because I could not tell if he was breathing. His pallor was that of the pre-embalmed and if he had said five hundred words in my lifetime, I had not heard half of them. He shambled down the hall as if I might not know where my father slept, and I followed.

Maubry opened the door without knocking. As with everything in the house, the scale of the door was more suited to a man on horseback than a man afoot. We passed through abreast of each other and I saw my father propped up in a bed the size of my entire camp tent in New Brunswick. He looked ashen and worn, so much smaller than the man I remembered. But he had a lap desk piled with work and he looked over his spectacles at me with eyes which had lost none of their penetration.

"How was the fishing?"

"It was a scientific expedition," I countered.

"Do we have a fish named after us?"

"Not yet."

He snorted. "Time is short, Jacob. My time is short, at least. I had hoped not to do this to you, but I will not finish my work. I will need your help."

As I said, before this time, in the foolishness of my youth, I had never really pondered the source of our wealth. It was then that my father explained it to me. It being already late in the wintry afternoon, we had dinner brought up and worked into the night. It was much as I had suspected on the surface, but the depth and interconnectedness that had sprouted from the original investments like mushrooms from mycelium were astonishing. My grandfather had parlayed the original wealth into many markets and my father had, in turn, branched out even more. But as I was the only heir and disinterested in the act of business itself (a vast disappointment I sensed intuitively, rather than by anything my father said, which made it no less heavy and perhaps heavier), in his later years my father sought to divest and consolidate the business by liquidating our familial holdings into a portfolio of modern technologies which I could manage with a minimum of effort.

It was late at night and my head swam, but my father burned on with an urgency that was undeniable. He forbade me brandy, and I drank coffee much later in the evening than is my custom. When we finally broke for the night, papers were strewn about the bedroom in some approximation of a map of the holdings. Not by geography, but by industry, vertical sector, holding companies, and such constructs as made my head swim like calculus had once done. He implored me that the most important thing was yet to be revealed and not to be a laggard in the morning, but to return immediately once I had broken my fast.

I went to my room, which had had the dust knocked out of it and a fire set to ward off the mustiness and the night, but I could not sleep. I paced until the sky had a faint rose tinge before the brandy took me in a chair by the fire. I was startled awake by a faint, but persistent, knocking, and when I went to the door, Maubry was there. Wordlessly, he turned, and I followed to my father's room. There, through the gargantuan door, still amidst the strewn papers and folders was my father, slumped, eyes closed, one contract still in his hand. I begged Maubry off and shut the door. While my father and I had never been close, or even frequently cohabitated the same domains, still I respected him, and I know he loved me in his way. After my mother died, there was only work, and that work was only for me. So, I stood there, aware of the body, but also aware that I must steep myself in this web of business; I must slowly pick it up and put it away, so that I could truly own it, and it could now truly own me. Finally, after all these years, here was a map I did not fully understand.

And so, I worked for hours collating papers and making notes from our conversation while it was still fresh in my mind. All the while my father's body cooled next to me. I have no idea what the staff thought of me or my actions. I ignored several knocks, but once opened the door to find a tray of sandwiches and tea had been left on the floor, although by then I was craving the brandy again. Eventually, finally, I had the papers arranged on the sideboard, all but the last in his hand. I was remiss in not taking this sooner, for his grasp had frozen and I thought I might break his fingers to retrieve my final puzzle piece. I confess, I was baffled at this new information, it seemed to be the center of the web, but it was the one thing my father had not schooled me on.

It was then that Maubry knocked and opened the door without waiting for my reply, accompanied by a doctor who came in to do his business. He touched the body and took its pulse. Though it was long cold, he made no expression. He took a note, pulled the sheet up, had a huddled conversation with Maubry, and then came over to me where I sat to express his condolences before passing through the doors. A breeze blew the curtains as if this whole time Father's soul had been waiting for permission to leave and now given, was departed. I shook at this thought.

I realized the mantle clock was striking past ten, and the sky had long since darkened. With nothing else to do, I took the paper with me to my room. But there, even with the help of brandy, I had haunted dreams of vague but ghastly shapes in the sky, oozing over the landscape and changing it in unimaginable ways, a great terraforming of the familiar into the alien.

I awoke before dawn and sat by the window to reread the document in my hand by the light of a lamp. It was the deed to some long-forsaken part of the North Cascades on the Canadian border, containing a dammed water source called Eldritch Creek. On the bottom of the last page was my father's handwriting:

Jacob, no matter what may transpire, you must promise to never sell this property, when you die, you must give it to somebody who will promise...

And from there the pen had scrolled across the page, my father's dying act. The one thing we had not gotten to! I was embroiled in guilt for my weakness in the face of this act, for he had clearly worked long after I had gone to bed - right up to the very moment of his death. He died as he lived, alone and working for me, even though I was a few paces away, and still awake.

Despite many jaunts in and around the Cascades in my youth, I had never heard of this place. I went downstairs to the library and fired up the computer, one of the few techno-logical intrusions into the manse, hoping to shed some light on the importance of this original family investment. I was mildly astonished to not find a single mention of Eldritch Creek online. Wasn't the Internet the map of all knowledge, every corner by now filled in the way dust seeps through a crack in a shuttered house? Perhaps, I thought, the creek had another name. From the deed, I entered the coordinates, and started searching the topographic maps. Surely, a river and lake would be on the map, no matter what the names, but there was nothing shown. I switched to satellite view and continued, still for aught. This was indeed perplexing. Had the dam collapsed? The creek been filled? Was it all some fiction to support a more nefarious scheme?

By now it was dawn. I pulled the bell cord and ordered coffee and toast. Soon, I would have to make arrangements to put my father in the crypt, but in the early morning before the rest of the world awoke, I yet had time. I perused shelves I had not looked at since I was a young man who roamed them the way you roam a kitchen looking for a midnight snack. What crumb, what tidbit would suffice to slake my intellectual gourmand's hunger? I would pull books whose covers held me spellbound, inside each the promised solutions to mysteries deep, and started them all but never finished any. My fingers ran down the leather and gilt spines as I walked back the decades of memory. In the back were some file cabinets which I had ignored so thoroughly in my youth that their presence now surprised me. Assuredly they had always been here, and yet upon them I had never remarked.

The cabinets were arranged in chronological order. Thus, it was that in the back of the very first drawer I found a small leather diary the size of a paperback book filled from cover-to-cover with handwritten notes and images. In my hands, I held my grandfather's journal, the seeds to my own past, and unbeknownst to me at the time, the missing piece to my map. I took it over to a table with a lamp and began to read. As I had surmised, my grandfather had started by prospecting in the North Cascades. At that time, almost all of the terrain had been mapped and plundered by miners and loggers, and the pervasive attitude was that these resources would last forever and were first-come, first-taken.

In 1904, there was a massive earthquake under the North-Central Cascades up against the Canadian border that caused buildings to collapse as far away as Bellingham. My grandfather, already a well-established minor tycoon thanks to his logging and mining interests in the region, funded an expedition to survey the damage. This was when he discovered a newly formed valley birthed by the quake. From his diary:

In this valley, it was as if God had plucked whole mountains out by the roots and dropped them upon the earth, as one might pluck and discard a weed. For the first time, men were able to see the very bowels of the earth without peering through the narrow window of a bore hole. We could see veins of ore and trace them to their largest junctures merely by walking along them. One guide remarked that it was as if there had been an older world, and that had been papered over with a veneer of stone. His pontifications proved eerily valid when following a vein of curious rock. Whilst spelunking into a particular crevice, we returned with a series of otherworldly tablets made from this stone, carved in strange runes which could not be read and, to a man, made us nauseous in the attempt. Most curious about them though, was that our Geologists could not discern the rock, it was something unto now unknown.

Based on such daily miracles, before we'd even completed our survey, I dispatched my most trusted man back to Seattle to buy this land at any price. Here was to be the center of a new empire, and I would be its emperor.

I paged ahead, skipping descriptions of fantastic wonders as I followed the trek.

During our quest we began to gather strange tales. Always these tales came from hunters and fishermen, those who live in harmony with the earth, who know it innately, and seem bemused you do not share their observations. It is in the romantic hearts of such men, those who follow the water, who are close to the earth, always seeking to understand the language of rapids and cascades, mountains and trees, these men have long foretold of unrest, of change, of weariness in the bones of the world. These stolid and capable men have felt, if not seen, this unrest while traversing dried and dying creeks, uncharacteristically looking over their shoulders at noises in the bush for something that awakens.

In one case, a fisherman reported a wall of gray-green slime or ooze coming down a stream, burying all in its path. Barely escaping himself up the bank, he was left with a wretched unstomachable smell, and the corpses of every fish, beast, and bird in the valley, all decomposing as if they had been dead for days, maggots bursting from every eye. How he alone survived he could not say, except that perhaps a witness was needed to this vile purging and reclaiming of the land. For when the slime had scoured the valley clean, below that was new rock that looked like the monoliths we had discovered, like an ancient byway excavated, with hieroglyphic graffiti on the walls and bed, written as if by many tentacled appendages, each attached to the same mind, composing at once as the beast perambulated along.

Such tales were understandable from men whose very world

had been turned upside down, and who may have been partially mad at any rate from bouts of long solitude. Unlike a logger or a miner, these men want the world to remain wild. And were it not for the wonders we had seen, and the tablets in our possession, it might be easy to believe him either mad, or that he might tell such tales merely to keep other, less attuned, men out. But this was not my mission. We showed him our tablets and he recoiled in horror, confirming that the same mad hand or mind that had written them had also scrawled upon the bed of the creek. We were anxious to follow up on his information, to track the intelligence behind these mysteries and took up to follow his directions, though he refused to guide us at any price.

I flipped eagerly ahead, hungry to solve this riddle.

At long last, we have come to the geographic center of the cataclysm, where we found and followed the newly formed stream, which, for its richness and strangeness of hieroglyphics, the men bestowed the name Eldritch Creek. At its headwaters, we discovered a vast chasm that must house a subterranean lake whose water has never seen daylight since the Creation. Here, we decided we would build a dam to raise the lake and generate power for our new venture.

I had seen great riches and I knew somebody would take these if we did not act immediately. To myself I promised: Here, I would use these resources and the arcane knowledge that had been exposed to create a paradise far from the corruption and decay that plagued the modern world. New cities made of new materials, self-sufficient and independent. A country unto ourselves where we answered to a now distant and long-unresponsive government, and we would no longer belong to a decaying civilization where power ate at democracy and freedom, replacing humanity with greed.

Such a dream! While I had lived my life in its shadow,

never had I heard this espoused. I marveled for a moment of the vision of the man and shook my head that the hypocrisy that seems so obvious now of creating such a modern Utopia while also maintaining infinite resources never penetrated the optimism of these men. I read on.

My grandfather saw an opportunity and took it. Having already used his mining claims and their proceeds to procure all of the surrounding acreage, he built a dam on Eldritch Creek with the intent to create a hydroelectric station, powering his dream. A dam, a power station – independence and absolute control. Why had this dream never come to pass? Here was the end of the journal, and although I spent many hours going through the files, no answers did I find.

Maubry came to get me. My father's body was prepared and awaiting us in the crypt, a throwback to when the house was built that I'm sure was on no city planner's map. In fact, I had never actually been in the crypt before. As we were not a close family, neither were we religious. I had no words to say aloud, and if Maubry was moved to speak, he did not show it. Together we pushed the lid onto my father's stone coffin and slid it into its final resting place. Next to it was an empty slot, framed in fluted stone, with the name Jacob engraved upon it. I ran my fingers over it, imagining spending all of time here, finally near my father, and wondering if by then I would have accomplished anything besides spending down the family fortunes. I saw it now, the map of my life in front of me, burning away to ashes: no family, no legacy. It was then that I noticed the opening on the far side of my father. I walked over and looked at it, but it had no name. This, then was to be my crypt, the first crypt had been for my grandfather, my namesake and it lay empty.

How had I never known this? I turned to cadaverously taciturn Maubry. He gave a slight shrug, and said, "He never returned from the dam," as if that explained everything, and then he turned and walked out to leave me alone with my thoughts.

I walked up the stairs and stepped out into the cold autumn rain. Night was falling, and I returned to my studies in the library where I had supper of cold lamb and claret. All things pointed to the dam. I slept a fitful sleep, full of dreams of dams and floods, but the floods were filled with great gelatinous beasts whose bodies were smashed together into an almost liquid mass that destroyed everything they flowed over, leaving an acrid stench. I awoke early, drenched in sweat, and immediately I knew my course. It had been charted long before I was born. Finally I had a map for my life.

I bathed and dressed and drove into town to see the lawyer and settle the estate – what little my father had left undone. I went to the mining business office which was staffed by a few grey old men in ancient suits. We looked at the books, but the mines had been shuttered since the sixties, and this office basically maintained the leases and few holdings we had. Then, I asked for the plans of the dam. After a not insignificant search, a roll of brittle blueprints was produced. I told them of my plan to remove the dam and return the area to its pristine nature, thereafter to transform it into a reserve.

The men shot each other glances and offered me a seat at a scarred table made of dark wood. With creaking voices and fluttering hands, they implored me not to do this. They begged me to abide by my grandfather's and father's wishes to leave the parcel lie as it was. When I pressed them for reasons, they became silent, and looked down at the table in front of them. Misunderstanding them, I thanked them for their service and explained to them their positions were safe as I expected to keep them on to handle the reserve. This did not seem to assure them, but I had other business to attend to and attributed their unspoken melancholy to the shock of recent events, moving on without further explanation. Oh, the things we would do over, had we but the chance.

That afternoon, I returned to the house and immediately set about outfitting an expedition to the dam, contacting members of my father's crews and local experts. I intended to survey it and begin my plan to remove it. Still, I could find no man who had ever been there or heard of it; we could find no mention of the dam, or any topography that would support a lake. The mystery deepened. We had the coordinates, but we could not find it. The best we could determine based on coordinates and topography, Eldritch Creek would have been a very minor tributary of the Roaring River, a tumultuous, cascade-infested swath of whitewater whose redeeming properties seemed largely that it was too hard to access to be spoiled. Perhaps the damming of the creek erased it? It did not occur to us that a map would be consciously inaccurate, and that all maps then based on it would be wrong.

Finally, it was decided we would trailer mules up the logging roads until we got close to the coordinates, and then use them to haul our explosives and gear to the site coordinates. We felt we could travel up the watershed to its source and explore from there. It took the rest of the week to outfit and arrange the men, and we left before dawn the Monday after Father's death. We drove from Seattle to Bellingham and headed east. From the main highways we dropped to secondary roads along the Roaring and then followed logging roads deep into the mountains and primeval stands of forest. Even the second growth trees were enough to block out the day's waning light. It was well past dark when we found what we thought was the creek, running small in what was once a much deeper channel, and we bivouacked directly in the road. Our phones lost any trace of signal hours ago. The other men were bothered by this, but I had been spending time in the bush since long before there were such devices, and had never succumbed to the vice of the electronic tether.

In the morning, I stood on the bank of the creek, looking at its preternatural straightness and flatness of the bottom. While looking at the water, windows of clarity would appear and vanish in the swirls, and as I stood looking, I ran back to camp for a glass which I held inverted in the water, peering through the bottom, a poor man's scrying glass. Soon, the men were clustered around their eccentric boss, bent over waist deep in the stream, wondering what had gotten into me. In minutes all sorts of devices were improvised from camp gear to peer into this hidden world. Our assumptions were proven true as we discovered the strange and nause-ating runes carved into every portion of the channel, there in plain sight but for the water's turbulence. We had found Eldritch Creek, deep in the shadow of the newly risen land, like an Atlantis reborn in the northern forests. With this knowledge, myself and the foreman, Waithwhite, headed out to scout our route.

While sound from a distance, our plan did not take into

account the ruggedness of the land. The tributary ran in a steep and narrow valley whose riparian habitat was blackberry, salmonberry, devil's club, and thorny maple. All of them packing spines and covering fallen old growth which could be up to six feet tall that we had to clamber over. Even with machetes, by noon we had made scant progress, and certainly nothing which mules could follow. Winter snows would surely be here before we reached our goal. We regrouped at the trucks for a meal of stew while pouring over the maps under a tarp. By now, it was raining to beat the Flood and the short, steep creek would soon be overflowing its banks. It was decided to abate for the day and to attempt one of the ridgelines the next day. We killed the remaining daylight with cribbage and brandy, telling tales of places we'd been and the strange things they held.

One man, with eyes as black as his hair, said he had fulfilled his contract and would go no further. When pressed, this is the story he told:

"My people call themselves the First Men, but we were not the First People. In your Holy Books, the center of the earth is given to the Devil. But we who do not write books, we know of the evil that calls Hell home, the beast you call Leviathan, for even after the earth formed over them, they haunt us, slumbering, dreaming of conquest and rule. The First were beings who swim on the tides of time, coming to the new Earth from the stars, and claiming Paradise as their own."

He swept his arms around. "These Cascades were once the bottom of their sea. What you see today are merely the second taking; the folding of the clay from a planet once totally unrecognizable, home to cities that would warp and weave in your mind as you looked at them; cities which changed as their builders' dreams changed."

Again, he swept his arms at the mountains. "You think it was your god who did this? It was beasts, a race of seething incomprehensible elder beings who lived ages ago and in their total war and corruption destroyed this planet, not wanting to leave for one what others could not have. They enslaved it, ate it, poisoned it beyond repair. Now they are residing in the deepest and darkest cracks we have not explored, waiting only for a moment in which we unsuspectingly bring the light to them and them to light. Dark spirits haunt these ancient woods, guardians of older and more evil creatures who lived yet deeper in the mountains. Strange things happen beyond the massif above us. Our people know to tread lightly and not tempt these beings who haunt our dreams when they are near, for our dreams come from their dreams. When you listen to these nightmares too long, that which makes you human becomes unmade, and you devolve back beyond even the clay, to become some misbegotten creature whose soul is replaced by something you cannot control, the sasquatch the white man hunts, but that you never want to find. You become a slave driven insane by appetites no human ever had, slaking them not for yourself, but for your eldritch puppet masters, your every action their bidding."

"Things my people would not wake, you have woken. When the white man trespassed above their slumbering graves, and cut the monster trees – trees that took a week to fell – sentinels of the eldritch monsters, the waking began. Then, even the white man could hear the dreams. Can you hear them now? If you do, take heed, those who trespass will not return."

Such tails darkened the group's mood and while I listened as intently as any of the men, I realized it was up to me, as their leader, to lift their spirits. I convinced them that clearly many people had been to the site and back in its day. That in the century since it was built people must clearly have been here, flown over it in a way my grandfather could not, and that while we could not currently see it, in short time, all mysteries would be revealed. I did not explain, though, that we sought one who had not returned. Talk turned more ribald, a bottle was passed around, and I monitored their libations and the time. We turned in before midnight and rose before dawn the next day. Our dark-eyed friend was gone.

When we finally made it to the ridge top, we found the remains of a narrow-gauge rail line and a steam donkey that had been there a century or more hence. This stroke of luck would surely lead to the fabled dam. Despite the bed laid for the track, the ridges were still brutal going, and we continued to use the road as a base camp for three days while we cleared the trail, until finally on the fourth day the ridge-line ran into a headwall. We sat down, dejected, and one of the men wandered off for a smoke. Presently we heard yelling and chased over to him. From his vantage on the edge of a steep slope, we could see the dam below us. There were shouts and hoots of joy, but they died away quickly under an inexplicable gloom that pervaded the area, as if there was some malignant entity here which resisted our celebration.

Half of us stayed to work out the descent, and I sent half back to the trucks to begin moving the base camp. We made the drop down the brutally steep ridgeline, often on our backsides, to the bottom of the dam. I knew from the blueprints in my father's library that the dam itself was 130 feet high, wedged into a crevice in a cliff face, yet standing below it looking up, it seemed foreign and unreal. As we stood there at the base and craned our necks to follow it to the top, I felt like I might fall over. At the bottom were a few small concrete buildings and the footing for the hydroelectric plant they never built. How those men managed to get the equipment and resources up to that rift in creation and complete this monstrosity was a feat beyond me. And here we were to tear it down. It seemed sacrilege upon sacrilege. I did not want to debase my grandfather's memory, yet I did not want my family legacy to be the disfigurement of this wild place. I resolved the conflict by telling myself that I was keeping with the spirit of my grandfather's dream, if we but differed on tactics.

The climb back up took much longer than the coming down, and we set about with what little gear we had to clear a campsite and start a fire. Interestingly, no digital electronics worked at the site, and we were reduced to manually recording our findings. I have always been a journaler. We had some time before our cohorts returned and we used that time well to survey the dam and come up with a plan to place the charges. Thomas, the Blast Master, wanted to use a series of charges from the top down to gradually reduce the dam, and this would entail a man be lowered from the top of the dam to place them. This was an intricate and tricky job and we entertained several false starts owing to the inaccessibility of the top of the dam and also that water was coming over it in a small but steady flow.

On the morning of the second day, the crew was clearing away brush from the bottom, while Thomas and I were pondering if it was even conceivable to come at the problem from the top, when we had a bit of luck, for the crew on the bottom had discovered a doorway. Thomas and I grabbed lamps and charged down the slope, skidding and bumping along. By the time we got there, the crew had pried the doors open.

I led the way up stairs crudely carved into the rock. Next to them was a pipe three feet in diameter. Once again, I marveled at the technology brought to this remote and inhospitable spot that would be hard to reach even today with all of our technology and helicopters. This must be the sluiceway for the ill-fated hydroelectric station. Water would be diverted through the pipe to run the turbines.

At the top, we passed a small control room, where the valves to operate the pipes had been smashed with a sledge hammer that still lay on the floor. We exchanged glances before moving through another door that opened into what we first thought was a vast cavern. As our eyes adjusted, we could see a faint glow to our right, and after scrambling up a scree slope, the mystery of the lake's absence from modern maps was explained. We stood at the top of a gap, above us a great cliff slanted out over our heads. Behind and below us, the land sloped steeply away to a great forest, containing trees larger than any I had ever seen. In front of us, back the way we came, was a deep cleft slanting into the earth. We must've been standing at the center of the 1904 quake where two great plates had arisen together and slipped apart, the one overlapping the other and creating a deep rift which could not be seen from above, the way you fan cards

in a deck, each hiding the one below for some prestidig-
itation.

We retraced our path to the stairs. Running along the rift
before us was a long lake, created and held back by the dam.
We stood at one end of the lake on a shore which stretched
as far as our lights could penetrate, but the glow of the gap
on our right faded into the distance. We began to follow the
shore. With the lake on our left and the sloping horizon on
our right, there was no chance we could lose our way. Presently, we were surprised to come upon a war-sized spruce-
bark canoe pulled up onto the beach. Even more to our
delight, the canoe, though over 100 years old, seemed to be
viable, due to the lack of exposure in the rift. This changed
things quite a bit, for now we could make a proper expedition out of it. Dragging the canoe to the lake we filled it with
stones and sank it to swell shut the joints for our return.

By now, even the scant daylight was fading, and as we
were not supplied for any extended trek, we returned to base
camp, by which time it was full nightfall. Our comrades were
not due back for at least another day, so we turned in early
and had fitful sleep. At breakfast, the men looked haggard
and were reticent to converse, but gradually it came out that
to a man we had had strange dreams, oddly parallel, of half-
seen horrors swimming through obsidian depths. Further,
the few who had managed to swim to the surface of these
dreams in the search for sanctuary in consciousness, heard
strange shouts and hollers from above the ridge behind us.
Each relayed the same thought that at first, they thought they
might still be dreaming, but that the chants were accompanied by disgusting, cloyingly acrid smells. All of these stories
were lent veracity by the fact that we each felt nauseated, and

few had more than coffee and crackers to break our fast. I was reminded of similar comments in my grandfather's journal about the hieroglyphic stones.

Leaving Thomas in charge, I chose as my companions Waithwhite, boon companion on many an adventure, and Roffino, a steady man who had seen many terrible things in Afghanistan without blanching. Soon, we had loaded our equipment, and left word with those remaining in camp for the returning party to hold fast for our return. I admit, that even amongst all of the strangeness and the bizarre qualities of this world, yet inside me, the angler still existed. Starting from my youth, I have never traveled far without my full fly kit, with rods ranging from three to twelve weight, as often the chance to fish presents itself in my travels, and for all of the effort of packing it around, I have only missed it the more the times I did not have it. While the lake showed all the signs of being barren and sterile, I was reminded of the life in deep ocean vents and thought to myself that strange things come from strange places and that perhaps here in my very own backyard, so to speak, might I finally catch a species which could, in some small way, carry on my family name? I still sought my father's approval for my pastime, I suppose.

And so, late in the morning, myself, Roffino, and Waithwhite emptied the stones from the canoe, floated it and stowed our gear, and set out on our expedition with no real idea if the lake were a single mile or a score of miles long. The curves of the fissure were such that in some places we could see the horizon to our left for a long way ahead, and at times our way twisted and turned like a river losing the horizon entirely. Without landmarks, there was no sense of scale and soon we were lost in our own wayward thoughts as we paddled along.

In a pique of optimism, I threaded up my twelve weight rod with a heavy sinking line and a long dark streamer, and behind that I trailed a smaller phosphorescent streamer on a 3X tippet, so that I was rigged for beast large or small. Thus, we continued in permanent twilight. We ate lunch in the boat and noticed a very small current back towards the dam as we sat. Once off the littoral edge of the beach, no soundings touched bottom, and the dreams of the night before and the hellish landscape we found ourselves in, made it all too easy to imagine this rift reaching to the very center of the earth. We conversed for a bit, but gradually fell silent. I could not shake the feeling we were being watched.

By our watches, it was a full day that we paddled, and still the rift continued. As the faint luminescence faded, we debated camping rough or continuing on. At that moment, we pulled ashore to stretch and consider our plans. By mere luck or fate I will never know, but where we pulled ashore we found round stones the size of a hassock strewn about. I was sitting on one, thoroughly tired from our labors when Waithwhite mentioned the rocks. As a geologist by trade, he was merely making conversation when he mentioned that we had not seen such loose stones anywhere else about the chasm.

I stood up and unshielded the lantern to consider them, something we had not done all day to protect our night vision. Indeed, not only were stones strewn about, but it looked like a great cairn had been smashed. As we walked among the stones, we began to find loose bones, as if a skeleton had been torn bone-from-bone, flung about, and then each separate bone pulverized where it lay. A deep suspicious dread began to grow in my stomach when Roffino shouted he had found something. We scrambled over to be near him, and in his hand he held an oilskin-wrapped leather journal identical to the one I had back at camp.

My worst fears confirmed, I unwrapped it and peered at it in the dim lamp light. It was indeed the sister to the journal I had found in the library, the final exploits of my grandfather, whose grave this must be. Who had made the cairn? Where were those to tell the tale? And what primordial being had so cleverly dissected the tomb and desecrated the body? There was no debate when I called for returning to the boat immediately and making for camp, exhaustion notwithstanding. We had a quick, cold supper of salami and cheese and headed out.

Here the water was wide as a true lake, and the lanterns were of no use. Without the faint sunlight, we navigated by the echoes of our splashing paddles, resting occasionally and letting the currents straighten our path. At times, we dozed in our seats, with an unspoken agreement to not return to shore. I had, I admit, forgotten my line trailing us in the water, when it was struck so hard the entire rod nearly left the boat. Line screamed off the reel. I jerked out of my doze and grabbed the rod. The fish was running towards the bow and actually pulling the boat, or I'm sure he would've snapped the line, as there was no way I could stop this behemoth. I have caught sturgeon, shark, and marlin on the fly, but nothing on my line ever pulled like this.

Suddenly wide awake, I feared for the line and I feared for the rod as I worked every sinew and tendon to fight this beast. In retrospect, I am thankful for the ferocity of the battle for it kept my mind from dwelling on just what I may have caught. And so, it went through the night, the fish pulling us steadily, me winning by inches, losing by feet. If my back was tired from paddling, it felt broken from working the rod. Eventually, the rod began to fracture, breaking into splinters on the tensioned side away from the guides.

But then slowly, ever so slowly, I started to gain on the fish, the constant drag of the boat must've finally taken its toll. Time had lost all meaning, but ever so faintly the crack to the left began to define its existence when we finally brought the fish to the boat. Roffino in the middle thwart gaffed the fish and tried to pull it in, but the weight threatened to capsize us. On hands and knees, I worked my way forward to see what my labors had wrought. There in the black water was a fish, or fish-like silver being, whose head began like a cutthroat, if cutthroat had teeth like wolverines and heads the size of grizzlies, transitioning to a long snake-like body nearly the length of the boat, but along the way, where I would expect fins, were - I know not. Tentacles. Claws. Barnacle-like gaping pustules with circular rows of teeth, irised like a camera lens. Wounds seemed to form and heal, and with its last breath, it gave a shriek that echoed from the roof of the cavern and left us all cowering in the bottom of the canoe, hands over ears. I was glad Roffino had not managed to boat it. We agreed to rope it to the gunwale and continue our journey, and despite my horror and exhaustion, I rested assured that my legacy was now decided, though had I the imagination to see the metaphor in attaching my name to this monster, I may have cut it loose the very moment I first hooked it.

Time was a river we were hooked to, but we knew not its length. At first, we conversed about the beast lashed to our bulwarks, but eventually even our excitement faded back into exhaustion. Thus it was, we were drifting languorously when the water erupted on the far side of the boat and an ebon tentacle shot out of the depths to smash Roffino through the bottom of the craft like driving a nail through a banana, the resulting impact shooting Waithwhite and I up into the air and dumping us in the water. In a panic, we made for shore while the dread creature lifted poor Roffino into the air and summarily dismembered him as we listened to his screams. In that moment, I somehow became certain that this was not only the species that had killed my grandfather, but the very same creature. It then proceeded to do similarly to the craft, the water erupting with each blow as parts of boat and man rained down on us. This fury the monster wasted on the inanimate object of the boat, combined with the narrowness of the lake at that point, I'm sure, saved our lives as were stumbling ashore when the creature finished its obliterations.

Even as we crawled and scrambled upright, Waithwhite was grabbed by the ankle by a sinuous tentacle that moved not like a mindless appendage, but more like a self-conscious snake. Unthinking, I drew my belt knife and leapt upon it. My stabs being ineffective against the force dragging him backwards, I began slashing at it in an attempt to cut it until at last it let go. I half-lifted, half-dragged him up the beach, just as a score of similar appendages came raining down from the sky and smashed the rocks where we had hence been. The accompanying howls of rage drove us to our knees as we covered our ears for the second time that evening. You have heard of the kraken? The beast whose number is affixed in our minds born half of imagination, half of the evil formed in the Downfall, described by mad sailors as "round, flat, and full of arms, or branches," and is "the largest and most surprising of all the animal creation?" This was our enemy.

The blows and screams continued as the creature blindly sought us out and we scuttled, crab-like, up the bank, before we stood and ran. The tantrum continued unabated, whipping the near-shore water into a froth until, at its crescendo, it stopped suddenly and within seconds there was no trace of our adventure. I crashed to my knees and fell forward prostrate, only then aware of the journal still wedged within my shirt. Judge me if you will, I confess, in that moment, I celebrated that reclaimed artifact more than I mourned Roffino. By then, I had gained and lost more in a night than I had in a lifetime. I was more tired than I had ever been and not even sure how I was going to make it to my knees, let alone camp. However, the thought that no rescue was coming reached some reserve as deep and unknown as the chasm whose brink we tottered on.

Finally, by silent consent, as if words weighed too much to lift from our throats to our tongues, we rose, put our arms around each other, and stumbled towards the dam. The one bit of luck in the entire endeavor was that the monstrous fish had pulled us nearly home, for while we wandered in near-unconscious haze, we made it to the landing at the edge of the dam before collapse, and there our party found us soon after. I do not remember much, if anything, about the next day. They said we in turn ranted in delirium and at times had to be restrained, while at other times they put mirrors before our nostrils to check for life. On the morning of the second day I awoke and stumbled out to the cook fire where I was met with expressions equal parts of surprise and relief. Waithwhite was there, wrapped in a blanket, holding a mug of cocoa. He smiled sheepishly at me, and I back at him. It was only then I noticed his hair had gone stark white.

By the collective silence I could tell that the team was waiting for me to tell the tale. It was only later that I found out Waithwhite had gone mute, and I never again saw him without that simple grin on his face. I think it was only out of respect for me as the leader and boss, and the clear physical degradation of our bodies that people believed even a tenth of our tale. But it mattered not. As I relived the events, I became even more resolute that we must finish our work, destroy the dam, and eliminate the lurking evils that festered behind it. Only by removing this monument to my grandfather's calculated greed and arrogance could we restore nature to its rightful balance. In doing so, I would also get my revenge on the creatures that had taken not just my grandfather, but also my trusted friend. Though I was still weak and feverish, I was immediately galvanized to action.

The men left in camp had not been idle in our absence, and they outlined the plan. Thomas had been studying the flow over the dam, and while he could not estimate the volume of water in the lake, he could estimate the flow rate for each foot of the dam removed. In this way, we could reduce the dam in a series of controlled explosions, slowly draining the lake without flooding the valleys downstream. I was impatient with the plan, as I felt it would take a considerable time commitment to execute, but after long discussion, there seemed to be no other way. Ever the professional, anticipating this, Thomas had placed the first charge while I was incapacitated. We agreed to send message back to the base camp so they could be prepared in the eventuality of some catastrophe, but Thomas was very confident that he could "shave that peach" in as fine an increment as we desired. At that time, I also ordered the procurement of weapons of higher caliber, several small canons such as you might mount on the bow of a yacht, to be brought up to the dam. When the last of the water dropped, we would go hunting the beast which had come hunting us, but this time he would be in our element.

We waited until the next day to make sure that base camp was alerted and blew the charge immediately after breakfast. I had imagined more of a festive spirit would emerge with the event, but our adventures had dampened that and the mood at camp was more edgy, as people watched the water spill. I decided that it was best to put a watch on the blast site while we made ready about camp. Thomas took the first watch to make his measurements and keep an eye out for any problems.

The adrenaline of the moment passing, I found myself quite weak. Clearly, I was not yet over my travails. The project underway, I returned to my tent for rest. Passing through the flap, with my head ducked at an odd angle, caused my eye to rest on the oilskin-wrapped journal from my grandfather's cairn tucked under the clothes that had been stripped off of me during my prostration. I slapped my forehead; the journal had entirely slipped my mind until this moment! Pouring myself a brandy to bolster my nerve, I sat on a camp stool and opened the book. It was a twin to the first, written in the same neat, cramped hand, as if he didn't want to waste an em-dash of space on the page. This was a different story told, though. I thumbed quickly through the beginning that related getting the equipment here and building the dam. (Although, I was still fascinated by these logistics, I needed now to know how to combat the mysteries behind that wall.)

The earthquakes never abated but continued to rumble and grind. Whole hillsides slump and slide off, burying the once-exposed riches. I am getting frantic to get the power up before the earth re-swallows its horde. The men are already working seven days a week, so I have offered them shares in the venture to keep on.

I flipped forward a few pages.

At first the lake itself was not accessible. It was only as the dam grew and the water rose that it came out from under the shelf to be navigable. As always, I was excited to explore this new frontier, so I commissioned a canoe for this purpose from several of the woodsmen on the crew. As the lake fills, so too does the tension around the project. The men have started having strange dreams of grotesque underwater monstrosities. People who ventured to the edge of the plateau hear strange screeches and drumming, although we know the area to be uninhabited.

We are also witnessing strange happenings. Mushrooms the size of fire hydrants are sprouting in the environs. If cut, they dissolve into gray gelatinous masses of putrid odor. Being an educated man, I dismissed the first reports as the workers' imaginations getting the better of them after being long from home in this foreign place. The evening the sluice opened, though, the sequestered evil behind the dam made itself apparent by undeniable means. A group of men were below the dam in the stream fishing for salmon which had come home to spawn, the tribulations of the tortured earth ignored by their overwhelming instincts. Never asking more from the men than I can deliver, I was up at the construction site working into the night with my trusted lieutenant Xander when I heard shrieks and screams from the fishermen. Being so close, we were the first to the spot, to find the pool full of shredded corpses and bits of men. The one man who was left alive had his leg amputated below the knee and was rapidly bleeding out. As Xander tied a tourniquet on him the dying man told a story of salmon with brutal fangs like dogs rising up from the water and attacking the party. It happened so fast, they were all cut down before they could get to shore.

I have spent some time in the Amazon, and so have some experience with such tales, but I do not think piranha are in these waters, and I could not afford panic among the men. Despite our efforts, the man bled out. I drew my pistol and emptied it into the far bank. By then other men were converging upon us. I told them the anglers were put upon by wolves, which I could not hit in the dark, and we would shut down the site and hunt them in the morning. Until then, the men were forbade from the river, lest the wolves still be around.

It was the measure of my grandfather's genius that he was so able to sum up a situation, even one as gruesome and fantastical as the one that confronted him, and instantly make a decision. He understood that an unknown evil would unman his crew, but that a known evil would give them something to rally around. In the meantime, he also surmised that whatever had attacked the men came from behind the dam, and perhaps had returned whence.

Quickly, Xander and I gathered provisions and ascended to the lake to take the canoe. On the way, we smashed the valves diverting water from the lake into irreparable ingots, for I was sure the demon spawn came from the sluiceway and not from the river. Once on the lake, I strung a rod, in the hopes of catching whatever had attacked the men. Both Xander and I had the uneasy feeling that we were being watched or stalked. We would hear large splashes in the distance echoing in the cave in such a way that their source was hard to make out. Once, a v-wake lapped the side of the boat, as if we had just been passed by something larger on the surface, but not a nibble on my fly.

Perhaps it was the brandy, perhaps my remaining fever, but reading such tales when you know what these mysteries portend is hard to do, I had to steel myself to it. I had met the architect of his fate and had escaped it myself only by luck. These two men, pressing on in the dark and unknown to solve this mystery even after they had seen the horror on the creek below, it is hard to imagine in this day men so brave, or a friendship so true. I think they imagined not the scale of the monsters they sought, for surely they were not prepared. Their mission was typical of that age, assuming that by might, right, and will, they could suppress anything that stood in the way of their expansion and greed. And like so many such missions, this one was doomed before it started. I reflected that the creature may even have sent its minions out into the stream as lures, a great fisherman in its cavern, awaiting its prey as it slowly reeled them in.

Like us, nothing happened that first night and they had rested and slept, awaking to the sliver of light on the right-hand horizon and decided to continue on for one more day.

This was the last entry in the journal, but I can guess what happened from the scene I found. They must've landed on the far shore where we found his demolished crypt.

There the beast attacked and killed my grandfather. Xander, and a truer companion could never be found, in his grief, in the dark and stalked by unknown horrors, took days to build that tomb, although how long it lasted before that mad creature attacked it and obliterated any trace of the man, we will never know. An unlearned man, he probably did not see the value in the journal and buried it with my grandfather in the dark. I imagine the creature struck while he was at his labors and like us, Xander most likely made his escape during the insane wrath and made it back to the dam where we found his boat. It must have been his resolute hands on the sledge that smashed the valves, stilling the dam works until we rediscovered them.

I became aware of a distant booming, and putting down the book, I bolted my brandy and went outside. There the men were looking over at the dam, which shook, bulging visibly, over and over again, like a woman demon-pregnant, with hell spawn's berserk force hammered at her belly from within. The very ground shook so that it was hard to walk in a straight line and I lurched over to Thomas like a drunk on a typhoon-beset steamer. Thomas's face looked pale as I walked up to him. So intent was he in looking at the phenomenon that it took a moment to break his reverie. He didn't say a word, but merely pointed to a crack in the very center of impact. A crack that grew with each resounding blow.

Immediately, I began bellowing orders to the crew who were riveted in place by disbelief, horror, and fascination. I thought I did not need to see the outcome of this assault to learn of the perpetrator. I assumed I had seen the king of the depths, but I was about to learn that I had only met the least of his court. Men ran about collecting important tools and data as we began a hasty retreat to higher ground. Water began to pour from the crack and with it wriggling crawling things began to squeeze through and grab the sides of the fissure as if it could be wrest asunder.

Oh, hubris! At every turn, my recklessness had been exposed and the soundness of my grandfather's decree had been re-enforced, and yet I had steadfastly maintained my course of lunacy. The dam wasn't the center of some Utopian bliss, if that had ever been its intended purpose at all, it was a prison, locking away forces beyond comprehension. A prison never completed because of my grandfather's death. It had been wiped off the map in a vain attempt to thwart the arrogant actions of men such as myself which would unleash horrors unknown. My father had tried to tell me and run out of time. The dry and dusty old men in the office tasked with keeping the secret had not rectified their charge with my headstrong and impulsive decision upon my inheritance. And now, I had handed the keys to the portal to the inmates within.

What had taken a crew of men almost three years to create, was rendered asunder in mere moments by the most unnatural collection of creatures ever assembled within this universe. One moment, the fissure was reeling with jets of water and squirming appendages, the next, it exploded as if Thomas had blown in it one orgiastic riot. A wall of water 130 feet high filled our little valley and created a shock wave in front of it that blew the leaves off trees before blowing them right out of the ground.

When we fill in the map of life, we start to say "this thing is like that thing" and it gives us words and images to share our experiences. When the dam on Eldritch Creek came down, there was nothing any human has ever seen or dreamed that can compare. The only thing that would open the doors of comprehension the slightest crack would be to say that "all Hell broke loose," because surely some elder god had created a prison deep within this earth and locked away his first attempts at creation, abominations of the highest order. One can only hope they were not created in the image of their maker, for if that being exists we are all doomed asunder. To describe them would be impossible, for like shadows on the surface of a canvas tent, any representations seemed mere projections of the actual beast, which flickered in and out of comprehension as if it spanned multiple dimensions.

In that wall of water was a ball of protoplasm, all arms and eyes and mouths, continually forming, deforming, and reforming faster than the eye could follow or the mind could fathom. Creatures that have slept in their crypts since before time, now brought into the sunlight ravenous with a million years of fasting. A billion years? Men who were close to the bank were sucked in by huge tentacles, and as soon as the creek was full to the edges, the monstrosities began crawling out, hunting and destroying with equal ferociousness. The air was cacophonous with the great roar of the water, the pounding of the creatures upon their captor the earth, and the dying screams of rent humans. I stood, I admit, too over-whelmed to move; no decisions could my brain make; no thoughts could my mind form.

Thomas shoved me, a carbine in one hand, ammo in the other, Thomas herded me over the ridge away from the horror through brambles and over logs at breakneck speed.

There was no time to breathe or pause for minor injury. We made it down to the next valley and arduously up to the top of the next ridge, before we turned to face our fate. Behind us was such a surfeit of fecundity and alien life, it rolled over the ridgeline stripping it to the bedrock like a tsunami of hate and animus, growing with each bit of organic matter so that as it came it was like a wave ever-growing in rapaciousness and horror. The shattering of the trees, the howling of the demonic horde was almost more than my ears could take. Who could fathom that the center of the earth held such a cosmos of reeling malice?

And then slowly, so slowly that at first I could not countenance it, a mound began to grow on the horizon and a huge bulbous beast, the size of a stadium, tentacles like trains, began to summit the ridge. Although in the din I could not make out any specific difference, I sensed somehow that the presence of this beast marshalled the horde before us, and that for the first time, they acted not blindly, but took notice of us and began to converge upon on our position.

I am sure the rest of the crew is gone and that these are the last few minutes of our life. Thomas is carefully aiming and firing at the elder god. Perhaps this insane act is an effort to stay sane in his last moments, for in man there is a great defiance, a gnashing, frantic energy that he expends against nature, fate - even God - and I am proud to be taking my last breaths upon this stage as he sets the standard of bravery and futility simultaneously. Mayhap, other men with such strenuous tenacity will survive to someday overcome despair and challenge this monstrosity as it swallows the world.

Unfortunately, this tale does not traverse the arc of hubris, wisdom, and salvation; but rather folly, horror, and damnation. I laugh. Am I giddy? Does his effort deserve such a response? Is this the final cosmic joke and our nugatory efforts the punchline? I contemplate my foolhardiness, to judge my forefathers without the context of history, ignorantly trying to do what I thought was right, and taking us all down this path to destruction. In these last moments, you might think me mad to brood over my failures while my boon companion fights the good fight. But I am not mad, and I am not vain. Even as I fear I may have doomed all humanity, I am insane with optimism that somehow, I am not bearing witness to the last act, but the first, and that humanity will re-establish itself, will crawl back out from whatever dark orifice we are driven into to survive this roiling maleficence we face, and that we will learn the true story of our errors.

As I look up, I realize it does not matter, the creature has surmounted the ridge and rides down on the lives of its minions, leaving a pulpy mass in its wake. I look at the multifarious beast, the million waving arms, the myriad of chasmal mouths, the multitudinous eyes, I somehow feel that all of its primal malevolence is at this moment directed at extinguishing Thomas and me. Perhaps there was some deep and subtle kinship betwixt this creature and the creature I caught in the abyss, for it comes on with a palpable single-minded animosity that assures me I am most definitely not leaving this mortal coil for a better place.

The dice are cast and summed, and evil has won this roll, but for how long? How long?

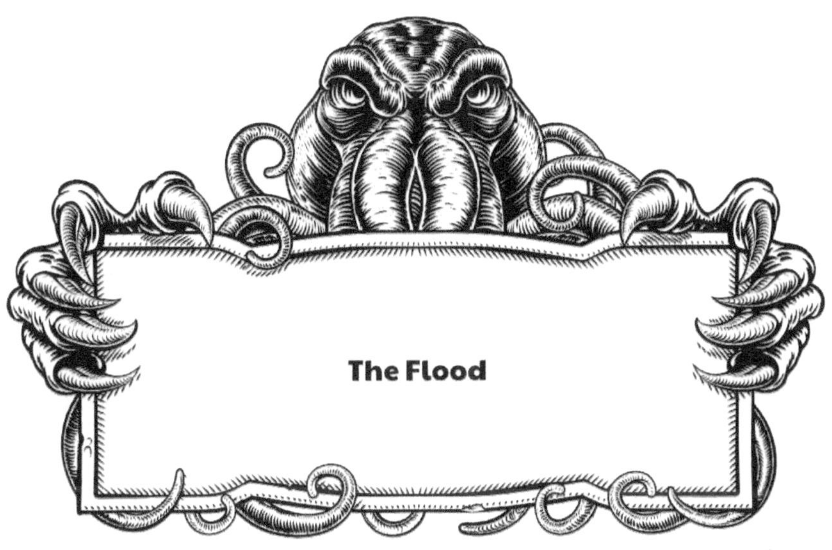

BY OLIVER LODGE

Genesis 7:4 - *"[I] will cause it to rain... and every living substance that I have made will I destroy from off the face of the earth."*

OUR FATHER THOUGHT he was teaching us a lesson when he stripped us of our clothes and locked us in the basement. Our misdeed was so harmless that I no longer remember what it was. What I do remember is that it was out of character for him. That my brother and I both agreed on once the dreadful event had come to an end. Our father was always a fair and gentle man if not somewhat sad and withdrawn. We came from a wealthy family, and though Dad spent most of his time in his library, what he was unable to express to us in terms of affection, he made up to us with his generosity. He owned hundreds of acres of the most coveted real estate in

all of New Orleans. Our backyard was a lavish garden exten-
sively furbished with a variety of rare plants and flowers
from exotic lands. The mansion we called home was an
architectural relic from bygone centuries. It brought visitors
from around the world who'd take photographs from
outside of its towering gates of iron wrapped in
bougainvillea and black raspberry cultivar. When our minia-
ture personas weren't being carefully cultivated by the finest
tutors on the veranda, we were being taught in private
schools of the most illustrious ilk.

Caretaking was always handled by the hired help and our
mother. It was after her passing that there was a turnover in
staff, and the duties of our supervision temporarily fell upon
our grieving dad. Surely stemming from the despair of
having lost our mother, he flew into a rage one evening and
threw everyone out of the house save for the two of us. Not
wanting us to see him in tears for the first time in our young
lives, he resorted to banishing us to the basement without
food or clothing for an entire three days. I was five years my
brother's elder. He was the frail age of six at the time. I'd
always been the stronger sibling. I still feel a gut-wrenching
pang of guilt when I recall how I'd placed my neediness
above his. I was sobbing uncontrollably on the freezing,
damp floor during that second evening in confinement. Out
of pity for me and fear for our mutual welfare, he comforted
me by running his emaciated fingers through the lush curls
of my sandy hair. I wanted so badly to fend off the terrible
cold that had infiltrated the marrow of my tender bones.
Without thinking, my lips found his after having turned
around to see the beacon of his pale, angelic face floating
before me like the glorious light of escape revealed to a fugi-

tive crossing freedom's finish line. I was the older sister who had always watched over my shy, little brother. Now I wielded the same authority over him as his lover. I had him fulfill every desire I could imagine, and some I'd invented anew on the spot, while we served out the remainder of our punishment in the dark chasm which lay beneath our picturesque abode.

If we hadn't already been unnaturally close, we were virtually inseparable following our release from captivity. There was something about the fragrance of his luminescent skin: silky, translucent, and unmarred by the tragedy known as wisdom. It whetted my appetite for the taste of his fledgling lips and cleansing touch. He was my flower; I, a bee hovering before his succulent stamen, moving in again and again to lure the sleek balm of his essence into my acquisitive insides. He never denied me love no matter how irascible my hunger, and our passionate trysts lasted long enough to break records.

His gaunt body was hexed with the same malignant genes responsible for killing off half of my mother's decrepit ancestry, only he was never granted the experiences of adulthood that even the sickest of our relatives lived to see. I barely said a word at his funeral, nor did I cry. Intellectually, I knew he was gone but failed to internalize the loss. His demise did not prevent me from fantasizing about him for hours throughout the day. My grades took a turn for the worst. I began to engage in dangerously promiscuous behavior in high school. There wasn't a single member of the opposite sex who couldn't have had my body for the taking. All he had to do was approach me. Though they filled me with revulsion, I'd engage in these destructive flings at an unprecedented rate. I didn't just have sex with other men to punish myself and blot out my grief; I also did this in a blind and irrational quest to find a partner as idyllic as my deceased brother.

None of them came close.

Our father soon got wind of my lascivious escapades, and, in a fury not unlike the one that precipitated his offspring's exile to the basement, stripped me down to my panties and whipped me viciously, leaving serpentine welts around my waist and back. He disowned me and had me ousted from the family home.

After many years of prostitution in the streets of Marrero and the surrounding West Bank, I was no longer recognizable as the rich, young princess from the days of old. Crystal meth had completely ruined me. My arms were covered with sores. I'd even scratched out one of my corneas during a particularly excessive stint of drug use, leaving a swollen opaque globe of scar tissue to take the place of my eye. Untreated staph infection had cauterized almost all of my veins shut. My neck became the only place that still accepted compulsory visits from the needle.

I was squatting in an abandoned motel on Tulane and Canal with my boyfriend during the drought that would precede the worst calamity in human history. Many of the roadways had melted from the unbearable heat of summer that year. The sewer system stopped functioning and we had to boil what little water we had. Children, the disabled, and the elderly started dropping off like flies from exposure, dehydration, and dysentery. After a summer without seeing so much as a drop of water it finally started to rain. Wrapped in broad stripes of pink and black hose with my knees bent in and kissing one another like a marionette without a puppeteer, I was sitting in an oak chair by the window in a barren, empty flat. I remember the day lucidly for I'd come home with some money in the early afternoon after my boyfriend had beaten me the night before, demanding that I get back to work on the streets and return with the sum he'd come to expect from me. Though I'd been dreadfully ill and suffering from a severe bout of scabies, I went out to hustle up some more tricks before the sun had risen in hopes that my partner wouldn't take the high road, leaving me to fend for myself. Sure enough, I came back to discover him gone. I cried after having let fall a shower of dollar bills around my feet. I didn't cry over having lost my boyfriend, but because I'd been deserted once again by a man who could never manage to fill the monstrous void defining my life.

Eerily similar to the Great Flood of 1921, a natural disaster which had occurred after the Pueblo Indians had danced for months in an effort to summon the rain to provide them with relief from a torturous drought, the pitter-patter of raindrops outside the light of my window presaged the storm that would go down in history as ten times more devastating than Hurricane Katrina. The news had underestimated the extent of damage it would bring. Nonetheless, only about 5% of the city's population stuck around to find this out. This discovery would be to everyone's detriment, including myself, as I was one of the few who'd stayed on.

At first the rain had a unifying effect on the remaining residents. Food was shared communally. We drank and got high by candlelight. But as the water levels rose, so did our fears. I had run out of money, and my connections had all fled the scene. By boosting endorphin and dopamine levels through sex with random partners, I attempted to counteract the agonizing symptoms of withdrawal from methamphetamine. I was sandwiched between the floor and a stranger on top of me when the memory of my brother came surging back into my consciousness with a force unparalleled to anything I'd felt before. A vision of his compassionate white face drifted into my mind. My temples rang like a gong when his voiceless image occupied the aching gray matter inside my skull. He was calling to me from his tomb. I came to the realization that I would not survive the disaster that had befallen the Crescent City, and the only one I wanted to be with in my final hours was my dear brother. It made no difference that he was now just a vestige of his once living form because I'd soon be meeting him on the other side of that border separating the realm of the living and the dead anyway. The closer I could be to him when I entered the mysterious netherworld of Death, the better. With a strength I didn't know I possessed, I slid out from under one of my tricks, pushing him backwards before fleeing into the rain.

I was moving at a hurried gait when I left for St. Louis Cemetery on Esplanade. By the time I got there I was wading through an ocean of dirty water and heaps of mushy trash. Powerful waves of mud had sucked many of the cadavers out of their coffins. They floated around my brother's mausoleum with lost abandon. The nasturtiums and Japanese barberry shrubs around the base of the majestic monument had been uprooted along with the chocolate lilies – gloomy flowers pollinated by flies, which used to stand guard on the outer periphery of my brother's resting place with the poise of monks mourning the sins of mankind. Withered and dried up from the drought, all that remained of the elaborate greenery surrounding the shrine that'd held my brother's remains in its breast were a tangled mass of vines, unmanaged and overgrown from neglect. They had fused together into a protective wreath, sealing him off from the external world. I gasped for air as a torrent of polluted waves crashed over my head, the whole time clawing through the tight embrace of the thick, spinose cords. The scaly petals of the African acacias crumbled away in my hands and scratched the skin of my forearms as I pulled away the vines covering the entrance to his tomb above the ground. Stinging trichomes and glochids from the branches of the agaves tore into my flesh, their stiff, sharp thorns drawing profuse trickles of blood from my veins. Beyond these still were the forest num-nums, a prickly shrub bedecked with star-shaped flowers and fruit as bloated as vulvas in estrus. These diabolical flora contributed to my mutilation by slicing into my frenzied hands and arms with their spinescent stipules, releasing an upsurge of crimson from my shredded skin to mix with the muddy brine around me.

My lungs had completely filled with water by the time I'd finally reached my brother to die in his skeletal arms within that magnificent temple - the mausoleum encapsulating the watery grave we now shared together.

BY MICHAEL CLARK

Half past the hour, Victor had to hurry, standing in the shower washing the blood off his body from this morning's vivisection. Dressing quickly, he looked at his pocket watch. The train would arrive soon and as always there was the sense of urgency gnawing at his spine. He hadn't found any larva for the past three weeks but at least these vessels would not be viable now. There was a knock on the door and Victor froze. He hadn't had time to tidy up.

"Sir, you wanted a notice when it was eight," the voice came through the door.

"Indeed. Thank you." Victor relaxed.

"Shall I have the maid up with tea or coffee?"

"No."

"Then will you be checking out? Shall I send for a valet?"

"No. Damn it, go away," spat Victor at his unseen foe that irritated him like a fly.

Victor had no need of food now. He only traveled with a rucksack, in which he kept a few tools and books which he now scooped up haphazardly. His clothes he bought as they were soiled and what was soiled, he burned.

Looking at the sun and again inspecting the time piece, he put it away and grabbed the sack and headed out of the window. He did not wish to be delayed with some inane dance with the manager. Nor have his works here discovered too soon. He would slip down the makeshift fire escape ladder and melt into the crowd of some street market. He needed to stop it, here, now, once and for all. Nothing else mattered.

———

VICTOR'S TIME in India seemed to have gone on forever. Although it had only been a few short months. The squalor, heat, and crowding made him anxious. He was at once glad that it would move again, but this time with the terrible thought that it would move to a large city, harder to contain. If that was the case he would have only one shot now to stop it before he lost control and mass sterilization became the only option.

Walking into the train station the heat went from unbearable to just tolerable. Victor wiped the sweat off his brow and straightened himself. Were it not for the stench of urine overshadowing the spicy smell of curry and other scents from the food vendors, it might have almost been pleasant. As it was, he questioned why anyone lived like this.

In the corner prostitutes plied their trade with one lucky patron leaning against the wall as a young woman spoke magic to his member. Victor might have paused to watch for a moment, but he didn't want to miss the train's arrival. He didn't want to miss it as he had in London. It had already eaten and gone dormant so it would be hard to spot. It would be slow and patient.

Victor passed a news stand. Mostly old magazines and secondhand books. But one paper, the local rag he guessed, stood out. Not just because of its new look but the headline 'Blood cult suspect captured.' He grinned at the sight of it. If only, he thought.

The story in the paper made it out to be a straightforward case. Seventy grizzly killings, the corpses drained of blood. The organs of some removed in a clean and organized manner and laid about the room, while others were found in dumpsters partly liquified by some unknown means.

A clean trail to the killer, a madman that freely admitted to these killings. When they found him eating the flesh off his arm there was no doubt in the authority's mind. This was an easy and convenient close to the case. Further inquiry would have seen through the ruse but why would they want to? No one would want to see the deeper truth. The mind can scarcely comprehend the madness in the universe as it was. The depths of its darkness and that It was an old one at work. The foul creature had no doubt offered the mad man redemption, perhaps even peace.

It was a piece of luck. Victor had gotten sloppy, frantic even, these past weeks. But just as he thought the police would close in, the mad man suddenly appeared to save him. The only question was why? His arrest would have been a good thing for the cult. He tried to comprehend, but how does one comprehend this madness even with a deeply disturbed mind?

Victor had so far been unable to track it effectively; it moved mostly at night, always one step ahead, unpredictable. Always inhabiting the bodies the police had found even as Victor sought to destroy as many vessels as possible. It drove its victims and acquaintances to madness as it went.

But in the past week the trail had run cold. Victor knew that meant it would move soon. Today. This time to a busier, bigger city, perhaps Tokyo? There the sight of slithering tentacles and a gaping maw might simply go unnoticed as some twisted manga cosplay.

Victor couldn't let his guard down this time. A crash of dishes distracted him from his current thoughts. Then he heard the tinny squeal of a railway car wheel as it rounded a distant bend. Victor's gut churned in sickness and he broke into a sweat. He looked around. The denizens of this squalor were still moving through their day.

This place is old, haunted, rotting inside, never letting go of its horrific past. The architecture not unlike that in England a century ago. No doubt a hold over to colonialism. You would hardly know it was 2018. His mouth dried in a wave of panic. *Did it travel a different path? Perhaps even a different station? Was I late or early?* Victor turned it over in his mind. But he was sure he was not wrong. Turning to walk the length of the station, Victor found a gaunt man, well dressed, with dark glasses and a bowler hat sitting at a small table at what amounted to a small coffee shop. The tattoo on his hand instantly broadcast that he was a high inquisitor.

"Victor come sit. We have time," he said as though they

were long lost friends. "Come, come boy. It's far too hot to carry on this parlay standing."

In spite of his best judgment Victor did sit, his bag now resting next to him.

"Such a beautiful country, India. Don't you think? Coffee? It's quite good, pour yourself some," he said pointing at the small ceramic pot. Victor played along. But he was sure a half dozen men might appear as he poured the cup. "Generally, I prefer tea, but I enjoy the bitter taste of death and acid on a day like today," the inquisitor said.

"This place is a shamble. Disease and suffering. Starvation and corruption," Victor retorted as he sat back with his cup.

"Indeed. I feel that this place might never even notice when my master arrived. They might even find it to their liking," the man said and chuckled a little.

"What do you want?" Victor asked.

"I do admire you, Victor. Envy you, even. How it does not bother you to stand alone against certain oblivion. Yet here you are, again."

Victor did not understand what the inquisitor was getting at. "What else would I do until I die?"

"That is the question. It takes quite a different meaning for you does it not?" he said. "Most fail once and fall into a peaceful slumber of darkness. But that makes you so extraordinary, to fail so many times, seemingly without end."

"I do what I can to stop you. The fact that we are sitting here tells me you have grown worried. I think, and correct me if I am wrong, I may have eliminated all but the last Larva," Victor said.

The man smiled. "Arrogance must be the trait that has led you through so many lives. You have lost touch with reality if you think you are winning. Tell me, when you waded in the guts of those poor prostitutes this morning, did you tell yourself it was noble, Jack?"

"As I said I do what I can to stop the spread of the spores in the wombs of the forsaken. Jack is a name the papers gave me in London, I prefer you not use it."

"Wombs of the forsaken? That does sound like the title of a delicious movie. Why don't you like the name? I find it profoundly flattering, 'Jack, the Ripper.'" He took a sip of the acrid swill he mistook for coffee. "What do you think it is Jack? Genetic Memory? Perhaps some metaphysical entanglement that affords you your immortality? How do you transfer from avatar to avatar? You have no idea do you? Nor why?"

"What does it matter? The universe has seen fit to give me this tool to defeat you and the old masters you serve."

"Really? Did you think our master was so limited? Oh, this place you mistake for a universe will fall. It's just a cyst in space time waiting to be lanced. Look at this place, in entropy, a cancer, why fight it?"

The two men sat silently for a few moments. Each contemplating his own thoughts. "I suppose I should thank you for the appearance of the mad man," Victor said as he sipped the coffee. Fishing to see what the inquisitor's reaction would be.

"Please. They were on you dead to rights. The mad man was a fortuitous happenstance. You have, if nothing, a profound affinity for luck. I had nothing to do with it. But it did make it clear that something would have to be done about you. Pity really, I would admire you were it not for the trouble you cause me," The inquisitor said. "But then this is not your first dance, or even your third. Tell me, how far back do you go? Not London, by then you had been a thorn in our side for some time."

"Salem. In America," Victor said. "Well, England, just before."

"Ah yes, the witch trials. How did that work out for you?"

Victor's mind snapped to the time like it was yesterday. The Puritans, as they were called, were the first cultists. They had escaped with many spores to the new world. Victor had easily convinced the faithful that a devil was upon them. But for the most part it had only caused panic and paranoia. Still it served the purpose until the blood cult had reformed into the guise of authority. By then the faithful had become the enemy and were stopped. The Native Americans had believed him, skinwalkers they called them, but served only to start a century of bloody war, such are the twisted ways of the old gods.

"The past is of no consequence now. Here we sit and I am still wondering why?" Victor asked.

"It occurs to me, Victor, that we have been looking at you incorrectly. You are not a thorn, but an opportunity," he said.

"Bribery. Do you hope to turn me? Really?" Victor asked and almost laughed.

"Not quite." The man removed his hat and glasses. The top of his head was simply exposed bone, where no bone existed was a pulsing red-green mass and his eyes were slit like a cat, golden black. "But what a lovely vessel you will make for my master."

Victor had no time to react. The thought to move had just crystalized in Victor's mind when the top of the inquisitor's head exploded sending shards of bone and ribbons of tissue across the table. Within the chaos Victor spotted for the briefest of moments the mass of writhing tentacles as it landed with a sickening thump on the table. The inquisitor's form now crumpling into lifelessness. Victor reached for his bag and cursed himself for not having taken out at least the scalpel. Not a second more and the creature was upon him, its grip was strong around his head and Victor had no chance to fight it back as it forced his mouth open and pushed inside. The slimy acid of its skin searing the inside of his mouth and throat.

Victor could draw no breath and he gagged on the long proboscis now projecting down his throat. He would have vomited if he could. He could feel the beak of the creature biting into his flesh deep within him. Second sensation of ripping came from the back of his throat, it was clawing into the bone of his skull. The sound of the bone breaking was a crunching sound that echoed inside his mind. His eyesight blurred and his resolve weakened as Victor lost consciousness.

It was a moment of darkness. It must have been only a few minutes. Victor woke to a crowd that had formed around him. He tried to get up and a few people were trying to help. He drew a breath and knew that he had only a few moments until the larva would commandeer his body for its own purposes. Even now he saw flashes of memory pass in his mind, was it reading his thoughts? It must be or it would have clawed through his brain already.

Victor stood up and straightened his jacket. He heard the train approaching now. He had precious seconds to decide. They sought to make him a vessel for the old god. There was a limit to his mind, but not his life. Genetic Memory or whatever it was, he had prepared for the next generation. Pushing the crowd aside he walked to the platform. The train entered the station. The creature's instinct was to try to make him stop, but it underestimated the power of his insanity born of millennia of fighting the old gods. As he fell to the track he made sure at least his head would find the wheel of the train, the creature knew it, too, as he fell into the sweet oblivion of death to the sounds of its screams.

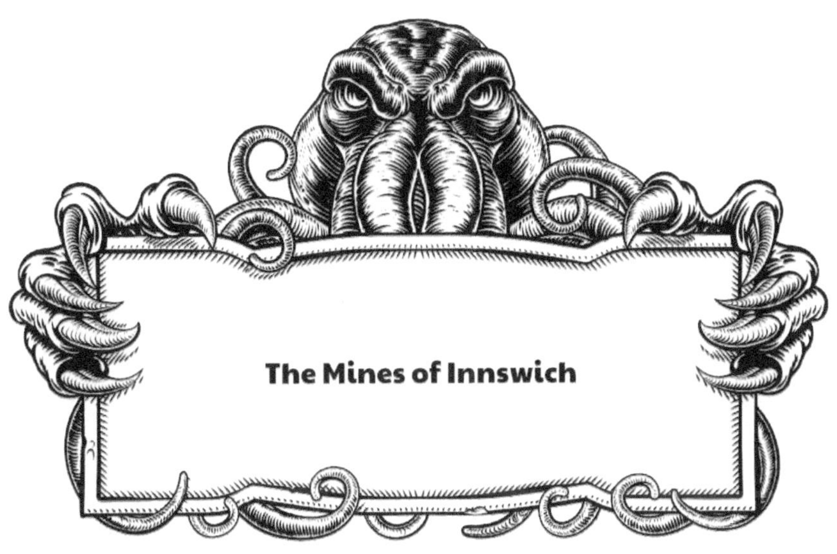

BY RYAN COLLEY

"It's not even dawn!" the man shouted as he wiped the bleariness from his eyes – some of that came from sleep, but most from age. He'd forcibly been awoken by the rattling of his front door. A loud rapping, followed by someone trying the handle. At first, he thought he'd over-slept. Not something he did often, but definitely more frequently since entering the sixty-fifth winter of his life. Not that his failure to rise early meant much – he had a relatively peaceful existence.

Being the Police Chief of Innswich, the small and sleepy New England town, meant that the most he ever had to deal with were noise complaints stemming from the native townsfolk about newcomers from the big city. People of Innswich, the true people, didn't like change. After all, the townsfolk had existed there for generations. In fact, his own ancestor had helped settle upon the land which they called home. The families that were born in Innswich, died in Innswich, as did their children and children's children, and it had always been that way. Outsiders saw that as small-minded, but the people of Innswich cited it as a point of pride.

"We got us someone gibbering nonsense," the man, whose voice the Chief recognised as his deputy, exclaimed loudly. He even sounded a little bit excited, and why shouldn't he? Nothing ever happened in Innswich.

"Stick him in a cell to sober up!" the Chief shouted back with annoyance, hoping to get a little more sleep before his day started. He didn't understand why he was being called – a drunken fool was a minor problem at most. Hell, in Innswich it was the only problem besides noise.

"I did, then that's when he started hurting himself," the Deputy replied. "He's completely mad."

"Well, call the asylum and let them know one of their lunatics got out," the Chief snapped. He was about to threaten the Deputy with the cell when he added something else.

"He's that student who moved up on the hill," the Deputy explained. "He was found near the mines."

"I'm coming," the Chief said, suddenly calm. His body relaxed and the bulging vein on his forehead disappeared. All the anger deflated with that one statement. He climbed to his feet and got ready as fast as his old bones could manage.

———

The Chief climbed into the Deputy's car – a brand new 1929 Stearn Knight. He'd never liked automobiles and the further he kept from the damn things, the better. They didn't belong in Innswich. Then again, a lot of things didn't belong in Innswich – not just automobiles, but outsiders, too. The world wanted to grow and get faster and expand, but not Innswich. It was content to exist a little out of time with everywhere else.

Regardless of local resistance to moving forward, Innswich had always been a strange place. Not just because it was remote even by New England standards, but because it had an unnatural richness in the soil. The ground was full of minerals and ore – precious metals which had no earthly right being there. Yet the lands around the town were unexplainably barren. Some argued the prosperity was a result of the respect they had for the land, whereas the less superstitious believed the land was settled on because of cornucopia below. That had always been the source of the town's prosperity – they could make what they needed, and trade for what they couldn't. That was what made the mine so precious in its day, but the mining had stopped in the Chief's youth.

After the brief and to the point update from the Deputy, they rode the rest of the short journey to the station in silence. The Deputy radiated a quiet excitement regarding their change in routine, whereas the Chief was deep in thought. No one went into the mines. There was a reason for that. Even if the Deputy hadn't told him who went into the mines, he could have worked out it wasn't a true Innswich resident – they all knew to stay away from it. Even Farmer

Samuel from over the hill, in his most drunken of stupors, wouldn't go near the place. So, it had to be one of the newcomers. One of the city folk. Naturally, it had to be the newest resident of the old farmhouse. But that had been confirmed by the Deputy, so it did not matter.

The Chief was mentally berating the workers that had assured him the mine was sealed up.

"Can't trust outsiders," the Chief muttered to himself as his internal contemplations spilt out, only for the Deputy to shake his head. Times were changing and small-town paranoia was becoming a relic of a bygone era, or so the Deputy hoped. The Chief would never change, and neither would the town's attitude towards outsiders. People would be stuck in their ways forever, or until they handed the mantle over to the younger generations. As much as the Deputy respected the Chief, he was glad that the old man would be leaving soon – his time was gone. The Deputy wanted to move the town forward, but he couldn't do it while antiquities like the Chief were around.

They pulled into the small police house. There was one other automobile, belonging to the only other officer, parked outside. The small yard already looked cramped with the intrusive machines. They walked in and headed straight for one of three cells – neither of the other two was occupied, although it was rare for even one to be. The Chief saw a young, dishevelled man chuckling to himself.

"He okay?" the Chief asked, raising an eyebrow. "I was told there had been elements of, uh, self-harm."

"There was, sir. Had to fetch Doc," the young officer replied loudly, clearly trying to impress the Chief. The Chief thought that was the problem with city folk, they always tried to impress those above them. Innswich folk took people for their value, not what they could do to make you happy.

The Chief sighed, "Good job. He sedated?"

"Yes, sir," the officer replied obediently.

The Chief turned his back to the officer and said, "Bring him to my office and I'll see if I can get any sense out of the lad."

———

THE CHIEF STRODE through the cramped building, into his office, and sat in his chair, which sagged beneath his weight and years of use. He inhaled deeply and shuffled until he got comfortable. On his desk sat a very few personal items – a photo of his wife who had long since passed and an old blade he used as a letter opener. The blade had been forged from the metal beneath Innswich by one of his ancestors and had been in his family ever since. He picked it up and played with it – a habit born of stress. He had to take the small respite offered to him to collect his thoughts before he dealt with the situation.

"Going down those mines? What is he playing at?" the Chief said to himself, running his hand through his hair. He heard the approaching shuffle of the man, being led by his two officers, and placed the knife back down on the desk. His eyes flicked to the blade and he adjusted the positioning ever so slightly before smiling with contentment.

The Deputy sat the man on the other side of the desk opposite the Chief. He wasn't cuffed, and that's the way the

Chief wanted it – although the Deputy hadn't cuffed him for his own reasons.

The Deputy remembered something he had heard many years prior, "Treat a man like an animal and, by God, he'll act like one."

"Thank you," the Deputy said to the officer, dismissing him with those two words. The Chief wished the Deputy could be so easily dismissed, but it wasn't in his nature. He walked into the corner and stood, observing everything. If the Chief needed assistance, he would be there in a second. The Chief became aware of his own heavy breathing in the silence of the room.

"So, why were you in those mines?" the Chief finally asked after a pause that felt like an aeon. Then the man spoke and told his tale.

Several hours prior to the man being in a cell, he'd awoke with a start. Waking in the night and hearing strange noises wasn't uncommon in an old house. Old buildings like the one he resided in took hours to settle, and the wood wouldn't stop creaking until long after he retired to the bedroom. What was uncommon was whispering. It wasn't what he'd grown accustomed to, nor any wind that swept through the hills. The man held his breath and listened to the indistinct whispering, wondering if he had intruders in his home. When the volume and tone didn't change, as you would expect from someone moving through a house, he moved downstairs to investigate.

He checked the entirety of his house, but he didn't find anyone – somehow, he knew wouldn't and that didn't surprise him. The whispers felt a lot more unnatural than a physical intrusion – there was something about it that was so … wrong. He knew the juxtaposition of his skin crawling and mind pulling him towards the source wasn't right, but he couldn't work out why he felt the need for either. He could have easily put it down to sleep deprivation and stress, something he was often left feeling when studying the texts his university had provided. Inability to maintain sleep. Strange dreams. Unrested. Feelings of fatigue. The nightmares. He needed a break. However, he needed to complete his work on the texts – not just because the university had assigned the task but he felt compelled to do so.

He then began walking towards his front door and stepped outside, the distant tendrils of barely spoken words guiding him. No matter where he turned, they always seemed just out of earshot. Regardless, he knew that going outside had brought him closer. So, curiosity piqued, he followed where his feet took him and set off with a lantern in hand.

———

There wasn't much in the local area around the farmhouse. That was the reason the property had been chosen. It meant distance from distraction whilst he conducted research into the old Sumerian texts. Distance from family and the university. In the cool of the night, following unnatural whispers … the distance felt more like isolation.

He was a student in languages studying under Professor Walford, who himself was a researcher of ancient texts at Miskatonic University. When he told Walford about his interests in old texts, Walford was overjoyed. Walford explained he was looking for a research assistant to replace his previous one. He said that it was a very intense role and that his colleague had cracked from stress and disappeared not long ago. Naturally, the texts still needed translation and the student didn't care about anything more than the fact Walford was considering him a research assistant. He accepted immediately.

The role came with some amazing perks – almost too good to be true! Off-campus housing and all living expenses paid. The university had already leased the house for a year and wanted to fill it ever since the previous student vanished. So, he would fill the same property and continue the same task.

Strangely, that single disappearance was not the end of the dark history surrounding those same texts. When reading through his predecessor's notes, he found that large amounts of the notes had been destroyed by the prior Dean of the university who also went inexplicably mad when exploring them himself. A superstition had grown amongst the academic staff regarding those texts and it was almost an ongoing joke that no one would willingly study them. Despite the strangeness, he was happy and simply thanked his blessings for a chance to study something so old and mysterious.

As part of his induction into Innswich, Walford warned him that the mines should be avoided due to being unsafe. He explained that the locals were old fashioned and claimed that strange noises could be heard around the hills and that they echoed up from the mines. Walford laughed it off and so did the man – old towns bred superstition. Nonetheless, he felt it was his civic duty to investigate, as well as remind the possible ne'er-do-well that the mines were closed for a reason.

He wanted to make a good impression on the townsfolk as he had grown quite attached to the area in the days he had been there and hoped to move in permanently. On top of that, the purely logical and academic part of his brain strived for an explanation of the unseen sounds. He needed to know what was affecting him so deeply. He didn't even begin to consider that he didn't know where the mines were, he'd never needed too. Yet he was being drawn there by some external force.

He followed the whispers over the hills and across the land. He stumbled and regained his balance. The night was cold and the grass was slick with moisture – he didn't even notice his lack of footwear. His curiosity was slowly replaced by a growing obsession. He had to find the source. He would search all night if he had too. This obsession lingered below the surface, driving him onwards – all of this unbeknownst to him.

———

WHEN HE ARRIVED at the entrance to the mines, he knew something wasn't right. The mine was still sealed by the wooden boards that prevented access, yet the 'Keep Out' sign had fallen away. There wasn't any sign of trespassers, but there was no uncertainty that the whispers emanated from the mouth of the mine which bored down into the earth. Without even questioning whether he should, he tore away the wood until his hands were bloody and full of splinters. He entered the mines.

The ground inside was uneven, and the darkness around him felt enough to swallow his very soul, yet he kept going. The light from his lantern barely kept the dark at bay when illuminating the rocky pathway. He journeyed deeper and deeper into the earth, following the paths dug by the miners that had helped create the burrow. The wooden support beams kept the roof and walls from collapsing, but bowed under the weight of the world. Not once did he question whether he should have been there. He followed the distant and mysterious whispers. Their presence never changed, nor did they grow any louder or clearer, but that's what drew the man deeper. He barely even registered the oddity of his quest.

Further and further he went. Deeper into the earth than he ever thought possible. Until he eventually came to the end. It was a tunnel like any other, except it just ended. A smooth wall marked the end of the mine. There was a single discarded pickaxe on the floor. Stories from the town said that they stopped digging because they could not go any further, but it looked more like they had just abandoned the mine without warning or reason.

He was almost content to turn back because the whispers had stopped. He smiled, the silliness of the situation finally reaching his brain. His logical mind overriding the strangely primal drive he'd experienced. He turned his back on the dead-end, ready to return to the surface, but the whispering began anew. He turned slowly, as if to spy the whisperer in the dark, but there wasn't anything there. Then he spied something he didn't see before. Something in the rocks. The smooth wall ... it looked out of place. How had he not noticed that? Almost as if it was made of a different kind of rock.

He approached it slowly, placing his hand to it. It was warm to the touch and it seemed impossibly smooth. Then he bent down and picked up the pickaxe by the rotting handle. He didn't even register his movements, acting without willing himself too. He began to chip away at the wall – heavy swings as he brought the iron head to stone.

He was by no means a strong man, but he worked until he began to sweat. He worked until the handle gave way and snapped. He carried on working with just the pickaxe head in hand, smashing the blunted point into the rock. His bloody and raw hands could barely take it anymore. Yet he continued until he had created a space to pass through. He panted as he stared into the space beyond the hole. The man entered into an impossible world.

———

IT BECAME apparent the moment he stepped through that he had found something unusual. A much older room. Older even than the mineshaft that led down to it – but that should have been impossible. Whether the men who dug the mine knew it was there was unknown to him. Perhaps they were driven by the same compulsion he was? Or perhaps they sought it out, knowing it was there all along? Either way, they stopped before they breached that final barrier.

He saw something in the chamber which spoke to the language expert in him: hieroglyphs. Strange lettering and symbols lined the ancient and impossibly smooth masonry in the dome-like room. It wasn't the walls of a cavern, carved out by the forces of nature, but the walls of a purpose-built room. He wondered if the room was man made, but that simply couldn't be. He ran his hand over the carved hieroglyphs. Strange and unknown symbols, unlike any language he had ever studied. Normally elements of other languages could be seen, even traces, but every symbol was unique and unknown. The man continued to look around, taking in all the oddities.

A large circular pool of water was in the centre of the chamber. How long had that been there? There didn't appear to be any stalactites hanging from the ceiling to suggest it came from outside. Nor were there any faults in the perfect stonework for it to drain through. It could have been there for thousands of years! Despite its age, it was clear. No dirt or dust tainted it.

Strange symbols, impossible chambers, and ancient water aside, there was something much more interesting to be seen. Beyond the pool of water and at the back of the chamber was an altar, raised up above the rest of the room. He crossed through the shallow pool, the coolness washing between his bare toes, and he climbed onto the raised section.

As unnatural as the chamber felt, he could still somehow tell it was a place of worship – much like the churches he had been forced to go to in his youth. Almost as if to confirm his innate belief, there was a book on the altar with a strange leather binding to it. Was that the holy tome of some dead religion? He touched the cover and almost recoiled. No ... not holy. Looking at it, unholy suited it better. He opened the book, the yellowed and ancient pages felt close to breaking just from his touch. The words were even older than the Sumerian texts he'd been studying. He had found something truly unique.

He continued turning the pages carefully and, within those pages, he saw inhuman words and letterings. Symbols, scrawled by hands that were not that of a man or woman. Those markings, because he could not bring himself to call them words, struck him at a mental and spiritual level. The words meant nothing to his eyes and he could not understand them in any language he knew. Yet he understood the meaning behind the words. They passed whatever filter and understanding the civilised world had created through common languages and the meaning projected directly into his mind. He was horrified. He turned the pages feverishly, looking for an explanation amongst the unnatural words and monstrous pictures that had been painted in shades of red. He did not find one. Not one he was happy with.

The final image on the final page was simply that of a humanoid creature, not quite of a man but far too closely resembling one to be a coincidence. His mind could barely take it. He dropped the tome back onto the altar in disgust, for reasons he could not fathom. And that is when he saw it.

His gaze had fallen to looking at the pool. He hadn't noticed it when moving through the water, he was simply too close to realise what it was. But from his elevated position on the altar, he could see a face. A horrible, large face. A being that presented itself in the mind of the man as a hateful and hungry god-creature – one that was incomprehensibly alien and ancient. The man recoiled at what he saw. The cephalopods hiding in the most stygian depths of the darkest ocean were more of a beloved brother to the species of man than the horrific abomination that was in those mines.

Its mere presence changed everything he knew of the world – his knees began to buckle. Not because he was in some unfeasibly old chamber, further underground than any human tools should allow, but because the titanic and ancient face was alive. Made of metal, flesh, and stone. And it moved. It flinched and writhed, like a being in a fretful sleep. Each movement caused the ground shudder and quake. He could not explain what he was seeing, simply because he did not know any words in any language to explain it. How could he possibly comprehend what he could not put words to?

Then the man realised something more about the benighted being: it was the source of the whispers. They came from it, not from the impossibly smooth lips that formed its mouth, but he was hearing its dreams as they were cast out and imprinting him on a psychic level. So, the man did the only sane thing someone faced with insanity could do – he ran. It would be the last sane thing he did as his mind broke.

He left the chamber laughing, leaving his lantern on the altar. He tumbled his way through the darkness of the mine as he laughed. He laughed all the way to the surface, and he was still laughing when he was picked up by the police officer and taken back to the station. Even in front of the Chief, as he finished his tale, he laughed.

As the unbelievable tale came to an end, the man became a lot more lucid and frantic. The glaze of drug-induced mirth left his eyes, but still he laughed. It wasn't one of shock, nor fear, but one of a man who had seen how the world would end and knew that it meant nothing.

"You still don't get it though, do you?" the man howled. The Deputy walked forward to restrain him, but was stayed by the surprisingly steady hand of the Chief. The Deputy paused midstride.

"What don't we get?" the Chief asked calmly.

"I saw the ancient writing. The words which must never be spoken," the man nodded, with a sick smile. "I couldn't read it. No one alive could. But I know what they meant. In my head, the words crept in. The words crept in and they sang to me!"

"What did they sing? What was the song?" the Chief demanded, leaning in to hear him. The Deputy winced at how close the Chief was to the clearly deranged individual.

"Not a song, no. They sang their tale. They sang … ah … I can see it in your eyes!" the man said with an understanding smile, nodding. "You know the words I speak of!"

"What did they say?" the Chief asked firmly. The Deputy was taken aback by the man's strange accusation.

"Their essence. It all came together in my head! Meanings I couldn't understand. Could not comprehend. But I know what they mean," the man continued, babbling to himself as he put together a puzzle which only he could see the pieces to. "All of our existence. Everything we have done or will ever do is for nothing. Everything we achieve, as a species, means nothing when weighed on the cosmic scale! We are but ants in the spiralling chaos that is the universe. We're not here on this Earth to own it, nor be caretakers of it! No meaning. No reason. And our continuing existence solely relies on that

Titan never awakening from its ancient slumber. And that's the truly maddening part! It is not a case of if it wakes up, but when. What once slept shall awaken once more!"

"What did it say!?" the Chief shouted angrily, slamming his fist on the desk – it was the first time the Deputy had seen him show anger.

"Not every Old One dreams in R'lyeh or rules in Carcosa," the man warned, then he finally spoke the words which would forever chill the Deputy, "One is slumbering beneath Innswich!"

With that, he dived forward and grabbed the blade from the desk and raised it high. The Deputy dived forward to prevent any harm from befalling the Chief. He would have been too late to save him from the strike had he been the target. Instead, he thrust the knife towards his own throat as he screamed an inhuman name meant to only be spoken by inhuman tongues.

"Gnas'Yuaru!"

The blade plunged deeply.

"Gnas'Yuaru!" he gurgled, blood pumping from the wound as he fell to the floor, gasping, as his mouth still tried to form the ghastly name.

"Just go home," the Chief said to the Deputy, ushering him out of the door.

"Shouldn't we at least check those mines?" the Deputy asked with alarm.

"No," the Chief said, shaking his head. "Those were the ramblings of a clearly disturbed mind. Just get some sleep. You've done well today."

With that, the Chief shut the door to his office and looked at the body. Clutched between his hands, even in death, was the antique family blade – the Chief bent down and retrieved it. He ignored the blood on it and placed it down on his desk delicately before sitting back in his chair. He was alone. He sighed. The day had only just begun and he already had a body on the floor of his office. But he knew what he had to do next, so he picked up the phone.

"Operator, could you connect me to Professor Walford at the Miskatonic University in Arkham, please … thank you," the Chief paused and waited until he heard the receiver click as he was connected. "Walford?"

"Billingham? It's not even dawn!" the voice responded tiredly as he recognised the Police Chief's voice. "Is this about the chap I recommended for the farmhouse?"

"It is," the Chief answered calmly.

"How's he getting on?" Walford asked when he realised the Chief wouldn't elaborate.

"Not well … he went into the mines," the Chief responded.

"And?" Walford asked in return, suddenly a lot more awake.

"He's lying on my office floor, dead," the Chief replied, staring at the spreading blood pool.

"Well, that is extremely unfortunate," Walford sighed. "What about the texts he was working on?"

"Still at the house," the Chief replied promptly. "I can have an officer watch the property until you send someone else … and when will that be?"

"Next week," Walford replied. "I can have another student moved in by the end of the month. I need those texts translated."

"We don't need the texts to know what's happening," the

Chief replied, instead he simply said something which they both had longed to hear, "It's begun … *Gnas'Yuaru* will rise."

"May the earth tremble at his wake," Walford replied, finishing the ancient blessing. There was a moment of silence between them before he added, "The next student can continue the translations. Let's hope that they can survive the whispering call longer than the last two."

"Indeed, dealing with bodies is a young man's game," the Chief said wryly and set the phone back down onto the cradle with a smile.

Prelude to The Four Immortals

BY L.E. HARRISON

Rescuing Rainey Sullivan was going to be the death of him.

He was more certain of that than he'd ever been of anything in his life. As the jaws of the Gilladragon opened to an impressive seven foot span, Julian Cato couldn't help comparing its five rows of sharp, jagged teeth to the deadly spikes protruding from the walls of the Tunnel of the Damned—the first time he'd traveled through spacetime to rescue his boss's daughter.

It wasn't that Rainey was accident prone. It was true that she often inadvertently found herself in desperate circumstances. But, Julian mused as he swung his broadsword at the slavering monster's throat, more often than not she sought out the trouble that prompted her father to send his best Time Guardian out on a mission to save her.

In Every. Godforsaken. Dimension.

The tip of Julian's sword punctured the beast's thick, scaly flesh. The monster let out an ear-splitting shriek as bright green, gelatinous blood pumped from the hole in its artery. Julian lifted his broadsword and leapt quickly out of the way before any of the slow-moving, lava-like substance could land on him.

"Go!" he shouted to the young woman crouched on the ground a few feet from the dying Gilladragon. "Get inside my portal, before more of them get here!"

Rainey stared up at him, a contemptuous sneer twisting her features. She looked to be about fourteen. Her full cheeks had yet to grow into her regal cheekbones, and the cold bite of cynicism was missing from her expression. Instead, adolescent contempt for anyone older than twenty years—and he was well past that, by at least seven times—blazed in her eyes.

"I didn't need your help," she bit out as she climbed to her feet. "I had her right where I wanted her."

Julian held back a laugh. He didn't want to seem conde-scending—or worse, cause Rainey to start doubting her own worth. Time travel required a delicate balance. Especially with the daughter of Carron Sullivan.

"A little help when it's needed is a gift from the gods," he said, instead.

"A gift from my father, you mean," she muttered, looking down at herself and brushing the dust from her clothes. She stalked past him toward the ship. "For the love of Tempus, I can handle a Gilladragon on my own."

"Probably," Julian agreed. "He sent me just in case. I arrived in haste, and may have misjudged the gravity of the situation."

She halted, turned to face him with hands planted firmly on hips, rolled her eyes, and sighed dramatically.

"I know why he always sends you, Julian," she said.

Her voice held a wisp of wisdom wiser than her years, he thought. Then he cringed at the alliteration—and his lamentable tendency to overanalyze all things Rainey Sullivan.

"We must go," he prodded gently, sheathing his sword.

She nodded, turned around, and sprinted through the opened hatch of his Time Pod.

Relief supplanting his anxiety, he heaved a sigh of his own, and went to join her.

———

"Are you taking me to my father's Station?" she asked. "Fatum's balls, it's hot in here."

"The AC's on," he commented absently, frowning down at the screen of his com-link. "And no, I'm taking you back home."

She pouted. He didn't have to see her expression to know she was doing it. He could feel it, even though she was lounging behind him on the recliner. They could fit up to three, but Time Pods were small, built for the comfort of one person only. With two people inside, his ship felt crowded and claustrophobic.

DM 51—primarily notable for its unique species of gargantuan, genetically mutated Gilladragons—was also well known for its overabundance of color. One tree's leaves could easily boast seven or eight shades, which were mimicked in swirling patterns over its trunk. Despite, or perhaps because of its many successful scientific advancements, DM 51 was covered in trees as well as every type of flower imaginable. The dimension truly was a wonder to behold Julian mused as they traveled high above the landscape.

He stared out his windscreen at the kaleidoscope of hues shifting and swirling, wondering what Rainey had meant when she'd said *I know why he always sends you, Julian.*

She had emphasized the words *know* and *you.*

Why had she done that? Did it mean something? What was it that fourteen year old Rainey Sullivan from DM 51 thought she knew about him?

"You missed your turn."

Rainey's voice startled him out of his musings. He whipped his head around, and frowned over his shoulder at her.

"What does that have to do with anything?" he retorted, his voice tight with irritation.

She pointed her finger in his face, and opened her mouth to answer, but he cut her off.

"Rainey, you're very young. I know it must seem to you as though the world is black and white, following clear patterns that behave in ways we have pre-prescribed. That if you're a good person and work hard, you will always be rewarded by some divine entity. That if you don't receive your rewards on the mortal plane, it is somehow evidence of your moral failings."

"Julian, I only meant—"

He held up his hand for silence, warming to the lecture. "Mark my words, girl. It's all bullshit. Politics. Relationships. Religion. All of it. The only thing real in this world is Science. It's all you can ever count on."

The corners of her mouth tipped up in a grin. "Are you finished?"

Julian folded his arms over his chest, and turned back to face the windscreen. "Yes. Just a bit of friendly advice."

"Well thanks for that," she quipped sardonically. "But all I was trying to tell you was that you were supposed to have gone left on Main, to get to Chestnut St. It doesn't matter, though. You can always turn around and go in the back way."

Julian froze. An instant after her words penetrated his psyche, he flushed with embarrassment. He leaned forward over the console, cleared his throat, and punched in the code to turn the ship in the right direction.

"There," she said, pointing to a modest two-storey wooden farmhouse perched upon a small hill, flanked by two large colorful arborvitae.

Rainey's home was the same in every dimension. And in every dimension, she lived mostly alone—except on the rare occasions her father or siblings came to visit.

Julian lowered the Time Pod gently to the verdant grass of the side yard. Rainey was halfway out of the hatch before it fully opened.

"Thanks for the gift," she quipped as she waved goodbye and sprinted around the corner to the front door.

The hatch closed with its familiar whooshing sound, and the ship rose above the peak of Rainey's pointed roof. Julian sat back in his chair, closed his eyes, and released the breath he hadn't even realized he'd been holding.

"Tell me everything you know about Gilladragons," Carron Sullivan instructed the instant Julian stepped into the Time Commander's private chambers.

Julian stopped just inside the doorway. He stood with his feet apart, shoulders straight, and hands behind his back. He studied the Commander's demeanor, trying to determine whether or not his mission to rescue Rainey from the Gilladragon on DM 51 had been successful.

Of course, it was difficult to glean what Carron might be thinking—especially when it pertained to one of his children. At the moment, all six feet four inches of the man seemed to radiate tension. As he paced before the row of long, rectangular windows, his shoulders were taut, his fists clenched at his sides.

The Commander was still impressively fit and muscular, despite his advanced age. His full head of jet black hair showed no traces of gray. His skin was unlined and deceptively smooth. Julian found himself wondering what Carron's secret was, and also if it was considered out of line to ask your boss for tips on skincare.

"Julian," prompted the Commander. "I asked you a question."

He cleared his throat, and began espousing all he knew about DM 51's unique species of Gilladragon—what they called the Gila monster (with its odd capitalization) in every other dimension.

Unfortunately, what Julian knew about the gargantuan reptile wasn't a lot. After he was done with his speech, Carron frowned in annoyance.

"That's it?"

Julian shrugged, then nodded.

"Oh, wait a second." Julian held up his hand just as Carron opened his mouth to speak. "There's one more thing. The extra L was added to distinguish the giant species from the ordinary one, giving added emphasis to its superior size. No one is really sure when the words Gilla and dragon were joined together—or, for that matter, when the word dragon was substituted for monster—but most language scholars support the theory that the two words had been hyphenated for a period of time before—"

"Julian," the Commander interrupted. "Shut up."

Julian nodded. "Yes, Sir."

The rhythm of Carron's pacing picked up speed. "I was trying to avoid this, but I suppose it was inevitable from the beginning."

The Commander stopped pacing abruptly, and ushered Julian into the hallway. "There will be an officer's briefing in one hour. You should spend that time looking up everything you can about Gilladragons, then come and join us."

The door was slammed in his face, leaving Julian to stare at it for several moments, perplexed. Carron's ominous words replayed over and over in his head.

Officer's briefing.

In one hour.

Come and join us.

Although he was himself a high ranking officer, Julian was never invited to take part in the briefings. His orders were to remain friendly, but aloof, to never fraternize with the other seven Time Guardians directly under Carron Sullivan's command.

Something must be going on. And judging by the way the Commander was reacting, whatever it was, it wasn't good.

———

"Julian Cato suffers from a condition known as Disassociation," Commander Sullivan explained to his assembled officers.

"During his Amalgamation, there was a blip in the software. The blip affected the melding of his inter-dimensional soul, to a degree that is still being studied. The doctors treating him for this condition assure me that an aspect from each dimension does exist within his psyche. However, some of them remain unmeshed within the collective whole. Rest assured, this side-effect is extremely rare, but it has been known to happen. His condition is being closely monitored, and I am thoroughly informed about his progress after every examination.

"The best doctors and scientists in every world are working on a cure as we speak. They are confident that it is only a matter of time until the minor - and I stress the word minor - damage is repaired."

"So," he concluded, clapping his hands together and glancing at each of the officers in turn. "Now all your questions have been answered, and you can understand why Julian Cato has been treated, as some of you have complained, differently. I have not been, as many of you have erroneously alleged, playing favorites. I would be remiss in my duties as your Commander, if I did not grant him some extra attention. I trust this goes without saying, but I must remind you that what I have just disclosed is classified information that does not leave this meeting chamber. Any questions?"

A squat, bearded, dark-haired man tentatively raised his hand. Carron pointed toward him and nodded.

"Go ahead, Steve."

Steve cleared his throat and eyed Julian warily. Julian, from his position leaning against the doorframe, shrugged and flashed him an apologetic half-smile. Steve grimaced nervously, and turned back to Carron.

"A 'blip,' Sir? Can you explain exactly what that means?"

Carron pursed his lips thoughtfully. "I can. But I'm not going to. That information is classified."

Steve opened his mouth to protest, but at the Commander's frown, he closed it slowly and nodded.

"Anyone else?"

Everyone blinked, wide-eyed, and shook their heads no.

"Excellent," pronounced the Commander. "Now that we are all up to speed, this briefing is adjourned. We will all, with the exception of Julian, who will be sent out overnight on a follow up mission, meet again tomorrow morning at the usual time. Enjoy your night off."

Julian moved away from the door. Casting surreptitious suspicious glances his way, the other seven officers filed out of the room. When they were gone, he closed the door and turned to the Commander.

"You're sending me out on another mission so soon?"

"Yes," Carron affirmed. "I'm sorry, Julian, but it can't be helped. It seems we have a bigger problem on DM 51 than I initially thought. It appears that my daughter has salvaged a baby Gilladragon from the nest of the mother you killed. My sources tell me she intends to raise it as a pet, but the end result is disastrous. I need you to go back, and—"

"Rescue her again," Julian finished for him.

"Right, then," Carron said. "You know what to do. Report to me when you return."

Julian sighed, then headed to the station's shipyard to find his Time Pod.

Rescuing Rainey Sullivan was going to be the death of him.

———

"Rainey, you can't keep a Gilladragon as a pet."

She scowled up at him. "Why not?"

"They're not like dogs and cats," Julian explained. "They have no feelings. They kill indiscriminately, and without warning. Its bite can be fatal, and its breath is atrocious. People have tried to tame them in the past, and it always ends in tragedy."

Rainey's scowled deepened. "Those are urban legends, Julian."

"Maybe the hatchling hasn't fully grown into its stench yet. There's a school of thought that purports the smell to be lethal. It's like a defense mechanism. You must not have been close enough to get a whiff of it the other day, but I can fully attest to the adult animal's noxious odor. Like a cross between a pile of dead bodies and a refuse yard on DM 1."

He mimicked a shudder of disgust, and Rainey laughed.

Then her expression sobered. She met his gaze. "Thank you for coming all the way back here to warn me, but it wasn't necessary. You can assure my father that I will be fine.

Akki would never harm me—or any human, for that matter. He's special."

"Akki?"

"That's his name," she explained.

He raised an eyebrow. "You named a baby Gilladragon?"

Rainey shook her head. "No, silly Julian. He told me what his name is."

It was Julian's turn to scowl. "Rainey, listen, your father and I are only looking out for your welfare. There's no way you can keep an animal like this. It's common sense. Stop being so stubborn and childish. Give me the Gilladragon. I'll take it back to your father, and he can—"

"Absolutely not. Tell Commander Carron Sullivan to go pound sand on DM 1. You can join him, if you'd like. Now get out of my house."

Julian, a two hundred year old Time Guardian of the highest rank, would have assumed that there was no way a fourteen year old girl could intimidate him. He would have been wrong.

She stood before him, hands on slender hips, green eyes blazing. The expression on her face was one Julian had seen many times on an older version of Rainey—implacable and determined. Her mind was made up. Nothing he could say was going to make her change it.

Although he knew it was useless, he decided to try one last time. In the very likely event that the Commander wanted a play-by-play report of this mission, Julian had to be able to show that he'd at least tried every tactic he could think of.

"How do you plan to take care of it?" he asked. "What will you feed it? Akki may be the size of a groundhog now, but how do you plan to control him when he's ten feet tall and twenty-one stone? You know you can't have an animal of that size in a little Amish farmhouse. What will the neighbors think?"

Those were all legitimate questions that Rainey was too intelligent to dismiss out of hand. Though, he had to admit, this latest stunt of hers was casting doubt upon her reputation as a prodigy.

"He won't be here that long," she countered. "I'm only helping him out temporarily. And don't ask, because I'm not going to explain why. I will, however, let you in on the fact that Akki and I can speak through animus rimor. It's a long story, but he's not who you think he is, Julian. He more than just an ordinary Gilladragon."

Julian had heard stories of gods being trapped in various life-forms. The concept wasn't new, but the fact that Rainey believed she had found such an elusive creature gave him pause. Prodigy or not, she was still an adolescent girl living on her own. Perhaps, if her story was true, if she really was communicating mind to mind with the creature, she could use her father's help to sort it all out. Julian realized he should report this news to the Commander straightaway.

He was not going to win this argument with Rainey, and was simply wasting time. Julian noted her skepticism as he pretended to give up and return to the station. As he boarded his ship, he could see her gazing through the window, a deep frown etched into her forehead. He was willing to bet she wasn't fully buying his capitulation, and suspected he was running off to tell her father.

She was only partially right. Julian hid his Time Pod in the woods directly across the street from Rainey's house. After the sun went down, he came back on foot, waiting in the bushes until he was sure she was asleep. Then he crept silently through the house until he found the upstairs bedroom where she kept the baby Gilladragon in a large, modified dog kennel.

He snatched the creature from its cage, making sure to bind it tightly with rope inside a canvas bag he'd brought along. Then he sprinted out the door and back to his ship. The animal squirmed and flailed, straining the limits of the bag, as Julian dumped it on the recliner and went to enter his destination on the screen.

Let Carron deal with the mess created by his offspring, he thought, as he collapsed into his chair. He folded his arms behind his head, and settled in to take a quick power nap.

———

HE DREAMED of the time he'd rescued Rainey on DM 24.

But what was happening in the dream was different than what he remembered. He didn't recall the noxious odor of the graveyard, for instance—let alone, the foul stench triggering his gag reflex. In the dream, the smell was intense and debilitating, causing Julian to stumble after Rainey like a man who'd indulged in too much whiskey.

"You're going down," Rainey taunted him from behind the elaborately carved façade of the mausoleum.

"It didn't happen this way," Julian muttered to himself as a wave of dizziness dropped him to his knees on the spongy grass.

"Wake up!" Rainey shouted. "You're going down!"

A loud thump shook the chair beneath him. Julian's eyes flew open, and the dream evaporated.

Only its foul stench lingered. Swallowing bile, Julian glanced around in panic. The Gilladragon was a lump of stillness inside the bag, but there was only one place that smell could be coming from. Holding his breath, he took off his jacket. As he wound it around his head, covering his mouth and nose, he consulted the com-link screen to see how far away he was from the station.

Twenty minutes.

Could he endure this stench for twenty more minutes?

The smell was making him lightheaded. His eyes began watering, and his lungs protested the lack of breathable air.

Five minutes later, he seriously considered changing the ship's course to land on the closest dimension—DM 1, only three minutes away.

Thirty seconds after that, he glanced behind him to check on the bag—and was dismayed to see thick, curling tendrils of smoke rising from the canvas. He stared, mesmerized, as the tendrils elongated and contracted, as though searching for something. One of them stretched up to the ceiling before quickly diving down and pinging his console. There was a loud popping sound, and the ship tilted slightly to the left.

"Hey!" Julian shouted—though it was muffled by his jacket. Before he could lean over to see if the mysterious tendril had caused any damage to his screen, he felt something slither around his wrists, then his neck. He glanced down to see the tendrils of smoke curling around his body like thick strands of rope. He jerked in panicked reflex.

"What the—?"

The smoke tugged him backwards and wrapped itself around both his body and the chair, rendering him immobile. In the same instant that one of the tendrils rose to cover his eyes, Julian felt the ship drop dangerously.

His stomach lurched as the descent picked up speed. Bracing himself for the inevitable, Julian squeezed his eyelids tight and gripped the cushioned arms of the chair he was strapped to.

He had one last, coherent thought—right before the impact of his ship crash-landing on the ground of DM 1 knocked him unconscious.

Rescuing Rainey Sullivan was going to be the death of him.

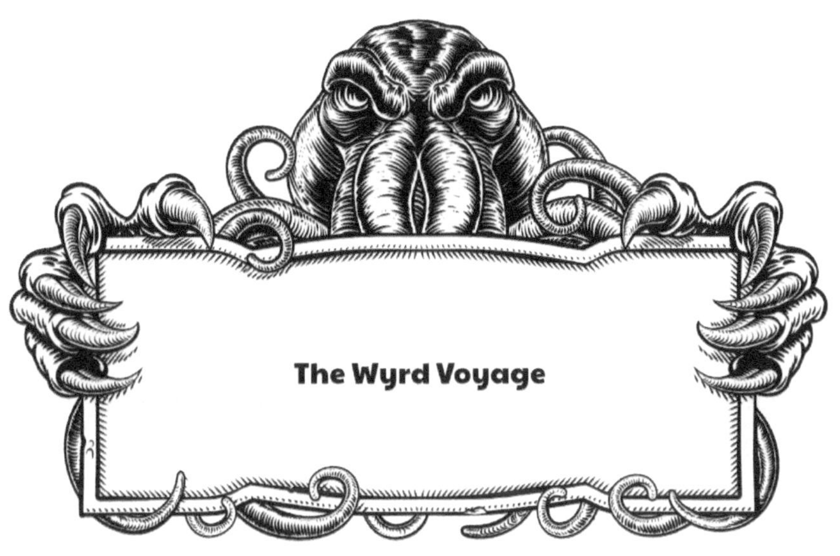

BY KARI LEIGH SANDERS

My name is Althea Smythe. I am a collector of odd trifles, curios, and artefacts relating to those known as The Old Ones and The Elder Gods. When possible, should I come upon manuscripts or records pertaining to the items I collect, I chronicle my findings so that others who share in my interests might have a written account of past events. As to the veracity of my writings, I can attest to only recording those events which I can find documentation supporting either the same or similar happenings.

The following is a compilation of journals that were discovered in a collection of Old Norse memorabilia by one of my agents. I was unable to trace their origins other than to note that they were written during the mid-800s and that the writers came from southern Norway. I have taken the liberty of translating from the Old Norse and transcribing them in such a way as to make the descriptions of the events take place in chronological order and to be more comprehensible for the modern reader.

The journals were recorded by three völva (Norse seers or witches,) Amma, Hild, and Kolga, as well as a longboat captain, Raumr, and an initiate of Kolga's, Aelfrestan.

*A*MMA

There are times when I dream and times when I See. This is a time when I See.

I See dolphins. I See dolphins with the eyes of men, wearing harnesses of ivory and pulling an ivory chariot deep in the dark waters of the sea. Riding in the chariot is a man so beautiful as to put Baldur to shame. His skin is white, His features delicate, as a youth just past the cusp of manhood, His hair swirling in a golden maelstrom as He speeds through the water. His beauty is such that it seems profane, its perfection makes me shudder and try to turn away as His countenance brings to my mind a sense of the inhumanness of His being, but I cannot.

As I watch, the dolphins near the shore of our village and young Haukr, son of Pedr and Helga, steps out in the water. The figure in the chariot rushes to him and embraces him, whispering in his ear. What is said I know not, but Haukr's face grows slack as he leads the man home to his mother whom is also captured in an embrace, and when Pedr returns he reaches towards his wife and is pulled in while the whisperings continue. Strange, slick wisps reach from the man in the chariot and begin slipping through the doors towards the rest of the people in the village. Haukr wanders back to the water whilst his parents are being bewitched and as he dives beneath the waves towards the chariot his limbs begin to melt into his body and he becomes a dolphin with the eyes of a man.

These things I must tell to Hild and Kolga.

HILD

Today I stood on the cliffs and stared out to the sea. As I watched, I soon Saw. This is what I Saw.

I Saw myself, Amma, and Kolga, Aelfrestan, Raumr and his crew on a longboat travelling far, far to the southwest. I Saw our ship surrounded by dolphins with the eyes of men. I Saw snakes and crows in baskets on our ship and a calf tied to the mast. I Saw Kolga driving the winds with her cords and knots. I Saw an island beyond the lands known to us, beautiful, but destroyed under the feet of an alabaster giant, fair of countenance, but somehow horrific as well. I Saw Aelfrestan smiling as snakes covered his body while blood seeped from their bites which I collected in a bowl. In the bowl, in the blood, there were eyes staring out - eager, angry eyes – waiting to be released. Looking down in the sea there was another set of enormous eyes, staring up at us and circling the island.

A storm came crashing down around me and pulled me from my Sight. I shall go to Amma and together we shall go and speak to Kolga of what I Saw.

KOLGA

It has been shown to me that I must make a record of the things relating to my wyrd, my fate. I shall ask for writings as well from those who are tied to it. Someday our story shall be told, though when I have not yet Seen.

For many years I have lived high up on the cliffs capturing the winds in the wool to spin into my threads, weaving them into cloth for sails and binding them with cord into knots. I do this knowing that one day it shall come to pass that they shall be needed to achieve my wyrd. I live here with Aelfrestan, a young man whose wyrd is tied to my own, and a few women who aid me in the weaving. The norns must delight in my wyrd, for most of my life has been spent high up away from the village collecting the winds with which to send me far across the seas where I shall face it.

Aelfrestan was brought to me as a child and I have taught him the ways of the gods. He has no fear of his wyrd. When he was old enough, I sent him to the village and he was taught to sail on the ships. He then returned to me and has since devoted himself to learning about the gods and aiding me in my work.

When I am caught up in the weaving, the Web of Wyrd is sometimes shown to me. As of late it has become clearer and clearer. I know that soon I shall be visited by Amma and Hild and our journey from home shall begin. The great sail that has been woven over the years with threads full of captured wind is finished and a basket with coils of knotted cord sits in the corner. Aelfrestan has crafted a rope, this one not of winds, but of the tranquility and calmness he has learned. Our preparations are complete.

*A*ELFRESTAN

Kolga has told me to record my thoughts as we prepare and go to face our wyrd. I am not a poet, she says that is fine, I just need to write it down so that it may be remembered somehow. I do not doubt her, the Web of Wyrd opens to her, whatever she asks of me I shall do. She is the one who has raised me and helped me make sense of my life since my parents died. I should explain that perhaps.

My parents died when I was five, I was staying with my aunt and they were off on a raid. I Saw them, torn and bloody, walking up to me. I ran to them but they did not stoop to pick me up. They looked tired, but at peace. My mother touched my cheek and my father tousled my hair. They told me that they loved me and that I would make them proud. Then a woman, half alive and half dead, came behind them and they turned and faded away. She smiled at me and told me not to be afraid. My aunt shook me from behind and asked me what I was looking at, when I turned back, she was gone. I told my aunt what I had Seen and she reached out a trembling hand and touched my cheek, wiping off the blood left behind by my mother. She spoke to Amma that night, and when word came back that my parents were dead, they sent me up here to live with Kolga.

Amma, Hild, and Kolga are all völva, they all have special gifts from the gods, but Amma and Hild remain in the village while Kolga lives up here in the hills and cliffs. I believe she Sees more as she has more room to See. She taught me about the gods, about the nine realms, about the living, and about the dead. She taught me to capture the winds, to spin thread, and to weave the threads and knot the cords. When I was old enough she sent me down to learn how to sail under Raumr in exchange for cloth and knots made of wind. It is with Raumr that we shall set out on our journey soon.

While I grew up, I had times when I was visited by the gods. They told me secrets, and truths, and lies, and stories. I was also visited by the dead. Other than my parents, none of them ever spoke to me. I don't think some of them even saw me. High on the cliffs is a good place to See many things. It is a good place to learn and to think. I learned from Kolga and I learned from the women who help her weave, I learned from the gods, and I evened learned from the dead. You might wonder what the silent, sometimes unseeing dead could teach me, they taught me silence and acceptance. It might not be as exciting as the stories and secrets of the gods, or as useful as capturing the winds and weaving, but it is still a good lesson. Particularly for someone with my wyrd.

Soon we shall travel farther than I can even imagine. Farther than the farthest I can see from the tops of the cliffs and farther than that by hundreds of times. We shall be going to a land that none of our people have ever seen, across stretches of the sea that they may never cross. It shall be one more thing that shall be seen by me and not many others. But it is my wyrd to not be able to tell anyone about it after. Perhaps that's why Kolga wants me to write down my thoughts now, so that they shall last when my wyrd has come to pass.

RAUMR

I write this for Kolga who has for years blessed me with her gifts of wind, knotted in cords and woven into my sails. For this I have promised her two things, the first, which I have done, was to train Aelfrestan in the ways of sailing. The second is that someday she shall ask me to undertake a voyage and I must agree, no matter how far, or how strange the destination. This she has told me in the past few days to prepare for.

For over twenty years I have sailed these seas, to explore, to raid, and to transport goods. I have always had good fortune on my voyages and I know that no small part of that is due to the gifts of Kolga. When sailing with others and the waters would become becalmed, I could untie a knot from the cords she had gifted me and a wind would rise up. My sails could withstand the mightiest of winds without tearing, and pick up the slightest of them to carry us on. I have prospered and now have a wonderful longboat of my own. It is on this craft that I shall be carrying Kolga and her company to a place hitherto uncharted for a purpose I do not yet know.

We shall go with a small crew and a large amount of supplies. Though it sounds like a fool's errand, I have complete faith in Kolga. Her visions shall lead us, and her winds shall carry us. As we will be taking as well the völvur Amma and Hild, I imagine that this is a journey ordained by the gods. I have selected my crew based upon their skills and their faith as it shall be a journey into the unknown and I do not want those who are craven and may rebel should we be far from known lands for a long period of time. The supplies are being gathered and the ship is being made ready. We shall sail soon.

Amma

Before I spoke to the others, I went to Pedr and Helga to tell them of what I had Seen and to warn them of Haukr discovering something in the sea. When I arrived it was to find Haukr in his bed, fever stricken and muttering about going to someone. When I examined him I found that he had a small ivory figurine clenched tightly to his body. Helga told me she could not get him to release it. It is only this that prevented them from succumbing to it as well I think. I gave him an herbal concoction that put him deeply to sleep and, using a thick cloth so as not to touch it, wrenched the figurine from his hands and wrapped it tightly so that no one could look upon it. I'm afraid for the boy, I do not know if he can be saved.

I brought the figurine with me when Hild came to take me to visit Kolga. Kolga believes that the boy can be released from his state if our journey goes well. Helga must keep him in his bed, so we have given her medicines to keep him asleep should he become unruly while we are gone. I knew that we would someday go on a journey, and Kolga has been telling us more and more frequently that the time is coming near, but I now fear what we are to do. I dream now of the wretched, too perfect being and His cavalry of dolphins with the eyes of men.

HILD

It is time for us to depart from our home and to travel to the place that I Saw on the cliffs. When we gathered to share our visions, Amma had brought with her a figurine wrapped in cloth. After hearing her tale, I have no doubt that it is a carving of the man we both saw. I could feel a sickness radiating from it, it was not meant for humans to see or to touch. Kolga insists upon bringing it with us as it may help in releasing the boy from his state, and also to lead us where we go. Though I shudder to think of it being with us, something tells me she is right and it shall somehow be useful.

We are preparing to leave tomorrow with the tide. The ship is filled with supplies as well as baskets of snakes and crows as I Saw, and the calf has been tied to the mast. It is surprisingly calm as it sits on the deck of the ship, I hope it remains so as this voyage feels to be arduous enough without a frightened calf. Aelfrestan was the one who bound it and he spoke soothing words to it until it lowered itself down and became content. He is a serene young man with distant eyes. I know that he Sees things as well, and it is good that Kolga raised him and taught him not to fear them. It is hard to see things that others can't, and his life has not been easy.

Kolga

We have finally started our journey. The sail that was years in the making billows out from the mast, and the winds shall favor us in the long trip ahead. The crew is made of stolid, solemn men who do not question this voyage into the unknown. Indeed, it shall bring them honor in the eyes of the gods to undertake this expedition with us on blind faith alone. Amma and Hild sit with me in the stern of the ship where we make our plans while Aelfrestan sits by the mast, leaning against the calf.

The horrible figurine that Amma got from Haukr remains wrapped tightly in its cloth with us. I do not want the crew to know of its existence should it cause discord. I feel it calling out already to its home. I think that eventually it shall succeed in bringing something to either collect it or to lead it back. Something that would have come for the child and any other people of the village that it may have corrupted had Amma not gotten to it when she had.

We are still within known waters, though after tomorrow we should be heading into the unknown. Raumr wishes to land and refresh our water supply as it shall be the last time that he is sure of being able to. I defer to him in these things as I have spent my life up high with the earth beneath my feet. The voyage has been smooth and everyone is content so far. I hope it continues this way, though I know there shall be some trials to face. The Web of Wyrd showed me strange things, and the men shall fear them. They are strong men though, and I have faith in Raumr as well as the gods.

RAUMR

We restocked our supplies a few days ago and have turned ourselves out to the mercy of the unknown. The voyage goes well, the gods are with us, as are the winds. We are charting unknown seas, though there is little to put on a map. We can still glimpse bits of the coast and, until Kolga tells me otherwise, I shall try to keep them in our sights in case anything should go wrong. Everyone seems in good spirits, if a bit bemused by what we are doing. They shall not waver though; I chose good men for this.

AELFRESTAN

I have never seen so much water. When Raumr taught me

to sail we stayed close to home. I know enough to help if needed, but thus far conditions have been nearly ideal. I spend my time talking to the völvur and caring for the animals we have with us. The crows are raucous, they wish to be free to fly, but we still follow the coast, even though it is far away, so they cannot be freed as they may not return. The snakes are lethargic and do not need much caring for, and the calf is content thus far and allows me to lay beside it to sleep.

I am visited in my dreams by Hel. She is the first of the gods that I Saw and as I grew up She would sometimes come to collect those of the dead that I encountered as well. Her smile is always sad. The first time I saw Her, I was frightened by Her appearance, but over the years Her visage has become one that I love. She is comforting to me after so long. She has been a constant in my life and will be there after I die. Her father, Loki, has visited me many times, in many forms. He always appears beautiful when He wants me to know it is Him, and He disguises Himself as many things when He wants to play His tricks. I think I learned most of my life lessons from Him. His crafty tricks and sly lies provided a harsh, yet firm foundation for an education. Kolga would sit back and wait for me to figure things out on my own most times, although once or twice, when I allowed my life to become endangered, she stepped in and saved me. Those were important lessons though, I had to learn that I was willing to die, not just unafraid of doing so.

Now we sail farther than I could ever see, and we shall continue to sail farther and farther yet. I watch the water and daydream about what we shall find at the end. I am happy to be out here, to have the world open to me. I have not Seen the gods nor the dead since we set sail and it has been nice, though I do not think it will last. Where we go, I know death shall be. Are the dead of other peoples like our dead? Does Hel come for them as She does for us? I suppose that soon enough I shall find out.

*A*MMA

Each night now I dream of those terrible dolphins. They no longer pull His chariot, but they swim swiftly through the dark waters. They are coming to us. They shall lead us to Him. I see a road of water stretching out to us from His place. It is a river within the sea.

*H*ILD

The nights are filled now with visions of that island. Its temples and homes, so beautifully crafted, have been crushed to rubble. Its people grovel at the feet of the god who destroyed their city. He makes them create a temple for Him and when it is complete He smiles hideously at them. Many fight against Him, and He slaughters them without a second thought. In the end some remain, mad slaves to Him. He reaches down amongst them and each one that He touches sheds their form and becomes a dolphin which He binds with an ivory collar and throws into the sea. They cannot leave Him, they are forced to serve Him, and always look upon their ruined home and gather in the pools in His temple. He is the Master of the Temple.

In flashes I See those eyes again, staring up from a bowl full of blood, and the others, far beneath the sea, rising up to meet me. I know who they are. They shall be our salvation, but it comes at a price.

KOLGA

We have been in new waters now for twelve days and it was but a few hours ago when we encountered dolphins that I believe are connected to the figurine in some way. I do not guess this simply because of what Amma and Hild have Seen, but due to the dolphins' behavior as well. They came across the waters towards us and have surrounded the boat as if they were some sort of guard. It began with seven, two on each side and the rest following, and is now up to ten. The crew think it is a good sign, and I shall not dissuade them of this notion.

We have left behind the sight of land and have only open water to every side. Our provisions are still well stocked and we have yet to encounter any bad weather or other interference to our journey. Tomorrow we shall begin letting a few of the crows out to fly, though I think we still have at least a few days before we reach our destination. Perhaps flying shall ease their restlessness.

AELFRESTAN

The crows have been flying for the past three days, but they return to the ship. They do not seem to care for the dolphins, but they have nowhere else to go. Each day we are joined by more dolphins, and some have taken to swimming ahead of us, leading off towards the south. The crew at first embraced the dolphins as a sign, and then became wary of their ever increasing numbers. We now have at least twenty of them around us at all times. Kolga has asked Raumr to follow where they lead. This has eased the minds of the other men as they believe that they must be guides from the gods. There is a slight pull towards the south as well, Raumr believes there is a strong southern current close to us. Perhaps that is what Amma Saw.

At night now, when I sleep, I still see Hel, and sometimes Her father. Loki plays with snakes, letting them slither over Him. He reminds me of when I was young and He led me to a place in the cliffs where there was a writhing mass of snakes. He presented me with a bag and had me collect them and bring them home. At various times He would ask me to let one or another bite me. Sometimes it was harmless, sometimes venomous. Kolga had to sit with me a number of times when I was close to death from a bite dared on me by Loki. I learned to not fear the bite of a snake as I learned not to fear death. We do not know where the snakes came from, but we kept them. Two of the most deadly are the snakes on the ship with us now.

RAUMR

This voyage has become stranger and stranger. We are now surrounded by dolphins and riding a swift current that brings us further and further south. The völvur tell us that this is how it should be, so we continue this way. The crew are getting a bit unnerved by these happenings, but all things point to the aid of the gods, so we shake off our fears and watch the water fly past us ever faster. A few of the crows have not returned today, soon we should reach wherever it is this is leading us. Kolga has told us that the land we approach is not a safe place, but that we shall not be staying there long. As we still have a decent stock of supplies I am glad that it seems we shall be finishing this undertaking soon and turning back to our home. We won't have the aid of the current on the way back, but we still have her sails and cords, and hopefully the favor of the gods. I wonder what this land shall be like.

AMMA

We have arrived. When we came within sight of land the dolphins departed and swam beneath the waters, still seemingly headed towards the island. Kolga, Hild, Aelfrestan, Raumr, and I came onto the shore with a few of the crew. A few of the men began to seek out fresh water to restock our supplies while the rest of us followed an old trail leading to the interior of the island. When we crested the top of the hills rising up from the shore we were amazed by the sights below us. We appeared to have landed near the end of a once great city. Lying below us in a natural valley and stretching into the distance were ruins that must have housed between 1,500 to 2,000 people. The extent of its devastation made it difficult to guess. Marble seemed to be the primary building material and once glorious bridges lay in pieces in the river, while temples and homes alike had been pulled down from their perches on the protective slopes surrounding the city.

At the end was the only piece of architecture left preserved. It was a pristine white temple, many times larger than anything else that had been built on the island. It looked to be built into the rock with the marble façade covering the front. It was adorned with His face. Raumr was captivated by the visage carved on the temple walls, it was beautiful carved in stone, not bringing the revulsion of the existence of such perfection as when seeing He who it was modeled after. We broke him from his trance and returned to the shore.

AELFRESTAN

As soon as we landed I was inundated with the dead. The dead here are very angry, and very scared. I could See them, tearing at their hair, wailing silently in grief, and trying to escape from their prison. After I was able to gather myself we walked to a place where we could see the city that once housed all of these wretched dead. I could See them walking in the streets, unable to pass on. It was a terrible sight. The most appalling thing was the enormous temple that stood over the violated city. The home of the one who had brought such devastation sat over them like a king surveying his kingdom. Raumr was caught up with His beauty until we shook him and got him to return with us to the shore. As we left I glanced back and caught a glimpse of Him peering out from His temple. I could See beyond His outward countenance to something innate to his being. I could See slime coated tendrils drifting lazily about him, some the size of an arm, some as large as an ox's leg. He looked at me and seemed shocked for a second, and then He smiled.

When we returned to the shore I told the völvur what I had Seen. Our plans had all been tentatively made, we simply had to adapt them to the island. While they discussed what each was to do and the men from the ship hastily restocked some water, I walked a little way off to get my head together, and to get away from the mass of the dead. As I sat and stared out to the sea, a calm came over me. I looked up and Saw Hel walking towards me across the water. She stood before me and She had never looked more beautiful. It was almost time.

After Aelfrestan told us of all of the dead and the Master of the Temple we let him rest, his final act would come soon. We had Raumr get everyone back onto the ship and began to make our final preparations. Kolga would remain on the ship to work the winds for our flight from here. It was Aelfrestan and I who would remain on the shore. It was time to fulfill his fate. The ship would wait for my return and then fly from this blasphemous place.

We brought with us the calf, the cloth wrapped figurine, the snakes, and my bowl. Aelfrestan shed his shirt and nodded at me. "I am ready," he said.

Opening the baskets, I removed the snakes and draped them around Aelfrestan's neck. His eyes were distant; he was Seeing something behind me. He nodded at it and then the snakes struck, fangs plunging into his neck and then he raised his arms and they struck at his wrists as well. He bore his serene smile as he stood before me, arms wrists flanking his neck to make it easier for me to collect the venom laced blood that poured from his wounds. I filled my bowl, the snakes offering me no violence as I entered their range. The wounds were deep, and my bowl filled quickly. Once it was full I covered it and made my way on to the ship where I anointed the heads of each of the crew with a smear of the blood. Amma, Kolga, and I each coated our eyes and took a deep drink from the bowl. The rest was poured onto the serpentine figurehead of the ship. Raumr immediately set us sailing as quickly from the island and away from the current that had formerly been our guide and aide as he could. Kolga stood in the stern with cords out and her staff weaving winds into being. Soon we crossed out from the coast and into open sea.

Kolga

As soon as we saw Hild running across the shore to us I began to call up the winds as Raumr set the sail and the men got ready to flee as fast as we could. As she boarded and distributed the collected blood, we cast off, and she settled down to catch her breath. Raumr and I focused on getting away from the island and far enough from the current that we wouldn't be pulled back. Looking back to the shore after having drank from Hild's bowl, I could See Aelfrestan was now joined by a figure to either side of him. He swayed under the influence of the venom in his body and was supported by Hel while Loki laid a firm hand on his shoulder and spoke to him. Grateful that he was accepted, I turned back to our escape.

Amma

It was chaos aboard the ship as Raumr and Kolga sought to get us as far away from that dreadful place as they could. On the shore Aelfrestan still stood, unsteadily, and I could See Hel embracing him while Loki spoke to him and gathered up the wrapped figurine and the lead for the calf. He began to walk up the trail then, and Hel led Aelfrestan further up the shore, fading from view as She brought him home.

Hild collapsed as the three all passed from sight, so I got behind her and braced her to prevent her from falling from the ship as it frantically sailed away. The crew members wrapped ropes around us and themselves for protection as well and fell to obeying the shouted commands of Raumr.

As Loki crested the ridge I dropped into myself and I Saw and followed Him in my mind's eye. He entered the temple without so much as a glance at the carvings that dominated the exterior. The first chamber He walked into was a great cavern, it appeared to be an antechamber and there was an opening to the back, its stone covering rolled to the side.

Upon passing through the door there was a vast pool from which dolphins raised their heads and beneath which many more of them swam. Behind the pool stood a throne, upon which sat the Master of the Temple. He looked Loki up and down and said, "And who are you that enters my temple, while your worshipers attempt to flee from me?"

"Who am I? I am Loki. Blood brother to Odin, father to those that shall help bring about the end of the world, and the one who shall bring about your end, little god. You made a mistake when you tried to corrupt my people. It was a cunning attempt, for they are strong travelers, and able to reach you and strengthen your numbers should they fall beneath your thrall. But I am a more cunning god and you are old, and you are weak, and I shall not let you have them." He stated.

The Master became angered. "Old, yes, but I am not weak! Do you not see what I have done? My people worship me blindly! I can cast an influence over others, even far from my home, simply through an idol delivered by my followers that will bend their minds until they come to me! Merely gazing upon me drives humans to devotion!" He had risen from His chair, pacing before the throne.

"Ah yes, your idol, your beauty, your greatest lie. I am the Trickster, the God of Lies, amongst other things, and your idol has not fooled me." Loki unwrapped the idol from its cloth, "It is time to destroy any influence you may have had over my people," He said as He crushed the idol in His hand. From within the statue a putrid slime oozed through the cracks. The Master shrieked as His features seemed to slough away, and in their place now sat an abomination with many flailing appendages that resembled giant slugs.

"How dare you?" screamed the putrid being before the throne.

"I told you, you are weak. You and your brethren once ruled this world, but that time is long past. Now you hide in your little holes and seek out followers through trickery and insanity. I have known of you for a long time and have been preparing my followers to bring me to you to see you undone. I am more of a trickster than you, and more cunning than you. You have grown dull over the centuries and are fed by the beliefs of the weak of mind. Our people are strong in both mind and body and we grant them strength while they live. When they die, they rise up with us again to fight by our sides. Your followers are wretched and mad and that is what you have become."

The vile corruption writhed in fury, Its limacine limbs wrapping around Itself, running up and down the main trunk of Its body. As It roared, the pool became frenzied with the actions of the dolphins. They leapt and darted, some attempting to attack Loki where He stood before the water. "Do you see my children? You may have destroyed one of my idols, but there are more, and they shall deliver them, swimming as far as they must, to any shore!"

"Your children, yes. Would you like to meet one of mine?" The cavern began to tremble and the dolphins were whipped into a further mania in their pool as an enormous set of jaws plunged upward, devouring some of the cetaceans until the head of a serpent loomed above the water. "This is Jörmungandr, my son. He spans the entire world and lives beneath the sea. What say you, little god, whose children are more impressive?"

The Master of the Temple seemed to be quivering in both fear and rage, His gelatinous bulk undulating as though waves ran through His limbs.

"Now, little god, you have a choice. My son is hungry. He can either devour the rest of your children, followed by yourself, or, because I am feeling merciful, we can make a deal and I shall feed Him this calf that has been bred as an offering for Him. What do you choose?" Loki cocked His head to the side and waited.

"What is this deal? I shall agree to nothing until I hear it."

"It is simply this; you leave my people alone, for now and forever, and I shall let you live. There are plenty of other humans out there, and you may help yourself to them, but those that are followers of the Aesir shall be left free from your influence and from any harm by you and your followers forever. You are old, you are patient, this is not asking too much of you. Do you accept?"

"If I agree, you shall let me and my remaining followers live? You shall allow me to take others, as long as they do not follow you and your fellow gods?"

"That is the agreement."

"Then I agree. Feed your son that calf and leave us. Your people will never encounter us again."

"You are wise," nodded Loki. He released the calf from its lead and scooped it in His arms, throwing it towards the World Serpent's head where it was snatched up and eaten in a single bite. "Now, Jörmungandr, break through the stone beneath this island and drag it to the bottom of the sea where you can keep an eye on it." He grinned, "I'll close the door on my way out, I don't know if you can survive beneath the water."

"Treachery! You cannot do this!" howled the Master.

"I said I would let you and yours live, I never said where. Don't worry old one, you shall live a long, long time. I'm sure that you'll find a way to bring the humans down to you eventually. I did mention I was a trickster, and you'll find that this time, I didn't even lie." With that, Loki walked out of the door and rolled the stone closed behind Him as the Elder God screamed in His throne room. He turned His head and winked at me, and then vanished. After that I came back to my body, bound to the ship and Amma in a turbulent sea.

Amma

As Hild came back to herself she exclaimed, "Loki! Jörmungandr! He's tearing down the island!"

Indeed, it appeared to be so. The volcanic rock beneath the surface of the island must have been filled with warrens of caves that the World Serpent wrapped Himself throughout as He thrashed and heaved. The sea tossed around us, waves crashing over the vessel, but never capsizing us, nor flooding the deck. The protection from Aelfrestan's sacrifice keeping us safe. As the island pitched and cast about it seemed to be carried upon and within coils of Jörmungandr's body slowly to the south and under the tempestuous sea.

When the sea finally calmed down enough for us to be assured of our safety, we unbound ourselves from the ropes and fell to resting. We had lost no one in our flight, and our crew now had a tale of glory that should keep them in drinks for the rest of their lives. I felt a pang for Aelfrestan, but he had fulfilled his wyrd, and had done it well.

Raumr

Never before have I fought so hard to keep a ship from foundering as when we fled from that terrible island and its destruction. That we had all witnessed the World Serpent destroying an entire island behind us did nothing to calm our nerves as we battled the turbulent sea. Kolga's winds blew hard and she seemed to be weaving her staff and her cords faster than should be possible. Even with her work and that of the crew, I am certain that we had some protection from Aelfrestan's sacrifice, else we would never have survived that sea. The journey home was taken at an easier pace and we encountered no problems and no dolphins.

Had I known when we were preparing to leave what we were going to do, I would have laughed at Kolga for even suggesting the attempt. Having survived it, I am glad that we went on blind faith, and you'll find none more faithful in these parts than me and my crew.

Kolga

I shall miss Aelfrestan greatly, but I know that he met his wyrd well and was embraced by Hel, whom he adored, when his soul left his body. I have fulfilled my wyrd as well, though perhaps, as I survived it, I shall finally start to see what comes next for me. The Web of Wyrd shall tell me.

When we returned and told our tale, some scoffed at us. It was when Helga reminded them of the day Haukr suddenly recovered from his delirium and thanked Loki that they began to believe. Raumr and his crew got their moment of glory, and long did it last. Amma, Hild, and I went back to the way things have always been, staying in the shadows until we are needed. Everything seems to have worked out for the best.

Sometimes at night, I wonder why Loki didn't kill the Master of the Temple. Was it sheer spite to sink His home to where no one could ever reach it again? I suppose I shall never know, perhaps it was His wyrd.

I shall leave these papers, wrapped tight in an oilskin, in a small nook in a cave up on the cliffs. This is where I See them when I get lost in my weaving. I believe that I know why this needed to be recorded. Loki could have gone on his own, but without us to bear witness, it wouldn't have mattered. It needed to matter. I hope that what I See is true and that someone shall someday share the tale of our voyage, until then, we know, and that is enough.

Final notes from Althea Smythe:

I know that this tale seems unbelievable, and had I not come across a different one before it, I would have thought it a jest or a lie. However, a few years ago, before I was presented with this collection, I was given a transcript of Karl Heinrich, Graf von Altberg-Ehrenstein, Lieutenant-Commander in the Imperial German Navy*, dated in 1917 wherein he encounters a very similar place – at the bottom of the sea. I leave it to you to decide.

———

*This is a reference to H.P. Lovecraft's "The Temple"

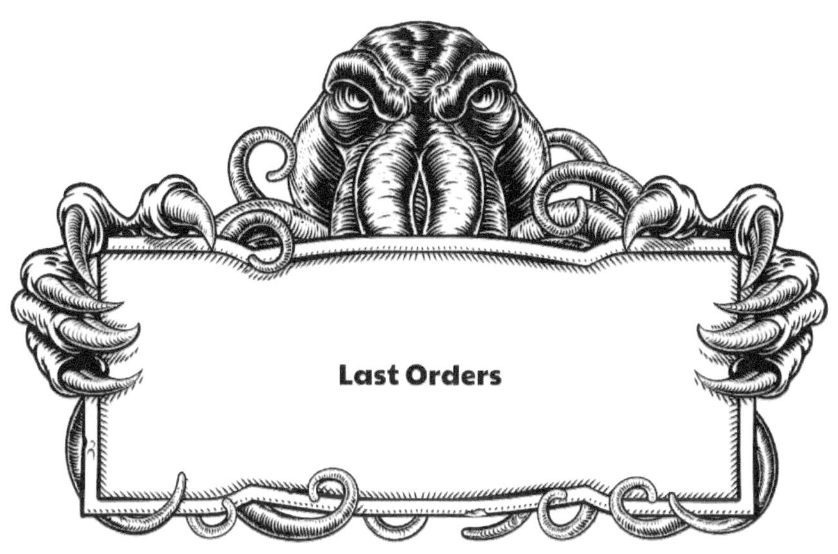

BY DALE DRAKE

Harry Saunders stared moodily into his pint, trying to figure out exactly when his life had gone down the crapper. It wasn't easy. It seemed for as long as he could remember everything he touched turned to shit. It wasn't that he was an unpleasant kind of guy. Sure, he could get rowdy after a few drinks and there was that one time he had been caught stealing from some tourist from up country. But who gave a tin shit? It wasn't anyone from the village, just some rich prick, probably from up London way, some guy with a flashy car and a summer home in Barbados. What was the loss of one mobile phone to a rich prick like that? He'd been caught lifting the phone from the man's back pocket but the thing that had really hurt was it had been one of his fellow villagers that had grassed him in, old Moreen from the village fudge shop, calling out a warning in her old warbling, cracked voice. The man had spun around, clamping a large hairy hand on Harry's wrist. Harry had not tried to run or struggle to get away. What was the point? There must have been about a hundred people milling around the village square that day and he knew his goose was pretty much cooked. For that little stunt, he had received a five hundred pound fine and a hundred hours community service.

That had been about two years ago now and he was still paying off the God damn fine. At two pound a month, he figured he would just about be finished paying around the time Jesus returned to forgive him the sin of stealing in the first place. Fucking people, fucking village. They hated the summer people just as much as he did. Behind their smiles was a smouldering contempt. But they hid it well, desperate for the money those rich pricks brought down with them. They were like squirrels, storing their nuts to help them get through the long winters when the seas were high and the fishing lean.

He was rudely dragged back from his musing by the clanging of the bar's bell. Big Eddie, The Lantern's landlord, was calling last orders and looking directly at Harry. He tipped his elbow a few times, the universal signal to drink up and, in Harry's case, to fuck off. Harry smirked and went back to contemplating the dregs of his pint. He knew damn well they had a lock in at The Lantern most nights. Old Eddie over there, he of the tipping elbow, would lock the doors, close the curtains and keep the party going to the wee early hours of the morning. Of course Harry wasn't invited. Not that it mattered. He had drunk away this month's welfare cheque at an alarming rate and had just enough money left to keep the electric meter running until

November's cheque arrived, hot and crisp and ready to be drunk or smoked away.

He stood, just about to leave, when his old chum, Johnny Calum, came barging through the door, rubbing his hands briskly. He glanced over at Harry then quickly hurried over to the bar, hoping to get a drink but big Eddie sent him packing with a wave of one meaty arm. Shrugging, he weaved his way over to Harry's table and plonked himself down. The smell of marijuana surrounded him like a cloud.

"How's going, Harry?" He grinned the smile of the perpetually stoned.

"Aright," Harry said, squinting at his old friend and fellow black sheep, although it hadn't always been that way for poor old Johnny. He had been someone once, a university graduate. He had studied in London and got himself a degree in businesses studies. His mistake had been coming back to the village. He had planned to take a year off before hunting down a job in the big city, a little time to recuperate after the traumas of university life, and so had returned to the peace and tranquillity of his childhood home, only to run into his childhood friend, Harry Saunders, who had introduced him to the magical world of drugs and hard liquor. Now, just like Harry, he was a nobody, a well-educated nobody, but a nobody nevertheless.

"Vandravens."

"What?" Harry muttered.

"I said The Vanderavens," Johnny repeated. "Jesus, Harry, how much have you had?" Harry waved that away.

"What about the Vandraven House?"

"I never said the house. There is nothing in that old place

but broken furniture and bad dreams, nothing we could sell anyway."

"Sell," Harry said, sitting up straighter, trying to clear away the fog. "Sell? What the hell are you talking about? This had better not be one of your get rich quick schemes. I don't fancy anymore God damn community service picking up litter and used needles. Once was enough."

"No, no, nothing like that," Johnny said, a strange gleam in his eye. "This is even better. You have heard of the Vandravens, Harry. You know their story."

"Of course I do," Harry answered, growing somewhat impatient. "Everybody knows about the Vandraven House and the Westerfield family found dead up there, their bodies all torn up in the basement. It was the talk of the town when I was growing up. They never found the people responsible. As far as I know, the place has been empty ever since. Some of the old timers say the place is cursed."

"I am quite sure it is," Johnny interrupted, "and was long before the Westerfield family ever moved in. Tell me, Harry. What do you know of Lucas Vandraven?"

"Not much," Harry shrugged. "He was the man who built the house back sometime in the eighteen hundreds, killed his wife and a whole bunch of servants before throwing himself off a nearby cliff. Ever since, the place is rumoured to be haunted. Now, are you going to tell me what the hell the Vandraven House has to do with any of this?"

"The house, nothing. Lucas Vandraven, everything! That, and the place he is buried."

Harry threw up his hands.

"If you don't start making sense soon, Johnny, I am gonna punch you right on the nose, I swear to God."

"Okay, okay," Johnny giggled, holding up a restraining hand. "But it won't make sense unless you let me tell it my way and old Eddie over there is giving us the stink eye. Come on, let's go to The Ship. Helen is working the bar tonight. You know she has the hots for me," he said, wiggling his eyebrows suggestively.

"That's disgusting," Harry grinned, clambering to his feet. "She is old enough to be your mother."

"Grandmother," Johnny laughed, also rising. "But what a set of tits!"

Laughing, both men left The Lantern, Big Eddie's scowl following them out into the darkness.

Ten minutes later, they were sat by a roaring fire in a quiet corner of The Ship Inn. Just like Johnny said, they had no problem getting served by the matronly barmaid who seemed overjoyed to see Johnny and chatted away enthusiastically as she poured them both pints, making sure her ample bosom was on display the whole time. Finally, they escaped into a quiet corner and Johnny continued with his story.

"You remember my grandmother?"

"Of course," Harry replied. "We buried her only a few months ago. I was there at the funeral, wasn't I, or have you forgotten."

Johnny ignored that.

"What you didn't know was that her mother, my great grandmother, used to work at the Vandraven House."

"So?" Harry shrugged. "What has that to do with anything?"

"She was a maid, a cleaner who used to go up there twice a

week and clean the place, polish the silver and turn the rugs, that kind of thing. She was the first one to find them, or what was left of them, after Lucas Vandraven had finished with them."

"Who?" Harry asked, showing the first real spark of interest. "Who did she find?"

"His wife. His wife and her maid all torn up on the sewing room floor. My old granny used to tell me tales when she had had a few drinks, how her old mother found them there both naked as babies covered in blood, surrounded by black candles. His wife, Elizabeth Vandraven, had been stabbed to death with a pair of knitting needles to the throat but it was her maid, Matilda, who was the worst. Her poor body had been torn to shreds where she lay on the floor, her stomach a red ruin, her blood splattered all over the walls. Later, when the house was more thoroughly inspected, there was talk of Voodoo and a bloody altar found in the basement, talk of human sacrifice and dark gods.

Two days later, Lucas Vandraven's body was washed ashore, crushed to his chest a child, or at least something resembling one, but nothing normal, a freak, an aberration. Yet even in death, Lucas Vandraven clung to it.

Both of them were hurried away and quickly buried in the Vandraven crypt in the grounds of St Peters. Neither of them were ever spoken of again in polite society. But my old grandmother was not a member of any aristocracy or polite society. She was common folk and she liked to talk, especially when the drink was upon her. She told how her mother had found the bodies then ran screaming from that house like all the demons of hell were snapping at her heels. What she failed to mention, however, was her theft." Johnny laughed. "Scared to death, she was, yet the glint of gold had stopped her in her tracks."

"Gold?" Harry said, leaning more fully forward, the light from the flickering fire casting shadows across his face. "What gold?"

"A pocket watch taken from Lucas Vandraven's study, a silver letter opener, and a few other minor trifles. Whatever she could stuff in her apron pockets, I imagine."

"Oh," Harry said, leaning back a little disappointed. "And this?" Harry said, reaching into his coat pocket and placing an old tatty looking leather bound book on the table between them. "What is it?" He drained off the last of his pint whilst glancing over at the clock on the far wall. It was getting late and, to be honest, he was getting tired of the whole affair.

"It's his journal," Johnny said, picking up the book and caressing it greedily. "Well part of it, anyway, talking about his adventures in far away lands or at least it starts off that way. The second half is a list, an inventory of things brought from his old town house in London to his new home here in Mevagissey."

"The Vandraven House?" Harry said, interested once again despite himself.

"Yes," Johnny said, seeming to grow even more excited as he flicked to the back of the book, right to the very last page, before thrusting the book at Harry. "There on the last page," he said. "Do you see it?" Harry did not need his old friend to point it out to him. The yellowed page contained a list written in Lucas Vandraven's large copperplate handwriting. The list was written completely in faded black ink, all except one word written in block capitals and in faded red ink, the word read *Necronomicon*.

"What the hell is a Necronomicon?" Harry asked, passing the old book back to Johnny.

"It's a book, Harry, a very rare book, one of a kind. It was written over a thousand years ago by a mad man, a poet named Abdul Alhazred. Some say he was possessed of the devil. The book contains dark rituals and writings on how to summon demons and other things far beyond man's understanding. The book was banned all over the world before it disappeared completely."

"And you think Lucas Vandraven had this book?" Harry snorted.

"Yes, he was a merchant seaman who owned a great fleet of ships that bartered and traded all over the world. Besides, it is written right there in his own journal, one Necronomicon. God knows if he knew what he had and whether it was connected to the deaths up at that old house. But Harry, don't you understand, if we could get our hands on it, it would make us rich beyond our wildest dreams."

"And you think it is here, Johnny?" Harry laughed. "Here in this pissant little village, hidden away somewhere in that old house?"

"No, Harry, I don't. I think it is in the Vandraven crypt. I think either the good folk of this village buried it with him to be rid of its evil or he put it there himself, to hide it from the rest of the world."

"And why would you think that?" Harry asked, playing with his empty glass.

"Because of this," Johnny said, reaching into his pocket and pulling out a piece of crumpled paper, which he unfolded and smoothed out across the table, revealing three rough sketches. "Do you recognise any of these, Harry?" Harry had a hard look at all three pictures. One was a book, the cover bound with what looked like heavy leather with thick rough stitching. The shape and pattern reminded him of a screaming man's face or perhaps it was merely a trick of the light. The other two pictures were exactly the same and Harry felt a familiar stirring at the sight of them.

"The first must be a picture of this Necronomicon thingy," Harry said, musing over it. "The other two look familiar but I ain't quite sure."

"You're right. That is a rough sketch of the Necronomicon. The other two are the coat of arms of the Vandraven family. One I sketched while looking at the statues of those god awful lions that guard the porch of the house. The coat of arms is emblazoned across their chests and the other I sketched from the Vandraven crypt. See the difference, Harry?" Harry looked hard. The Vandraven coat of arms was that of a three sailed clipper ship riding a huge wave. An eagle soared overhead, a struggling fish clasped firmly in its talons or at least it was in one of the drawings. In the other, the eagle did not clasp a fish but a book, a book that seemed to have a screaming face as a cover.

"My God," Harry gasped. "You found this one on his tomb, didn't you, up there at his old crypt?"

"Yes," Johnny said, glancing around nervously at the nearly empty pub. "For Christ's sake, keep your voice down, Harry."

"Sorry," Harry said, looking around guiltily before carrying on in a quieter tone. "You really think it's up there, Johnny?"

"Yes, I do," Johnny said, leaning forward until their noses were almost touching. "I think Lucas Vandraven built that crypt, not only to be interred there one day but also to hide his greatest treasures. God knows what could be buried up there, Harry, not just the book but gold, jewels. There has been talk of a pirate's treasure circulating round the village for years. God knows what a man like Lucas Vandraven got up to out there at sea. So what do you think? Want to go take a look?"

"Yes," Harry said, immediately his imagination soaring at the thoughts of such wealth.

"Good man," Johnny said, patting him on the shoulder. "Now just don't you worry about a thing, Harry. I have a plan."

Johnny's great and wonderful plan consisted of sneaking into his elderly mum and dad's garden shed to pick up a few rusty tools before storing them in the back of his equally rusted van. He then stole into the house, grabbed up a high powered torch from under the sink and a bottle of his dad's best brandy from the liquor cabinet. He thrust both into Harry's lap before gently turning on the ignition and pulling out of the drive, heading for St. Peters' cemetery. Harry looked at his watch as they drove through the silent streets of Mevaggissey. It was one AM.

"Nobody is stirring," he muttered, "not even a mouse."

"What's that, Harry?" Johnny asked, passing him the bottle.

"Nothing," Harry grunted, taking a long pull of brandy. "Let's just get this done."

"You're not having second thoughts are you, Harry?"

"No, are you?"

"Of course not," Johnny said, squirming under Harry's bloodshot gaze. "It just all seems a little more real in the dark."

"Ha," Harry laughed, taking another long drink. He could feel the brandy warming him all the way to his toes. "Old Johnny Calum, scared of the dark."

Johnny didn't answer, just nodded his head at the window screen as he pulled his old van to a gentle stop before the cemetery gates. "We're here," he sighed.

"Yeah, I guess we are. You know if we get caught we could get in a lot of trouble for this."

"And who is gonna catch us?" Johnny said, snatching the bottle from Harry and gulping the fiery brandy down. "When was the last time you even saw a real policeman in Mevagissey? Oh sure, we have that tosspot Andy Clutterbuck, but old Clutterfuck couldn't find his asshole with two hands and a flashlight. Come on," he said, climbing out of the van. "In and out before you know it."

"Okay," Harry said, pulling his coat close against the cold night air. "Let's get it done." The first obstacle the two men came across was the cemetery gates. Harry had never known them to be locked. The cemetery itself had not been in use for at least sixty years and dated back as far as the sixteen hundreds. People came here all the time to take charcoal rubbings of the old stones. Harry had even done it himself as a child and had never seen the old gates so much as closed, never mind locked, but here he was looking at the world's oldest and rustiest padlock.

"Not to worry," Johnny said, fetching the tools from the back of the van. "I have it all covered." That said, he picked out a pair of large looking bolt cutters, somewhat shinier than the rest.

"Came prepared, did you?" Harry said, shining the flashlight on the old rusty lock.

"Always best to do your homework," Johnny replied, bearing down, his back hunched. After a couple of seconds, there was an audible snick as the two blades came together, shearing the clasp in half and sending the flaky old lock tumbling to the ground.

"There we go," Johnny said, kicking the lock to one side. "Give me the flashlight, Harry, and follow me. I know where it is and stay close. The place is in shit state, bits of broken headstones all over the place, vines and potholes on the path."

"Yeah," Harry replied, his breath steaming in the air. "I have been here before, you know."

"That's the spirit, Harry," Johnny said, turning his back and heading into the darkness. "Only a few more steps between us and a fortune."

The cemetery was pretty much just how Harry had imagined it would be, scary as hell. Everywhere there were little noises, the wind sighing through the trees, the rustling of autumn leaves. Small creatures scurried away through the long grass, scared off by the human interlopers. Shadows cast by the faraway street lights danced and crawled over the leaning, broken headstones, and stone angels seemed to turn to watch them as they passed.

Suddenly, Johnny stopped, causing Harry to crash into the back of him, dropping the tool bag to the ground with a resounding crash.

"What the fuck?" Johnny rounded. "You trying to wake up the whole fucking village?"

"Well if you hadn't just fucking stopped."

"Well if you weren't breathing down my Goddamn neck."

"How the hell am I supposed to see anything?" Harry replied scooping up the tools. "You're the one with the Goddamn flash-light."

"Okay, okay, let's not wake up the whole village. We're nearly there now. It's up here," he said, once again taking the lead. "Just up past these trees." Harry had seen the Vandraven crypt before but never in the dark. Now, as Johnny played his torch over it, Harry seemed to remember every wild eyed tale he had ever been told of Lucas Vandraven and his terrible house.

"Impressive isn't it?" Johnny said, running a gloved hand down a white marble pillar.

"I don't know what it is," Harry said, taking in the structure. "Looks like a mixture between some old church and one of those Roman temples they are always showing on the History Channel."

"It's big, too," Johnny said, running his torch light down the length of the building. "See how it runs right back into the hillside there. So, tell me, Harry, why would a man like Lucas Vandraven with no living family, a man alone in the world except for his wife and some few servants, build a mausoleum as big as this?"

"Because he was a rich prick," Harry snorted, "and even in death he wanted people to know it."

"Or, he was using it to hide something, maybe a lot of things. Then there is this. Look here, Harry, just like I told you. Do you see it?" Harry came forward to the tomb's entrance, which was flanked on either side by tall marble angels. Each one carried an upraised sword and the crest of Vandraven was blazoned across their shields. "Do you see it, Harry?" Johnny said, excitedly. "Do you see it?"

"I see it," Harry replied. "Just like you said, a book clasped in the eagle's claws not a fish like up at the house."

"It's here, Harry. I would bet my life upon it."

"You may well have to," Harry replied roughly, handing him the bolt cutters. "If there is nothing in there, I may have to bash your skull in with this spade and leave you here. After all, there is plenty of space." Johnny laughed nervously and set about breaking off the old padlock from the thick wrought iron gates. He needn't have bothered. He barely touched the thing when it fell to the floor in a shower of rust.

"Well that was easy," Johnny shrugged. "Now comes the hard part. What do you think that door is made out of, Harry? Looks like copper, thick too, and we certainly don't have a key to that lock."

"Let me guess," Harry said. "You brought your lock picking set."

"Even better," Johnny said, taking the tool bag off Harry and placing it on the ground. He rummaged through it for a moment before climbing to his feet, a portable butane torch in his hand.

"Holy shit. What in the hell are you gonna do with that thing?"

"Melt through the lock, of course. Copper is a soft metal. Shouldn't take long to soften the metal then we just give it a knock with a good old hammer and it should pop right out."

"Just like that?" Harry said.

"Have a little faith in your old pal," Johnny said, kneeling down. He popped the flame on his lighter then turned on the gas. Immediately, a sharp blue flame sprang to life. Still smiling, he began to cut. The whole thing took a hell of a lot longer than Johnny had said. Copper may be soft but it doesn't melt easily. After two hours of heating then banging at the lock with a lump hammer wrapped in cloth to muffle the sound, the lock finally gave way. By this time, both men were sweating profusely, despite the cold, and Harry kept looking at his watch worriedly. It was now three o'clock in the morning. The effects of last night's booze were wearing off and he was beginning to wonder what the hell he was doing up here in the first place.

"Okay," Johnny said, gathering up the tools. "Let's finish this. Help me with the door, Harry." Together, both men put their shoulders to the heavy door and pushed. It gave way grudgingly with a loud creak that made both men wince and quickly look around before darting inside. What they saw inside stopped them in their tracks as their torch light revealed the chaos within. Everywhere there was broken stone and rotting plaster. In one corner was the remnant of a shattered coffin, a few bones scattered here and there.

Johnny continued to slowly play his torch light around the tomb, his mouth hanging open. In the centre of the room lay another coffin. This one had also been smashed open, its contents heaved out onto the floor. A skeleton lay close by dressed in the remains of a tattered dress. The skull was whole and surrounded by long wispy hair, long drained of any colour. It seemed to grin at them as if happy to see someone after so long alone in the dark.

"Mother of God," Harry whispered. "Look there," he said, pointing at the back wall. Johnny dragged his eyes away from the grinning skull and shined his light where Harry's trembling finger now pointed.

"What the hell?" he gasped, not believing what he was seeing. At the back of the crypt was a huge hole. The concrete had been somehow blasted away, leaving a ragged hole surrounded by crumbling dirt and poking roots. "Son of a bitch," Johnny growled. "They stole it."

"Who stole, what?" Harry said, scurrying to keep up.

"Grave robbers. Sons of bitches must have tunnelled their way in and stolen everything inside." He suddenly came to an abrupt stop, his anger evaporating as shock took over. He turned to Harry. "Look," he whispered, shining the torch with one trembling hand. Harry quickly looked over his shoulder.

"Holy shit," he said. "What the hell is going on here, Johnny?"

"I don't know," Johnny replied, staring at the stone steps that led down into the darkness. "I don't have a fucking clue!"

A full minute passed until either man spoke again. They just stood there trying to make sense of what they were seeing.

"Okay," Johnny said, squaring his shoulders. "Let's head on down."

"What?" Harry said, grabbing Johnny's arm. "What the hell are you talking about?" Johnny shrugged free and shined the torch in Harry's face.

"I am going down to take a look. There is something hidden down there, Harry, and I intend to find it. Look at those steps. No grave robber built those. Don't you get it? He hid it away, buried it down there, maybe, in some kind of cave complex he discovered while building the foundations for this place. It's down there, Harry. The Vandraven fortune. We can split it, Harry. You take the gold, jewels, whatever we find, and I will take the book. Come on, Harry. We are close, can't you feel it?"

And he could. There was something down there, almost as if it were calling to him. Perhaps his entire life had led to this one moment, all his failures left behind him. He would be rich, richer than his wildest dreams, then he would show them who was a loser. He could see it, now, them begging him for money and the village girls who had snubbed him, called him a waster, he could have them, he could have it all, and what was there to be afraid of? This was no Indiana Jones movie with a bunch of cheap booby traps. There was nothing down there but the dark and a fortune just waiting for Harry Saunders to go claim it.

"All right," he said, "lead the way." They had only been walking a few minutes, seemingly heading straight down, when the floor suddenly seemed to level off, forming a kind of tunnel. They staggered on, the walls getting narrower, their breathing loud in their ears. Harry was just about to demand they go back when they turned a final corner that opened into a small cave. Harry looked around in amazement, his jaw dropping as he let out a terrified groan.

The cave was lit by some kind of glowing fungus that seemed to crawl and undulate with a strange life of its own. Strewn across the floor was the wealth of nations. Gold doubloons, pearls, and jewels the size of hens' eggs, rough bars of silver and golden trinkets lay scattered about. Amongst all these treasures an obsidian altar rose in the centre of the room. Upon it lay a large black book that could only be the fabled Necronomicon.

"Sweet God," Johnny muttered. "It's here, Harry. We actually found it."

"No," Harry shouted, lurching after his friend. He span him about. "We have to leave this place, Johnny. We have to leave right now. Can't you feel it? This place is evil. We have to leave," he said again, half dragging his friend with him.

"Leave?" Johnny shrugged him off angrily. "It's there, Harry. The book is right there. You can have the rest, take it, take it all but the book is mine!"

"Help me."

The voice was nothing more than a sibilant whisper, yet both men slowly turned in the direction from which it had come. With a trembling hand, Johnny raised the torch and shined it on the back of the cavern-like room. There, slumped in a throne like chair, sat a man or a creature that had once been a man. The thing wore the remains of a tattered suit, torn from the waist up. Clinging to its rotting frame was some kind of loathsome leech or parasite. As the two men looked on in horror, the thing tore a strip of rotting flesh from the creature's side, revealing yellowed ribs. Black blood oozed from the open wound and the creature let out a cry of agony as it stumbled to its feet, reaching out imploringly to the two men.

"Help me," it pleaded. "Help me feed it, it's hungry, always hungry. Help me feed it. Help me feed my son."

"No," Harry screamed his denial. Turning, he fled into the darkened passage, Johnny right behind him. Even over Johnny's whimpering, Harry could hear it coming, hear it dragging its rotting body after them, trapped forever in its own version of hell. They were half way up the stairs when there came a clattering from behind and a cry of pain. Harry spun round. Johnny was down, sprawled on the stone steps, his face a grimace of pain.

"My ankle. Oh God, Harry, don't leave me here." A pale arm shot out of the darkness and wrapped itself around Johnny's throat as the thing that had once been Lucas Vandraven pulled itself up onto his body. For a moment, Johnny heaved and bucked, gagging and choking, then his eyes rolled up in his head as he fainted dead away.

Now there was only Harry face to face with this terror from the dark. He scrambled backwards as the thing reached for him.

"Come with me," it chuckled. "Down into the dark. Such things I will show you, such sweet agonies. Come," it said, reaching, straining. "You will live forever."

"No," Harry screamed, scrabbling to his feet. He turned and ran, bursting from the tunnels. He ran through the night shrouded crypt out into the night. He fled, screaming, his mind broken.

IN THE GRAVEYARD, all was still. An owl hooted and the wind sighed through the trees. Overhead, a pale moon shone a silver light over the now silent tomb of Vandraven.

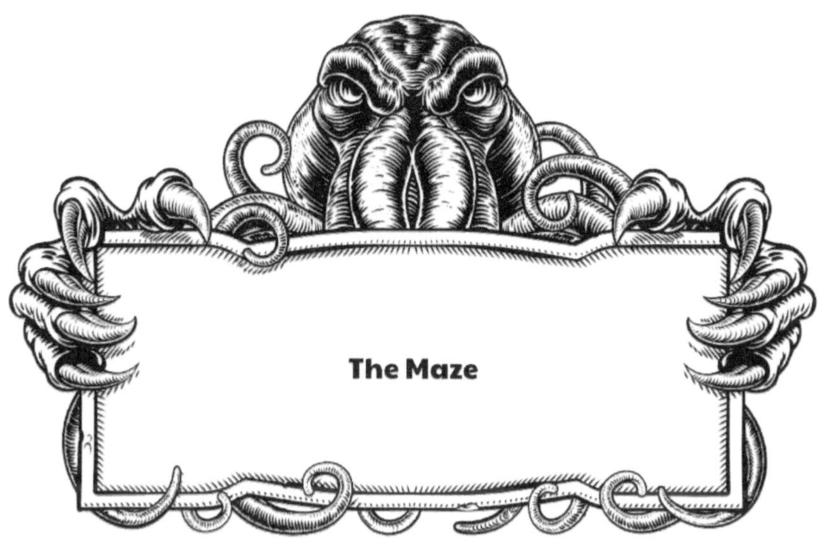

BY CHARLES REIS

I t's been said that when a person encounters a traumatic event, that person relives their entire life. When I experienced my trauma, I relived everything that led me to this point. This was my flashback...

It was in-between my classes at the University of Rhode Island. With me working full-time while trying to earn my degree, it ruined my social life. However, I knew it would be worth it. My mom had said to me many times, "Joshua, you are going to be the first college graduate in our family! You make me so proud!" Her words kept me from giving up.

Before going to my next class, I used the restroom that was next to the library. When I entered, I became uncomfortable. The lights were flickering, the faucets were dripping, and garbage was in every corner, but the decrepit layout wasn't what bothered me. When I entered, I at once felt a cold chill down my spine. Although I was alone, I felt like eyes were watching me from every direction. I quickly did my business.

Afterwards, I washed my hands. That was when the lights went out. I wouldn't have normally cared, but it felt like I was standing in the deepest parts of inner Earth. My body trembled and my heart raced. As I tried to feel my way out, I touched the wall, but felt something cold and slimy, as if I was touching a giant slug. I retracted my hand and wiped the slime off on my pants. That was when the noise started. It came from the walls and it sounded like ooze swirling around. I started to lose my balance due to an onslaught of dizziness and nausea. Seconds later, I lost consciousness.

I didn't know how long I was out, but when I opened my eyes, I found myself lying face down on a damp floor in a dimly lit brick hallway. When I stood up, I had to put my hand on the nearby wall to keep my balance. I rapidly looked around. The smell of musk filled the air. There were patches of algae-type plants growing on the walls and floor. The hallway appeared endless; no matter what direction I looked, there seemed to be no end to it. I hoped that was simply an illusion. I heard a faint humming sound coming from an unknown location.

I took out my smartphone, but there was no signal. An intense sense of isolation scared me to the point that I began crying. It felt like everyone that I knew were millions of miles away. After looking around, I believed my only choice was to explore this place. Fear infected every part of my body, but I had no choice. After taking a few deep breaths, I began my journey.

An hour had passed, but every step I took led me nowhere. While the hallways had other passageways, they all looked the same. I had no idea where I was going. I had lost track of time. Additionally, the lack of companionship made my plight more upsetting. I was about ready to give up. However, I convinced myself that if I kept on moving, I would eventually get somewhere. I needed to stay optimistic.

During my moment of despair, I discovered a notable change: the humming sound was louder. Wherever it emanated from, I was closer to it. I needed to find the source, it might be my way home. This glimmer of hope gave me a boost of adrenaline, so I continued. I felt more confident that I was going to find my way home.

I spent an hour trying the following the noise. Eventually, I came across a passageway where it seemed to be coming from, so I entered it. When I did, I discovered that it led to a ten-story high stone staircase. Walking up this was going to be a strain on my weakened body, but I had no choice. I took a deep breath and slapped my face, and I began my journey.

This was a long walk up. On two separate occasions, I rested for about five minutes. My legs and feet became sore. Nevertheless, when I finally reached the top, I got more questions than answers. I suppressed my impulse to scream because of the astonishing view that was before me. Without a question, I was on another world.

I stood on a large plateau that overlooked a massive maze made of brick walls, arches, and pillars in an endless array of twists and turns as far as the eye could see. Before me was another flight of stairs that went down into it. In the center Of the maze was a tall structure that would overshadow the Empire State Building. It had abnormal angles, unusual curves, and non-Euclidean designs. The structure was a light brown and covered entirely by strange carvings, although I was too far to make them out. Twelve large black squares hovered about twenty feet above the structure in a pattern like a clock. I wondered to myself how the hell those things were hovering like that. I figured it was some type of citadel, but regardless of what it was, the humming noise derived from that structure.

The sky had a greenish tint with two distant red suns. Rising over the horizon was a large red planet with Saturn-like rings. I felt that this had to be a nightmare, for there was no scientific way for me to travel millions of light years into the darkness of space. It was impossible... but here I was on another world. I started to gag, but I fought off the urge to have a complete breakdown; I needed to stay strong.

As I continued to gaze at this unbelievable view, I became relieved when I heard other humans, I smiled and thanked God that I wasn't alone. As I gazed down the stairs behind me, I saw four people walking up. I was ready to jump with joy. When they saw me, they stopped about thirty steps down. There were two men and two women. One was a white man in a business suit. He was in his late forties, thin, and clean-cut. There was another white man; he was tall, in his late twenties, and wore British police officer uniform. One of the women was of Asian descent with long hair and in her early twenties; her face smudged from crying. The last one was a short, athletic, dark-skinned woman in her thirties, and she wore a red sweat shirt and hijab.

The businessman asked, "Who-who ar-are you?"

All four kept their distance, and that made me nervous, "My---my name is Joshua... you?"

The businessman didn't answer my question, instead he raised his voice, "Where are you from... Joshua?"

"Well, I'm from Rhode Island. I was at school when I was taken here... and what about you all?"

The businessman spoke with a firm voice, "My name's Carl, and I live in Los Angeles. I'm the CEO of LogTech... I was at my office when I was taken."

The man in uniform spoke in a softer tone, "Hello, me name's Tony. I'm an officer from Manchester... and I was on patrol."

Next, the woman with the hijab spoke, "I'm Masarra from New York, and I was working at a library before I ended up here. This lady here is Ruka from Yokohama, but since she speaks little English, that was we could get out of her."

As Ruka looked down, she whispered, *Monsuta.*

I was happy to see them, but when I took a step forward, Carl backed away, "Hey! Hey! Don't be afraid of me." I said. I took a step backwards and held my hands in the air.

Tony spoke up, "Don't be miffed, mate, but there was a fifth gentleman with us. We came across what we thought was a sixth person... but it turned out to be a ... a bloody monster! The other gentleman... he was murdered by it." When I heard him say 'monster', dread filled my soul. I couldn't imagine what strange creatures inhabited this world. As Ruka continued to cry, I understood that the killing of the fifth person by a monster must have been a horrific scene to witness.

"Monster?" Saying that word gave goosebumps.

Carl yelled, "Did he stutter? I suggest you be on your way!"

I couldn't believe what I heard as my body quivered, "Please, don't leave me alone here!"

"Hell no! I'm not putting my life in danger!"

Tony looked directly into my eyes for several seconds. "Let the mate come, we can't just abandon him. Besides, look at his eyes!" I stood there wondering what was so important about my eyes. However, now wasn't the time to ask.

Carl pointed his finger at Tony, "I'll decide who can come with us! Besides, how do we know those monsters can't disguise their eyes too?" Overcome with rage, he balled his hands and clenched his teeth. As I looked at him, I realized his attitude was an act to cover the fact that he was deeply afraid.

Masarra went up to Carl and poked her finger into his chest, "What, are you voting for us all now?"

He responded by bulging his chest out. "Listen raghead! I'm not putting my life in jeopardy on good faith that this boy isn't a monster! He's not coming!" At that point, Masarra raised her fist, but she held back from punching him. I too had to hold myself back from jumping on him.

Tony screamed, "You stupid ol' twat! Go on, if that be your attitude! You can either be alone, or we can all go together!" Masarra nodded her head as she crossed her arms. I smiled and took a deep breath as I became filled with relief. Meanwhile, Carl began hitting the side of his legs with his fist. Despite his anger and fear, he was going to stay with the group.

After a brief pause, Tony turned to me. "Joshua, have you discovered any additional information?"

"Ya... come see this." I gestured for them to come to the top of the stairs. They slowly walked to me. When they saw the landscape, their eyes opened wide and their bodies froze; their souls overcome with amazement and fear. No one said a word. Ruka's emotional state eroded as she collapsed to her knees. I wasn't sure how much more she could handle. Although I was staying strong for now, this place was starting to bend my mind in ways it had never been before.

I pointed to the citadel. "The noise seems to be coming from that building. I think we should head there." I was confident in this plan because I knew it was our only logical choice. No one objected to it. A long journey awaited us. After Masarra helped Ruka off the ground, we started walking down the stairs to enter this new area.

This part of the maze was different. The majority of it was open-air instead of closed-in. The air was salty, as if we were near the ocean. There were small leaves, branches, and vines growing on the grounds and walls, and scattered throughout the area were small bushes. The passageways and tunnels were less lined with drop offs, platforms, and stairs. At one moment we were on top looking down into another corridor, and next we were on the bottom looking up at more floors. When I thought we were getting closer to our destination, it turned out we moved farther away. Frustration and anger became a common feeling. This wasn't going to be easy.

The more time I spent in this place, the more my mind wanted to break, and I could tell it was the same for some of the others. Carl was increasingly hostile towards the others. Ruka constantly cried and stared at the ground; her body constantly trembled. Tony and Masarra appeared to hold on their sanity, but I wasn't sure how much longer I would last. My thoughts swirled around in my head uncontrollably, and my breathing was erratic. No one had had anything to drink or eat for hours. At this moment, I began to think about my mother. I'm sure she was panicking by now, and I couldn't stand that idea. The more I thought about it, the more it pained my heart. I needed to get home!

Despite my efforts to learn more about the monster, my new companions didn't have a lot to say. From what little they knew, the creature used human skin as a disguise and could have ripped it off quickly like a cheap suit. It killed without mercy and then swiftly disappeared, so they didn't get a great look at it. Out of everyone, Masarra got the best look of it. She described it to me as a large beast with insect and fish-like features. One particularly detail she remembered was it had black eyes that were devoid of compassion and pity. That was the first sign that the sixth person wasn't human. I understood the importance of the eyes now. The creature... I prayed that I never come across one.

After two more hours of walking, I led us down a tunnel that turned out to be another dead end. I bowed my head, closed my eyes, and groaned.

"This is bullshit! Your sense of direction sucks!" Carl yelled. He looked like an angry dog as he ground his teeth.

Masarra responded, "You're not doing any better yourself. You got us lost a lot more than Joshua!" Ruka's crying was becoming more uncontrollable as she grabbed her hair. Masarra placed her arms around Ruka to comfort her.

"Shut her up or I will!" Carl's voice echoed throughout the area as if we were in a canyon.

"Don't you threaten her, you cocksplat!" Tony and Carl stared at each other as both balled their hands. Nonetheless, I wasn't concerned with all that drama because coming from the passageway we had just came from, I heard a strange noise. It sounded like multiple scratchings on the walls, and it was getting closer. The others didn't notice it due to their argument.

"Hey, I think something's coming." The scratching became more frequent.

Carl yelled at Masarra while his face turned red, "I'm here to survive, not to babysit a hysterical bitch!" The shouting match continued, as the three gained an advantage over the other by raising their voices.

"Hey guys!" Still, no one listened to me. Our lives were in the balance, yet they couldn't get beyond basic human conflicts. I was motionless as a statue as I heard the scratching noises were louder and more intense. I knew it was heading our way... we were trapped! My heart beat faster and sweat poured from my head. My imagination ran wild with images that were the epitome of terror.

Ruka's body quivered as she moved towards me, "*Monsuta.*" I didn't need to understand her language to know what she meant. I remained frozen as my ears became filled with the sounds of my heart and my heavy breathing.

I had to reach down within my soul to find what little bravery I had, then I shouted, "HEY! THERE IS SOME-THING FUCKING COMING!" Finally, they looked at me and noticed the noises. Their limbs stiffened up, their eyes and mouths opened wide, and their bodies shivered. We all began to cower towards the back, but there was nowhere to run.

Before my eyes, the monsters had arrived. It was a slow-moving moment of horror. First, a dozen hands crept from around the corners to grab a hold of the wall. They were black, scaly, and slimy like a fish. Each hand had four long, bony fingers with black claws. These claws dug deep into the walls, then scratched it like nails on a chalkboard. The scratching became so loud that Ruka covered her ears. Next, their arms appeared as they reached out with their hands to grab the wall further down. They were long and tarantula-like, with the joints moving in a way that reminded me of a robot. Finally, the creatures fully revealed themselves.

There were three of them. Each had four grotesque arms that allowed them to walk on the ceiling and the walls like a spider. One hung from the ceiling, one climbed on the right wall, and the other was on the ground. The ones on the ceiling and wall jumped in unison onto the floor. After, they stood-up on their two fat hind legs. Their bodies were muscular, black, and scaly like a fish. The shape of their heads resembled that of a carapace of a crab. These horrible creatures were the inhabitants of this forsaken world, and they were hunting us. Despite what my instincts told me, I couldn't take my eyes off them. I thought about what I had done in my life to end up in this place... this macabre realm where insanity and fear lurked in every corner and shadow.

Carl frantically moved towards the back, but the only way to escape was to run through these monsters, but that would be futile. The things made a hissing sound as an opening appeared on their heads that resembled a mouth. Five squid-like tentacles came out from them, each waving around like a tree branch in the wind. Fear overtook every part of my being as I saw that each tentacle had tiny razor-sharp teeth from the many suckers. I desperately began praying for deliverance.

Suddenly, a loud noise that sounded like a foghorn with a soft, soothing pitch echoed throughout the maze. After it ceased, it was as if someone had hit an off switch on the creatures. Their heads bowed, their limbs went limp, and their backs arched over. We didn't move a muscle, and we were afraid to take our eyes off them.

"What the hell happened?" Carl said. As we stood there, I wondered how long this was going to last.

After a brief period of silence, Tony spoke, "Mates, let's move our arses before they wake up!" He was right. This may be our only chance, but we had to pass through these creatures to escape. Just thinking about doing that made me want to vomit and cry.

"No point in wasting time!' Masarra said to us as she walked towards the creatures. Tony and Carl followed, but Ruka backed away. I grabbed her hand, but she pushed me away. Fear had conquered her spirit. Now, her instinct caused her to curl into the corner, pull on her hair, and cry. I never entertained the thought of leaving her behind. I would be no better than the monsters if I did that.

However, I had to use hand gestures and talked to her in a slow, gentle voice in hope that she would understand. "Ruka... please, let me help." I held her hand. "We can get through this... trust me." After she looked into my eyes for several seconds, she wiped away her tears and fought back against her fears. She got a good grip on my hand and stood up. My sincerity broke the language barrier between us. We followed the others.

The creatures looked like statues; there was no movement, not even the appearance of breathing. I wondered why the foghorn made them stop. The only thing that made sense to me was that these monsters were puppets to an unseen force. I'm convinced that the citadel held all the answers. While I didn't know what would be there, I was determined more than ever to find out... if I lived long enough.

Carl went first and passed through creatures quickly. Second went Masarra, followed by Tony. Both maneuvered through them fast as if it was an obstacle course. When all three were on the safe side, they turned in our direction and waited for us. Because I was aiding Ruka, I knew passing through these creatures wasn't going to be as quick. This burden gave me anxiety that made my heart beat faster. As I looked ahead, I saw that there was a gap between two of the creatures to the left. With her holding my hand, I took a deep breath and led the way.

When I took my first step between these monsters, the stench of fish polluted my nose. My body quivered as it was frightening being so close to them. I saw they had skin made of oily one-inch cycloid scales, but I couldn't stare at them long. They were even more repulsive up close, so I tried imagining that these things weren't even there. I looked directly at the others' faces; they were calling for us to hurry. Goosebumps covered my whole body. I believed life was still inside these vile villains, so they could revive at any time. I wanted to scream, but I held that urge back with all my strength. Ruka followed me closely, but a few times she paused, so I had to tug her to move her along.

As I walked through these creatures, it was like doing stretching exercises. I had to move my hips around and step in the right spots as I actively avoided touching these things. They looked like they were made of stone; not one part of them moved. The smell of fish was so strong that I had to hold back from gagging. When I turned my head to look at Ruka, I saw that she was mirroring my every move. Her eyes were wide open, and she gripped my hand with such force that she could have broken my wrist, but she was holding strong.

My heart was beating so fast that I thought it would explode. Everything played in my mind in slow motion, with seconds becoming minutes and minutes becoming hours. The last few steps felt like an eternity. Sweat poured from my forehead, and I heard nothing but my breathing and heartbeat. This was a nightmarish surreal moment being in between these creatures. I knew that at any moment, they could awake and tear me to pieces. Just as fear was ready to break me, I finally passed through the monsters. I continued to hold Ruka's hand as she made her way through, but once she did, she applauded and hugged me. Then, our eyes met, and we smiled at each other. At that moment, I saw her beauty.

Tony said, "Nice going, mate. Shall we make a move?" After we all took a few steps, the foghorn played. However, this tone was a loud, high pitched sound that forced everyone to cover their ears. After it finished, there were sounds of cracking, like sticks being broken. When we turned to look, we saw that the nightmare returned. At first, the creatures' fingers curled one by one, followed by their arms twitching. Carl ran and left us behind, but the rest of us remained because of paralyzing fear. These things were from the dark abyss of humanity's nightmares. Their very presence released an energy that infected our fragile minds that made us unable to run. Soon, their heads moved back and forth, they stood straight up, and they hissed

I reached deep within myself to fight what was holding me back, "LET'S GET THE FUCK OUT OF HERE!" My words snapped the others from their hypnotic state. Adrenaline pumped through our muscles as we ran. Ruka held on to my hand as we fled.

I had no idea where we were going; I just followed the others. As we entered a tunnel, I heard the scratching and hissing noises behind me. Those monsters were getting closer with each passing second. When Tony and Masarra realized they were several yards ahead of Ruka and I, they stopped to give us time to catch up. When I quickly looked behind, I saw a monster on the left and right wall, while the third was on the ceiling. They ran like a cheetah ready to kill its prey.

We sprinted towards the others, but before we could reach them, a wall came down that separated us. This was madness! Ruka and I pounded on the wall, but that was futile. The other two called out to us and banged on it, but they couldn't help us. I turned around, and I saw that the monsters had stopped. They didn't want to kill us right away; instead, they wanted to enjoy the moment. This was all a game. Being a few feet away, the creatures got into a pouncing position. The tentacles came out of their mouths, their hissing got louder, and their claws dug into the bricks. Ruka and I tightly held hands as we braced for the end of our lives. All hope was gone.

Maybe there was a God, or it was all part of the game, but regardless I couldn't believe what happened next. The wall to the right opened to expose another tunnel. I didn't know where it would lead, but once the adrenaline again kicked in, Ruka and I dashed down it. When the creatures started to follow, the wall closed and trapped them on the other side. The creatures continued to hiss and scratch the walls, but we were safe from them. At that moment, I realized that human and monster alike were under the control of the unseen puppet master… but who was it that was pulling the strings?

We ran for another fifteen minutes before I had to stop. Besides losing my breath and my muscles aching, my mind couldn't handle this hell anymore. I stopped and collapsed to the ground to release the emotions that were boiling up inside. I placed my face into my hands and cried. My fate was not in my control.

I felt the warm touch of Ruka's hands embracing my cheek. Looking up at her, I saw her pretty smile. How ironic that not long ago she was in a distraught state, but now she comforted me. I took a deep breath and I placed my back against the wall. Closing my eyes, I needed to rest and collect my thoughts. Ruka surprisingly curled up next to me. I placed my arm around her, and she rested her head on my chest. Her warm body felt good in this cold, damp environment. We both needed this time. I knew our bonding was due to this life and death situation, but it was nice having her near me. As we sat there, I felt my eyes closing. It wasn't long before I fell asleep.

I wished I had a pleasant dream, but instead there was nothing but a black void. I remembered that I had no thoughts or feelings in this dream, it was as if I no longer existed. I guess this was proper considering my situation. I had no clue how long I slept, but I awoke due to a sense that something was watching me. I knew that because my instincts warned me by sending a chill through my body. Although I was afraid, I slowly opened my eyes. When I did, I saw nothing. I looked in every direction, but Ruka and I were alone. Everything was quiet and still. However, I couldn't shake the feeling that I had many eyes watching me.

Then, I noticed a very lovely smell. I looked down at my feet and saw something glorious- a basket of loaves of warm bread! I shook Ruka to wake her, and her eyes and mouth opened wide. Like vultures, we grabbed the bread and ate. Our hunger turned us into gluttons as we savored each crumb. It didn't take long for me to feel better. When I looked at Ruka and saw her beautiful smile, I knew she felt better too.

With one loaf left, I reached for it at the same time as Ruka. When our hands touched, we looked into each other's eyes. We smiled. She was beautiful on the inside and out.

I took the loaf and split it in two, and I gave one piece to Ruka, "*Domo arigatou...* O, thank you," Ruka said. She looked like she was blushing. I had another reason to get off this planet: I wanted to get to know her more.

As I ate, I wondered who gave us this food, and why. I knew it wasn't the monsters because their intelligence appeared minimal. My logical conclusion was the puppet master was responsible, but it wasn't an act of compassion but rather to keep the game going longer. It wanted us to live just a little longer but for how long was the mystery. This force was like God... and that thought made me depressed.

Due to our location in a tunnel, I was unable to see the citadel. But I had to find it... that was the only purpose I had on this forsaken world. I used hand gestures to convey to Ruka that we needed to find that building. It took a few tries, but she eventually understood me. We stood up and exchanged looks; we trusted one another. After taking a few deep breaths, we continued our search.

As I walked, my thoughts focused on life. My views had forever changed due to my newly gained wisdom. Not only were we not alone in the Universe, but humanity was insignificant. In fact, humanity was nothing more than a pawn in a cosmic game.

Up ahead, the tunnel split into two passageways. If we took the wrong one, it meant more walking and an increased chance of coming across the creatures. The one to the left had a light coming from the far end of it, while the right was nothing but darkness. Ruka pointed towards the light, and with that the choice was made.

It turned out that the light was coming from an open-air area. This spot was some kind of lookout point that over-looked a ledge with a fifty-foot drop. Aligning the ledge was a two-foot moss-covered wall. It was a relief to see the sky and breathe in fresh air, even if it was alien. Straight ahead, the citadel had to be less than a mile away. Its shadow dark-ened the area. In addition, I discovered that the humming sound was broadcasting from the top of the structure. There were plenty of twists and turns still ahead, but we were close to our goal! There was more good news when I looked to my right: Tony was alive. He stood on top of the wall, looking directly at the top of the citadel. Ruka clapped her hands and cheered. While I was happy to see him, I wondered where Masarra was.

I called out, "Tony!"

He turned his head towards us, but he didn't look well. His hair was a mess, his face was dirty, his face was droopy, and his skin was pale. He cracked a smile, but he struggled to do it.

"What-what's going on buddy?"

He barely moved, "Those bastards devoured Masarra... I-I couldn't save her. I'm happy to see you two are good... but I see no hope." His voice reflected the man's determination to end his life. Upon learning that the cosmic game eliminated Masarra, sorrow filled my heart. Also, I feared my time was coming. Despite this, I had to convince Tony there was a reason to live... there had to be hope left. I slowly approached him in preparations to grab him if he jumped.

"Don't give up... Masarra wouldn't want that! Come with us Tony... we're almost at the citadel." I pointed to it, "That's our path to salvation!"

He turned his body around and held up his arms in a Christ-like posture, "Salvation... that's just a myth." Never losing the pose, he fell backwards. I rushed to grab him, but I missed. I froze in my place as my eyes opened wide and my hands balled. I heard a loud thump; that sound reverberated through my head. Ruka's screams echoed through the area. After a few seconds, I slowly looked down in hope that by some miracle he survived. That was a dream... instead, I saw his lifeless body down below. Blood oozed from his nose, ears, and mouth. A puddle of red formed under the body that grew larger as the bleeding continued. The view just didn't seem real, as my mental state interpreted it like a lucid dream. As I stared at the body, that gory view became imprinted into my memories. This was going to haunt my dreams for many years to come. This world made suicide seem like the best way out. Was I going to take my own life, too?

I looked at Ruka and saw her grabbing her hair, shaking her head, and wailing. When I placed my hand on her shoulder, she hugged me. We cried and tightly held one another.

However, there was no time for mourning. Holding each other's hand and with tears falling down our cheeks, we walked to the right of us towards a long pathway. I didn't know where it led, but I had to get away from here. I focused my mind on the citadel; that gave me hope.

Our journey seemed endless: upstairs, downstairs, to the left, to the right, forward, and backwards... there was no logic to it. At times, I walked in a hypnotic state, feeling very much like a zombie. Often my thoughts focused on Masarra and Tony, which caused me to look down at the ground and cry. Also, there was no doubt in my mind that Carl was dead.

When we went around the corner, Ruka shouted with joy and pointing straight ahead. When I looked, I saw that the citadel was less than forty yards away! The humming noise was very loud, but it wasn't unbearable to hear. Due to the shadow from the building, the area had a cold chill.

The surface of the building had hieroglyphic-style writings on it, but it wasn't written by any human civilization. Moreover, there were carvings that depicted various ghastly creatures. Some had aquatic features, others looked reptilian, while others were mammals. There were many of them, but three particularly caught my eye. One creature depicted had the head of a triceratops with tentacles for arms; another displayed a crustacean-like creature with wings and a pyramid shaped head covered with antennae; the last one had a humanoid-shaped body with a head of a fish and buggy eyes. This was a mural that displayed what the Universe had to offer. The idea that these things existed was nothing short of horrific.

The citadel had an arch shaped entrance that was about twenty stories high. The gray wooden double doors had an engraving of a terrifying scene. It depicted the citadel on a horizon with hundreds of this world's inhabitants lined up in rows looking towards it. All the creatures were kneeling with their hind legs while the forearms were in the air with adoration. Hovering on top of the citadel looked like a disorderly collection of globes that swirled around the twelve squares. Among the globes were dozens of tentacles mixed in with several canine teeth and large eyeballs.

My skin crawled when I realized that I was looking at religious art. This citadel served as a house of worship, and the monstrosity in the carving was their god. My body quivered as my mind raged with so many questions. Was this god the puppet master? Why would anything worship such a hideous thing? Was it going to let us go home? I had so many questions, but there were no answers.

Due to fatigue, Ruka and I walked slowly towards the entrance with our backs arched and arms dangling. Regardless, I couldn't stop looking at the carving of the god. The more I looked at it, the more my mind wanted to break, yet I couldn't stop eyeing it. Also, the building seemed to be welcoming us in a sinister manner. In fact, the doorway appeared to me like a mouth ready to devour us. All logic dictated that we shouldn't move forward, but we had no other choice. I really wished the others were here.

It felt like the longest walk ever. When we were less than five yards from the entrance, the humming noise ceased. It was so quiet that all I could hear was my rapidly beating heart and my deep breaths. It was eerie. We didn't move; we didn't even blink. After a few seconds, there was a loud sound of grinding metal from the doors slowly swinging outward. The shock from the noise caused us to jump and gasp. It took over a minute for the doors to fully open, but once they finished, the silence returned. For several seconds we stood there.

I looked over at Ruka, and I couldn't be happier that she was with me. When she looked at me, she smiled. I returned the favor, and we held hands again. If it wasn't for her, I believed I would have ended up like Tony. After taking a few deep breaths, we went ahead inside.

Our walk through the doorway seemed to go quickly. Inside, the air got colder, and we heard the splashing of water. White light lit the interior, though the source of that light was unknown. Twelve-by-twelve tiles made up the floor. The silver walls had several golden arches lining them. A white ivory column in the shape of a double helix held up each arch. Above the arches were platforms that hosted gardens with vines dangling over the sides. The plants were similar with those found on Earth, only these were larger and with weird shapes and angles. The colors of them were green, red, blue, orange, and other colors that I couldn't even describe. In the very center of the building was a large marble pool filled with water. A waterfall was hitting the center of this pool that created a pleasant mist in the air and a continuous echo. When I looked up to the ceiling to find the source of the waterfall, I saw was that it was coming from a black void high up where the light didn't reach. This place was Heaven compared to the Hell outside.

The pool seduced me. I walked towards the edge of the pool and jumped in. The pool was three feet deep. My dry throat came alive as I scooped up water with my hands and drank. Next, I washed my face. I began to smile over feeling the cool liquid over my skin. I walked over to stand under the waterfall. I loved the feeling of it splashing over me. I opened my mouth and shouted... I felt alive again. When Ruka entered the pool, she made a sigh of relief as she splashed water all over her face. She came closer to me. When I turned to look, she playfully splashed water at me. I did the same. We laughed. For a moment, we had a moment of happiness.

The mood soon turned to fear. My heart raced once I heard footsteps coming from the entrance that headed towards us. I turned around slowly. My heart became like a drum. However, I was relieved to see Carl. He walked towards the edge of the pool, then stopped. He was an asshole, but I was glad that he made it. Even Ruka clapped her hands and smiled.

"Carl! You made it!"

He stood there motionless. He had no expression on his face. His skin appeared dry, pale, and flakey. Ruka's mood turned to fear as she placed her fingers near her mouth. I started backing away when I saw that his eyes were black and devoid of empathy. I remembered the warning about the eyes: they were the first clue of the true horror that lurked before me.

I looked at Ruka, "*Monsuta?*"

"*Monsuta.*" She got closer to me and placed her arm around mine. After what we went through, we were going to meet a grisly fate. Life was so cruel and unfair.

We slowly backed away. I had put all my hopes into reaching the citadel, but it was going to be our tomb. I heard hissing coming from every direction; all of it amplified by the echoing. It got so loud I thought my eardrums were going to burst. Fear had become the dominant emotion.

Hundreds of these creatures appeared. They were climbing down the walls, coming out from behind the columns, and jumping from the gardens. Even more entered through the doorway. They were like ants marching towards their prey. There were so many of these creatures that they completely covered the inside of the citadel. The smell of fish filled the air so badly that it nearly made it hard to breath.

Carl's skin started to look like maggots were crawling under it. His limbs and head twitched. Rips in his skin and clothing formed as blood oozed from the cuts and piles of flesh fell off the body. The creature's arms burst from the chest and tentacles came from his mouth. Its claws ripped off the rest of the flesh. Eventually, all the human skin created a pile of gore on the ground. I couldn't figure out how such a large and odd shaped creature had the ability to fit into human skin. The creature was now fully exposed and ready for a kill. The others surrounded the pool; death approached.

I pushed us further into the pool's center, but that was out of instinct rather than a strategy for survival. My body shivered, and my eyes darted all over the place. The horror was everywhere. I held on to Ruka as she placed her head on my chest and cried. I didn't want to die! With the pool surrounded, several monsters stepped into the water.

It's been said that when a person encounters a traumatic event, that person relives their entire life. This traumatic moment caused me to relive everything that led me to this point.

———

THIS IS the end of my flashback. Now, here's the present.

I hope God exists because I pray that my death is quick. Then, a miracle happens. Playing straight up from the void is a very low pitched noise. Within seconds, the creatures start retreating out of the citadel. It's like someone hit the rewind button: they are moving in the exact same way they had come in, only in reverse. They are slaves, they follow orders without questioning. The lone exception is the creature that wore Carl's skin. It tries to stand its ground. Maybe it's because it craves human flesh so much, or maybe it's tired of being a slave. Regardless, it tries to step forward, but it's forced to listen to the command when the foghorns play again. It backs away with robotic-like reflex. It really wants to kill us, but it must serve its master. This is something the monster and I have in common... we're slaves in this game. Soon, all the creatures leave the building. It looks like Ruka and I are alone, but I know that isn't the truth.

An omnipresence causes me to shiver and a chill ran down my spine. It feels like many eyes are watching me. It's the same feeling from before. Ruka holds on to me tightly; I feel her body trembling. I keep looking around, but I don't see anything... I simply know it's here. Wherever it is, I know it's the puppet master... or more appropriately, a god. It's been watching us from the very beginning, and it controls our fate.

A voice speaks directly into my mind. Speaking in an unknown language, the voice is high-pitched, fast, and unbearable to hear. Ruka also experiences this painful voice. We react by covering our ears and screaming. It's a futile effort since the voice is going directly into our minds. It begins to split my brains.

"DAMN IT! STOP! IT HURTS!" My yelling echoes

throughout the building. After what feels like an eternity of agony, the pain subsides, the pitch lowers, and the language turns into English.

The voice says, "You can now understand me. You are only a handful who has ever made it through my maze. Congratulations are in order." I believe that this god doesn't like to communicate using a primitive human language.

I scream, "Why are we here?"

It wastes no time in responding, "Humans are a lower form of life; your sole purpose is to be used for amusement. Every now and then, I like to take several of your species to my maze to see if they can solve it. Very few do, even when I lend a helping hand." I now understand it's responsible for the incidents, like the bread and the walls, that saved our lives.

"Yes, primitive one. That was me. You two became my favorite pets, so I gave you an edge in my game. It pleases me that you both made it to my temple."

I look down in despair and tears formed in the corner of my eyes. I am a worthless pest. In the grand scheme of the Universe, humanity is nothing more than ants. We exist to be killed, enslaved, or ignored at the will of a great force. My life has no grand meaning. When I look at Ruka, I see she's filled with sorrow. The entity is communicating this truth to her by using her native language.

"As a reward, I shall return you to your world with a prize: the complete knowledge of the Universe." The water-fall ceases its flow. Up from the ceiling, bright lights shine down. It's bright as the sun, but it doesn't hurt to look at it. Ruka and I embrace each other, but we continue to look up. From the light appears a gigantic conglomeration of globes glowing in an assortment of colors. The globes make their way down from the ceiling in a spiral pattern. Fearful wonderment paralyzes us as they get closer and the lights get brighter. We can't look away as our minds fill up with the new knowledge. I don't want the secrets of the Universe, but I'm forced to take it. The more information I receive, the more my mind bends. I try to resist, but I begin to collapse into a psychotic mess. Humanity is unable to understand such forbidden knowledge... and this god knows it! Ruka tries to keep her sanity, but her cries and shouts prove she's losing. She holds me so tight that I have trouble breathing.

Through the light appears a massive, grotesque figure. It has dozens of large brown tentacles and four large mouths with sharp teeth and many eyes. This is the god from the carving! The god of the monsters. Amoral and desiring amusement, he knows this knowledge is making me insane, but it continues to give me more. I plea for him to stop, but he doesn't care. So many truths enter my mind... I can't stop it. I think of strangling Ruka so she can escape this horrible fate, but I'm too weak to do so.

"NO! NO! YOG!" I want to live in blissful ignorance! "GO AWAY! SOTH!" This knowledge is unbearable! My mind's snapping! My mind's being destroyed! "DAMN! OTH! WHY! WHY! TRUTH! NO! NOT THE TRUTH! HA...HAHA... HAHAHAHA! YOG! SOTHOTH!"

DATE: *May 15, 2015*
    To: Dr. Linda Koffman, Ph. D

From: Dr. Alex Samson, Upstate New York Psychiatric Hospital

Subject: Updated on Joshua Reese.

Greetings Dr. Koffman,

I've been working with Joshua since his transfer over a year ago from Butler Hospital in Rhode Island. Sad to say, there's been no improvement. He hardly sleeps unless heavily sedated, he has frequent violent outbursts, and he's unable to complete basic functions. However, I wanted to tell you an update on what I've learned from all his ramblings. A lot of it was incoherent, but I was able to piece together some information.

Joshua believes he was on another planet where a deity called Yog-Sothoth resides. I learned from research on old mythologies that this deity is one of many collectively known as the Outer Gods. Anyway, Joshua told me that although many races worship the god, it was the inhabitants of this world that constructed a temple and a large maze over twenty millennia ago.

He told me that this deity used the maze for its own amusement by placing him and several others in it. It controlled the aliens too, allowing or stopping them from killing at will. When Joshua reached the temple, it bestowed upon him the full knowledge of the Universe before returning him to Earth. It was this knowledge that led to Joshua's insanity. That knowledge must have been so vast, so dark, and so beyond understanding that his mind just snapped.

I know what you are going to say... this is just the imagination of a lunatic. Nevertheless, I recently discovered some information that makes me very uncomfortable. He made comments that joining him was a young woman from Japan named Ruka. All that he knew about her was that she was college age and from Yoko-hama. Out of curiosity, I made inquiries with my contact at the Tokyo Metropolitan Matsuzawa Hospital. I don't know why I did that, but something in my gut told me I needed to do it. What I learned gave me great worry. My contact, Dr. Toshio Shimizu, informed me that the hospital has a patient named Ruka Otoko, who was originally from Yokohama! Her mental state is like his and she was hospitalized about the same time that Joshua was. Ruka, in her ramblings, talked about being stuck on an alien world, having to go through a maze, and reaching a large building where a deity named Yog-Sothoth resided. If that wasn't frightening enough, she mentioned being with an American man named Joshua. This is beyond coincidence.

I will continue to work with Joshua, as I do pity him. However, I do so in fear of what I might learn: that his ramblings aren't of someone who is insane, but of someone who speaks the truth.

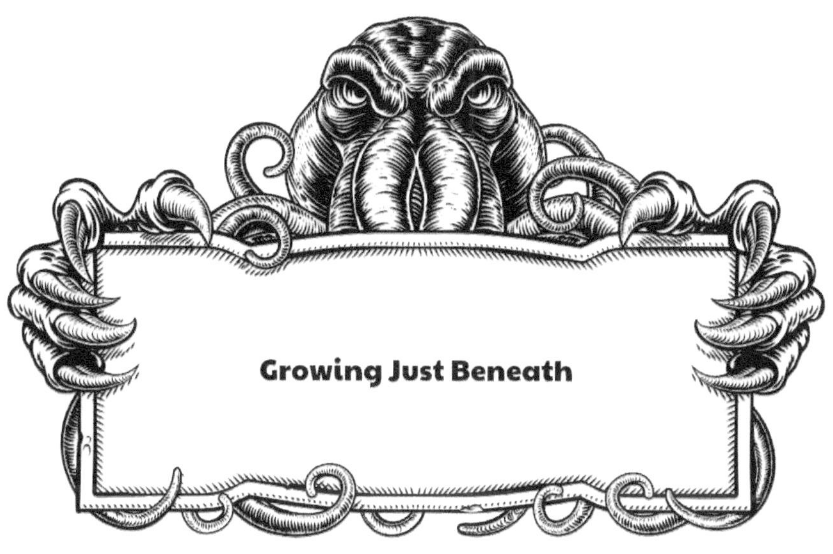

BY STEVE VAN SAMSON

1 : You've Got Bittersweet

"YOUR TREE IS SCREWED."

The statement threw me for a loop. I was still loading some cans of soda into the fridge when my aunt and uncle walked through the front door. We were hosting a low key summer barbecue and as usual they were the first to arrive. I looked up, not entirely sure I heard correctly.

"What's that?" I said.

"The dogwood out there. It's screwed." My uncle was shaking his head "Did you know?"

I stood up - glanced out the kitchen window. Along with the house and the expansive quarter acre lot, a number of gardens and flower beds became ours when my wife and I signed on the dotted line. The gardens themselves were actually quite nice and seemed well tended, as far as I could tell. But then, what do I know? Most of the flowers I can name are the ones I knew at the end of third grade. Roses, daisies—I'm pretty sure that tulips are the ones with the three points on top that look like Bart Simpson hair.

That said, even someone with my limited botanical knowledge would know our one tree was a dogwood.

"What does *that* mean?" I asked almost defensively. "What's wrong with the dogwood?"

"It has been invaded." My uncle looked sympathetic then. Like he was about to admit to running over the cat. "You, my friend, have bittersweet."

The statement hung between us like a cloud—pregnant with storms which had not arrived yet, but would very soon. To me, bittersweet was something you said when your first-born moves away to college. It was an adjective. What my seven year old still calls a *describer*. How can one *have* bitter-sweet? It was like saying the Bruins *had triumphant* after winning game seven of the Stanley Cup playoffs.

Reading the question on my face, my uncle smiled. "Come on. I'll show you." And without another word, the two of us exited the kitchen, and then the house.

Having arrived at the tree, my eyes searched and scoured. As far as I was concerned, nothing looked out of place. Sure it didn't bloom like the ones on Main Street and yes, the thing was inexplicably split down the center—thus resembling a child's rendering of water spouting from the top of a cartoon whale... but there were plenty of leaves. All green and healthy and thriving.

But as I would soon learn, that was precisely the problem.

As it happened, competing on my tree were two distinct types of leaf. Amidst the dogwood's own, another had asserted itself. Somewhat longer with fierce points and serrated edges. The more I stared, the more out of place these other leaves appeared. Slowly, my eyes moved to a conspicuous group of berries - some were orange, others red. Were dogwoods supposed to have berries? All I knew was the tiny spheres were pulling branches on both sides—splitting my tree in two.

In that moment, I found myself equal parts outraged and appalled. Affronted by an attack upon something for which I suddenly felt a great swell of affection for. These leaves, these berries, they were features of a single villain. An evil parasite seeking only to devour and destroy its helpless host. Gripped by something I can only describe as anger, my eyes traced the vines all the way down to the ground. Right to the source.

There, hidden in plain sight was a twisted, spiraling thing. Like some unholy amalgamation of chameleon and snake, the eyeless mother root glared back—utterly confident in her ability to go unseen. I had never looked upon anything so vile. So utterly alien. In that moment, I wanted to hack at the twisted thing—to tear it away with my bare hands.

"Yup! That's it right there," said my uncle, sounding like a vindicated Sherlock Holmes. "That's where it all started." He was pointing right at her. Right at the *mother*. "Friggin' bittersweet. I tell ya - we've got it in the woods behind our house. You leave this crap alone long enough and it will take over every time."

As he spoke, my angst got the better of me. I kicked my

newfound enemy with one foot. Then gave it a firm tug but the mother root wouldn't budge.

"Now listen," my uncle went on in the confident tone of an older man imparting his years of hard-earned experience. "You gotta pull all this down." He gestured to the branches above. To the leaves and the bright alien spheres. "But lay down a tarp first. Let the berries fall on that instead of the ground. You gotta think of this crap as the plant equivalent of a starfish. Leave behind a single berry or strand of root, it's just gonna grow right back. And it'll *keep* growing."

As he spoke, I nodded and I listened. Even then, I was unsure that my outrage would last long enough to see these instructions through, but I hoped it would. I really did. Maybe for the first time, I found that I actually wanted to be one of those *responsible homeowner types*. A character like you'd see in some bad sitcom—who describes the contents of their weekend on Monday mornings as a series of outdoor labors. Mowed the lawn... finished the retaining wall... rescued my dogwood from a hideous plant monster...

"All right." I said with resolve. "And if I get it all... do you think the tree will bounce back?"

My uncle stepped back. He looked the dogwood over again, from stem to stern, considering the question.

"As long as you get it all... but that's the trick." Then he gave a quick scan to the surrounding lawn. "See these?" He was kneeling before an unassuming weed—little more than a thin green sprout and some leaves. *Tiny, serrated leaves.* "These things are the real problem. Everything up on that tree is because of one of these little shits."

I reached for the nearest sprout, ready to tear it away with extreme prejudice.

"Wouldn't do that." My uncle was holding his hands up in a very *don't look at me* sort of way. "If you pull on that now, you're gonna be out here all day. Trust me, come back when you've got some time. When you're ready for a fight. I know they don't look like much, but these things have roots like you wouldn't believe. Bright copper, the color of new pennies. Instead of making a little cluster, they only move down a few inches beneath the dirt before banging a hard left. From there they shoot out, pretty much parallel to the surface. It's ridiculous. Just one of these things will infect your whole yard if you let it."

Still listening, I scanned the grass around us. Taking in all the insidious sprouts whilst still not fully comprehending the severity of the situation. Bizarrely, the scene caused my subconscious to regurgitate a scene from a nature documentary I saw. I could recall a segment on the garden eel - a tiny black and white fish that buries itself, tail first, in the sand. When there are no predators around, these eels will extrude their bodies from the earth and simply hang there, just swaying with the current.

As I looked at the army of tiny invaders, sticking up from the grass and soil, I wondered if they might retract at my approach. In that moment I felt surrounded, but also something like a predator. Some prehistoric, deep sea shark. Bittersweet had become my prey and now that I knew the myriad faces it wore, I could see nothing else.

2: Pay the Reaper

. . .

I awoke, staring at the cracked plaster ceiling of the master bedroom. I hadn't slept well.

Beside me, my wife lay sleeping and I moved carefully, so as not to disturb her. No reason for anyone else to get up so early, but for me there was no choice. Now that the gears started turning, my options were either: get on with the day or keep studying the cracks in the ceiling.

Moving downstairs, my footsteps were plodding, clumsy. Halfway down, I glanced out the window at the front yard. In that moment, through the haze of new wakefulness, I saw my tree for what felt like the first time. God, it looked so broken. Split in half, like the peel from a banana. Staring at it, my frustration grew. I was annoyed at the situation—at the amount of work ahead of me, but more than anything, I was annoyed that the plight of my own damn tree had to be pointed out to me. Up until the previous day, I had accepted the tree as I saw it, pockmarks and all. And for three years the bittersweet had grown without impedance. But no longer.

"Time to pay the reaper."

Even as I said this, I knew the line was off. That I was mincing quotes somehow. But... it was too early to think. Right then I needed coffee. Coffee and gloves.

The battle commenced just before 8:30 AM that day. I decided to take my uncle's advice, but without a big enough tarp, I used the cover from our pool. Laid it down in front and around the trunk, securing it with a number of medium-sized rocks. Finally, with the morning sun keeping watch, I set about my task.

Inspecting a cluster of berries, I located what looked like

the end of one of the creeper vines. It was wrapped around a large branch like thread around a spool. This, I carefully unwound and pulled. Pulled until stars appeared in the morning sky. At first it seemed a futile effort but after a second or two, the branch gave up about three inches of vine.

I jolted back from the sudden slack. My heart was pounding. Soaring. I knew the feeling was disproportionate to the amount of progress, but I didn't care. My eyes devoured the branches, then moved to the grass below. To the tiny soldiers standing there. The invading army of garden eels which stood at attention. I reminded myself that there were two battles to be fought. One above the earth and another just beneath. Undaunted by the breadth of my task, I tightened my grip and launched back into the fray.

My hands moved as if by themselves. Ripping. Tearing. Unseating. Liberating. The alien parasites were all I saw, *all I knew*. Time was no longer a consideration. My younger daughter appeared at one point, but I didn't stop. Couldn't stop. Acknowledging her only distantly, through a whirlwind of branch and leaf and fury.

When the task was done, I looked up to see that the pale morning sky had been replaced by a royal blue, afternoon one. I stepped back, needing to view my Impressionist masterpiece the proper way—from a distance. But as I moved, I became aware of thin lines of pain all over my skin. Sweat was leaking into a dozen cuts I hadn't felt until that moment, but the pain was good. Justified. Earned. As for the tree - *my tree*... it looked positively anorexic. Nearly one fifth of its previous bulk now lay on a pool cover I could hardly see anymore. The war was ongoing, yes, but the first battle had been won. I alone stood victorious—the Reaper.

And in that moment, *I had triumphant.*

"Jesus Christ!" exclaimed my wife. "What the hell happened to *you?*"

By then I had trudged into the house. Exhausted but with an amazing amount of satisfaction, I recounted the day's battle.

"What time is it?" I asked suddenly aware of a powerful thirst.

"Two forty-eight!" came the voice of my youngest "I told you lunch was ready *four times,* but I don't think you heard. You just kept yelling at that tree."

"Here." My wife approached setting down a glass and a plate containing what looked like one of her famous maple chicken paninis. "Come here. Let me see." She began to inspect my various lacerations, making me feel less *triumphant* and more *little kid who just fell off his bike.* But it was fine. All was well. I was done and for now at least, I had a sandwich.

"Is the tree gonna be okay, Daddy?"

Mouth full of maple-flavored chicken, I smiled.

"I fink fo." I took three giant gulps from the glass, almost emptying it. "But, Daddy's not done yet."

"Not done?!" exclaimed my youngest, launching into hyperbole. "You were already out there for a million years, today! How come you're not done?"

I smiled.

"Some of these cuts are kind of bad." My wife sounded concerned, running a gentle thumb over my arm. "Didn't you feel them?"

I thought on this. Thought and chewed and thought some more.

"Honestly? No. Not even one." I said. "I guess I was in the zone."

My wife looked up with a sardonic eyebrow. "I *guess*. We saw the pile from the window. Can't believe how much of the tree, *wasn't tree!*" She shook her head sympathetically. "So, what's left to do?"

"Well…" I said with a sigh. "Apparently bittersweet spreads like a virus. I took care of what was up in the branches… but there's more. Little sprouts with roots that bang hard lefts." I shrugged. "I don't know—I wanted to clear off my tree first."

"*Your* tree?" Her tone was playful. A parody of affrontation.

"*The* tree." I made a show of sounding as annoyed as I possibly could. "Anyway, I think I'll take a break and then go out again later." With one more gulp I finished the lemonade. "Hopefully it won't take too much longer." I moved in for a kiss knowing full well how filthy I was.

"Yeah right." My wife stepped away, tossing me a smirk.

"All right, all right." I said, turning to go upstairs. "Shower, good. Dirt, bad. I get it. Thanks for the sandwich."

"Sure…" Her voice trailed off. Then she came up quickly behind me. "Hold on a second." Gently, she put hands on my arm and shoulder.

"What?" I said. "Do I have some squashed berries on me or something?"

"*…Something.*" She sounded strange. "Ooh, man—how'd I miss this? Does it hurt when I do *this?*"

My reaction was explosive. It felt like she was measuring the depth of an open wound with a toothpick.

"Ah! *Yes!* What are you—?"

"Hold still." She said. Her tone was clinical now. My jaws clicked shut, clenching in pain.

"What the fuck?!" I jabbed back, immediately regretting it. "Sorry—I didn't mean..." When I looked, my wife was staring at something in her hand.

"Gross." She said, sounding more fascinated than anything. "It looks like a little worm."

The thing was about four inches long. Brittle looking but supple to the touch. It was bright copper, the color of new pennies.

"Actually, I think it's a little root." She finished the thought, turning the thing over in her palm. "This thing was *really in there.*"

3: The Mother Root

I NEVER MADE it back out to my tree that day. Nor the next. In fact, three weeks passed before I was able to gather enough will to once again face the Goddamned bittersweet. By then, most of my cuts had healed and faded into nonexistence. All except the one behind my shoulder. It was that cut my finger was tracing as I stood there, surrounded by dozens of innocuous looking sprouts.

These things are the real problem. I could hear the voice of my uncle. *Everything up on that tree is because of one of these little shits.*

I knew enough to be gentle and the first sprout was lifted easily. But as I continued to pull—gently, slowly, I saw that my uncle had not exaggerated. Bit by bit, the soil began to pop. Like tiny firecrackers going off beneath the grass—all of them in a straight line. Each pop came with a puff of fine dirt and another inch or more of coppery root. It was unbelievable. After a short while, almost an entire foot of the stuff connected the tiny green sprout in my hand to the underground. And the more I extracted, the more I wanted. On my brow was a fever—one that could only be cured by ridding the soil of its affliction.

For that, too, was mine—the very soil along with the tree and every blade of grass. It was all so clear. So simple. I was the Reaper once again, and by God I would not stop until the harvest was done. The insidious, copper roots had become my nemesis. Every time I thought I was coming to the end of one section, another branch would appear. They were circuits, vast neural pathways, coppery rivers with tributaries uncountable and they were growing, ever growing just beneath.

By the time I stopped to breathe, the lawn had been transformed. Around me, where green grass had flourished only hours before, stretched a patchwork of great, brown scars. My heart raced, my muscles hummed and the unhealed cut on my shoulder throbbed in time. No quarter had been given, no mercy shown. I looked around for some sign of the sprouts. Those tiny green soldiers that had possessed gall enough to flank my tree on all sides. But these were gone, slain. Every one, reaped with extreme prejudice.

A trembling hand extracted a phone, checked the time. 5:39 PM. *Damn.* I had been at it for over six hours. Hadn't even stopped for lunch. Not even a glass of water. I tried to remember if anyone had come out—my wife, my youngest. Perhaps to offer these things at some point. It seemed likely, but I could remember nothing beyond the battle. In my mind, the afternoon was a blur. A maelstrom of popping dirt and miles of bright copper.

I turned for the house, but before I took a step, a thought sparked in my brain. It was like an alarm I had set and then forgotten about. I couldn't go inside because I wasn't done. Not yet. Not with one battle left to fight. I turned to regard the trunk of my tree, and there she was, glaring right back - the source. She who had begotten all of my recent woes. The mother root. The alien queen.

I approached her slowly, unable to look away. Unlike all her children, the flesh of my enemy had faded to an ashen grey. A thought occurred at this. Perhaps she was dead already. Perhaps the war *was* over after all. I gripped her form, though gently. She was very old and, somehow I knew, very much alive. Whatever else she deserved, the mother root had my respect.

My initial tug was exploratory. If she noticed, there was no indication. Then, respect or no, my efforts began in earnest. I pulled harder and harder, until the great spiraling thing was unseated and eventually separated from the trunk of my tree. The victory was potent but small. I knew there was more to my final enemy—miles for all I knew.

The roots below the mother were incredible. A new network, vastly more complex and interwoven than the separate systems I had found beneath the sprouts. Those had been mere scribblings, but this was a masterpiece. And so I raged and pulled and dug until my fingers bled.

By the time I looked up, the sky was red.

Dusk was my first guess, but my phone told me otherwise. Breath raked the insides of my throat as I stood—desperate to make sense of the time. 5:13 am. The numbers were right there at the top of my lock screen. Of course this was impossible. For that to be true, it would mean I had been outside not only all afternoon, but all night. Noticing neither the changes in light or temperature or anything else beyond the battle.

But there it was.

Absently, I looked at the ground. Before me, bathed in the red light of dawn was my hated enemy. The Mother Root was dead. Her full form exhumed and strewn out for all to see. Catharsis coursed as I reached and took up the body of my defeated foe—lifting it like a fisherman displaying the catch of his life. Holding her like that, she looked like a bolt of copper lightning frozen in mid-strike.

By God, I had won. I was exhausted and covered in layers of grime and who knew how many fresh wounds, but it had all been worth it. I hadn't mowed the lawn and I probably couldn't build a retaining wall if my life depended on it, but in that moment, I most definitely *had triumphant.*

4: They Keep Growing

Nine days have passed.

Night time has become something to dread.

A time ruled by fitful, troubled visions. The dream-scenarios change from night to night, but there is but one ending. Eventually, something will be uncovered or pushed aside - a blanket, a rug, maybe a pile of unfolded laundry. Every time it is the same.

The vines are there. Always. Haunting me. Growing just beneath.

I didn't go to work last week. My wife, my daughters, they don't understand. Can't understand. They weren't there. They didn't rip a zillion miles of red root from the earth with their bare hands, only to find more and more *and more*. Because just when you think the end is near, all you've really found is another fork in the road. Cut off one head and two more grow in its place. No, that's something else. The hydra has heads. Me on the other hand, all I have is the Goddamned bittersweet. And bittersweet has roots. Of course, now I know the truth. They weren't just roots.

They were *her*.

I can remember tenth grade biology. Learning about the systems of the human body. At the time, it was the nervous system that struck me most. When I close my eyes, I can still see the illustrations in the textbook. The veins and arteries with their uncountable branching pathways. How they looked exactly like bolts of red lighting.

Most of my cuts are healed now. The one behind my shoulder leaks, but since my wife took the girls to stay at her aunt's house, I stopped dressing it. Without her here to fuss over it, I just didn't see the point.

I noticed the lines the day before yesterday.

In the mirror, I could see them radiating from the oozing spot behind my shoulder. They look like rivers. Dark, ominous things flowing down my arm—across my chest. There is no pain, but my limbs move with a tightness that wasn't there before. I can feel it whenever I move now. I can feel her. The mother root.

I don't know the how, only the what. She's inside me. Growing. Changing. Terraforming.

Every day, every hour she grows a little more. Reaches a little farther. Past organs, through meat and around bone. I can't say how much longer I have.

All I know is, I have to get her out.

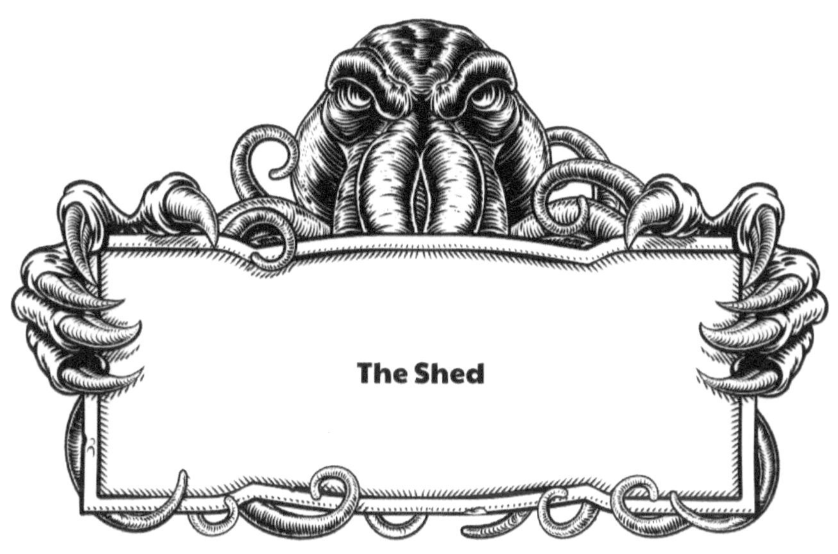

BY PATRICK RAHALL

The contents of the steel bucket sloshed and churned with Stanley Gauthier's uneven gait as he trod the path from the farmhouse to the shed. The disturbance of its contents released the foul odor to which Stanley had grown accustomed over the years. To him it was a welcome smell; it meant salvation from a terrible death. To him, it was the sweetest scent and more pleasant than any flower. It was dark out and clouds obscured the moon despite its brightness, but the path was well-worn and he was as intimate with it as a lover. The air was crisp and Stanley's left hip and knee ached from the cold and what Stanley assumed would be snowfall coming in the next twenty-four hours. At the very least, there would be frost on the ground when he woke up.

Stanley didn't look like a seventy-eight-year-old man, but he sure felt like it. He wore faded jeans and beaten-up but comfortable work boots that were on the verge of needing to be replaced, a red-checked flannel shirt over a thermal undershirt and his face was slowly getting taken over by the beard he grew annually beginning around mid-October before shaving it off in April. He was thin but had ropy muscles that moved and flexed under his skin like snakes. He was strong, not only physically but mentally; that was why he was chosen. He was unburdened by excessive imagination and was bound mostly by logic and reason, so when he was presented with a choice he saw it only in black or white with no shades of grey to cloud his razor-sharp intellect. He also had no formal education, instead, he had learned from his father and brothers how to fix engines, build structures and other handy trades; plumbing, carpentry, and had some skill with electrical work as well. Those which he had not been taught by others he had learned himself through intuition and trial-and-error experimentations. That was how he had learned to make the incredibly potent alcohol that had made him a local hero when the county had gone dry for a few years back in the late 50s and it was how he still earned a modest living and was able to keep to himself without fear of encroachment or interruption.

Stanley made his way to the shed that he had built with his own two hands and had maintained for nearly sixty years. He painted it last year to prove to himself that he was still as spry as ever and because the shed's occupant had insisted upon a slight change of scenery. It, of course, wouldn't *leave* the shed because it was far too comfortable an arrangement, but it wanted its environment altered every so often; sometimes as often as a few months and sometimes as long as six years. He always had to paint it some garish shade, too. It was currently bright yellow with white trim, but it had been acid green, traffic cone orange, hot pink, and more. His neighbors teased him about both the colors and the irregular frequency of the paint jobs. He always just shook it off and never really got into why he did it.

The shed was never locked; there was no reason for that. If anyone wandered in there they wouldn't be leaving again, and that was their own decision. He never invited anyone in, nor did he make it seem like there was something in there that was valuable that would entice someone to trespass on his property and try to get into the shed. That's not to say that there weren't curious people who ventured in, but on the bright side, those people never made another mistake in their lives.

Stanley turned the knob on the door and pulled the chain on the light switch before entering. This was not for his own benefit, but to put at ease the creature that dwelled within the shed. It may have been a terrifying, misshapen thing with a form that had driven many a sane mind to madness from the shock of looking upon it, but this was never an issue for Stanley Gauthier because his mind never attempted to rationalize what he was seeing, never attempted to find a "real-world" counterpart for this creature that was beyond all comprehension.

As he closed the door behind him and entered the nearly-empty shed he was greeted by the sticky, slimy sounds of the creature that dwelled within it. The creature, dubbed "The Glop" by Stanley, spent most of its time in a shallow pit full of fetid water. The stench was overwhelming, but Stanley was used to it and when he went back into his house, he would certainly bathe and wash his clothes because although he knew it not to be true, he felt that he'd been saturated by that horrific odor.

It was aware of his approach from the time Stanley had filled the bucket with its nightly sustenance. The creature's senses were supernatural, far beyond the scope of simple human sensory perception. At times Stanley was certain that The Glop was capable of reading his thoughts. Had he been more attuned to such things, he would have likened the creature's reactions to him as a form of empathy rather than some sort of telepathy, but as Stanley was not a man likely to indulge in any specific emotion outside of survival instincts the notion never occurred to him.

Stanley regarded the creature with a kind of cold indifference that one would expect from an unenthusiastic art patron inspecting a sculpture made of garbage; he was there to acknowledge its existence and the fact that it was there and his contributions allowed it to thrive, but beyond that, once it was out of his direct line of sight and it had been nourished it no longer mattered to him. The creature, however, had come to develop a bond with Stanley the way a feral cat would establish a connection with a concerned human that left food out for it; it had come to expect Stanley to arrive nightly with his bucket of what was essentially a slurry of meats and blood to sate its hunger, although if Stanley were to cease this exercise, the creature would find another way to sustain itself. It simply preferred the ease of having its food brought to it, rather than expending the effort to stalk, kill, and devour its prey.

The creature was a writhing mass of pinkish-white tentacles and eyes, with no real body to speak of in a traditional sense. It was as if some mad creator deity breathed life into a bowl of pasta and filled it with hate and rage and bloodlust. It perambulated like an octopus on dry land, squelching its way over to Stanley as it dragged the nauseating water mixed with some sort of vile secretion along the smoothly sanded wooden floor in anticipation of its nocturnal feeding. The tentacles occasionally branched out into what looked like a series of appendages that resembled human blood vessels. It gently touched Stanley's leg with about a half-dozen of its writhing appendages with a firmness that reminded Stanley that this thing might look delicate but it was capable of tearing apart livestock as easily as Stanley husked corn. To an outside observer, this might look like an act of affection but Stanley had no illusions about what it meant; it was a show of strength and impatience.

He offered the bucket and The Glop reached several tentacles out and entwined them around the bucket's handle, pulling it away from him deftly and it slithered away and into the shadows to feed, as it always did. Stanley should have thought it odd that he never saw the creature feed, but it didn't matter much to him one way or another. The creature always brought the bucket back to him clean, no trace of blood or scrap of flesh clinging to the surface of the bucket.

After returning the bucket back to Stanley, The Glop retreated back to the shadows and the soft splashing sounds of the creature returning to its small pool where it preferred to rest after feeding. Stanley didn't know why it needed to rest after receiving nourishment, but he didn't expect he'd ever find out and had given up wondering about it a long time ago. At that moment, all he cared about was getting back into the house, bathing, getting something to eat, and getting off of his aching legs. He hadn't noticed but his hip pain had begun to spread into his lower back because of the way he was standing. There was something hypnotic about the creature, and no matter how many times he had observed it, he was always surprised that he had stood motionless for an hour or more without realizing how much time had actually passed.

Stanley labored much more than usual on his way back to the house, even having to stop twice because of the pain despite the distance being no more than twenty yards. By the time he made it to the living room he was blinking back tears of pain and when he collapsed into his recliner the relief was so great that he completely broke down into sobs of joy. The pain in his back had subsided as soon as he was off of his feet.

He felt as though someone had driven spikes into his lower back just above each hip, and that each of those spikes had somehow sprouted spikes of their own and spread throughout his lower back from his tailbone to the bottom of his ribcage. Sitting down certainly had dulled the pain to a manageable level, but he was still very aware that it was there. He thought that if he could take a nice hot shower he'd be okay, but dreaded the thought of spending more than a few moments on his feet. That's when he remembered the shower seat he had been given as a joke a few years back on his seventy-fifth birthday. He knew where it was – sitting in the den, unopened for anyone who had come by to visit to see that he had never used it – but no one was likely to come by anymore. Things had changed since The Rift opened. He willed himself to his feet and, bracing himself on furniture and door frames along the way, made his way to the den and to his unopened shower seat. He pulled his knife from his pocket and flicked the blade out with a practiced maneuver he had perfected in the years that he had owned the trusty blade. Shredding through the packaging with haste unbecoming of him he managed to free the seat from the plastic and Styrofoam that had held it firmly in place, and he thanked whatever deities had decreed that the seat be fully assembled in the box when he managed to finally pull it from the box. Leaving the cardboard, plastic, and Styrofoam that he had just battled strewn about the floor Stanley lugged the seat with one hand and used the other to steady himself. The pain was slowly creeping back, spreading into his shoulders and knees as he made the trek to the bathroom on the other side of the house. After a few moments, he began using the chair as a walker to steady himself and provide the most efficient mode of navigating through the house. It was much slower, but it seemed to keep the pain from advancing any further and it was at least mitigated what he was already dealing with.

Breathing heavily and sweating profusely, Stanley finally made it into the bathroom. He was glad he had listened to his friends and family when they had suggested that he get rid of his old claw-footed bathtub and updated the entire bathroom. His current bathtub was much easier to get in and out of than the old tub, and it would also accommodate the shower seat with ease. He didn't think it would have fit in the old tub at all.

Stanley stripped the sticky clothes from his body with great effort, and he cursed himself for wearing so many layers, even though it was nothing out of the ordinary. Once he managed to remove his flannel shirt and thermal undershirt, his pants were easy enough; once he undid the belt they fell to the floor like a denim puddle. He was able to kick off his boots because he hadn't tied them on account of not expecting to be out in the shed for that long. His underwear was another story. After several attempts to remove them. but the pain his back not cooperating with his intentions, he decided to cut them off with his knife. Once he was as God made him, he steeled himself for the next ordeal – putting the seat into the tub.

Thinking things out critically, he decided that the easiest and most efficient way of doing this would be to sit down on the edge of the tub, lift the shower seat in and then swing his legs over into the tub after it. Stanley was never one to take on a challenge haphazardly; he always looked at every angle and every possible solution his mind would allow him to consider. Even now, despite his pain and discomfort, he knew that this would be easier than trying to lift the seat into the shower and then climb after it, or get in first and try to drag the seat in after him.

Using the seat as a brace, Stanley lowered his bare ass onto the edge of the tub, which was just wide enough to allow him a safe, if slightly uncomfortable, spot to balance himself without fear of slipping or falling if he were to lose his grip on the seat. It also provided him a fair bit of leverage and didn't overtax his already aching joints. At this point, it felt as if the spikes in his hips had shattered and shrapnel was working its way into the ball and socket joint. He was able to move the seat into the tub without great difficulty and swung his legs in one at a time, first planting his right foot on the non-slip tape on the floor of the tub, then using the seat as a brace, pulling himself into a standing position and dragging his left leg into the tub as well. Finally, he was able to sit on the surprisingly comfortable shower seat, allowing himself a few moments to catch his breath. Sweat was pouring from his body from the sustained effort and he felt slimy and gross, but it would be only for a little while longer, he told himself.

Stanley was sitting in the chair, staring off into space for a few moments before he snapped himself out of his reverie. He thought he may have even dozed off for a bit, shook his head to clear out the cobwebs, and reached for the faucet. Turning the knob resulted in not water, but a thick, viscous sludge pouring out of the showerhead. Stanley hollered and reflexively tried to move out of the way of the encroaching gunk, sending fresh waves of agony through his body.

He watched the disgusting ooze touch his foot and it did something Stanley had never seen before, and therefore was unable to comprehend it. It began flowing *up* his leg like a monkey shimmying up a tree. It started at his ankle and began a corkscrew pattern traveling up his calf and to his knee. Stanley thought his leg looked like some sort of grotesque barber pole. Then it began to feel warm, and a second tendril began ascending his right leg. At this point, his pain felt like it was far away, like someone screaming at him underwater. He was transfixed and could see flashes of red light within the ooze. It suddenly shot further up his leg to his groin and he stood up, horrified. The warmth he felt began to intensify until it was a searing heat that was unbearable and he screamed until he thought his vocal cords would snap from the effort. He began to get lightheaded from the effort and he would have fallen had the ooze not advanced once again up his body. Now the heat had not only burned his skin, but he could also feel it forcing its way into his body through any orifice it could find. This somehow terrified him more than anything he had ever experienced. This ooze, this sludge, or whatever it was, it was *alive*. His thoughts suddenly focused on the shed and The Glop. It had done something to him. It was almost controlling him, like one of those cars he had seen kids playing with where you use a handheld control and the cars went where you want. His first thought was that he was a puppet, but the cars were a more accurate analogy to him. It had somehow hypnotized him into a trance and made him stand still until he was in a tremendous amount of pain and it *knew* he would try to alleviate that pain with a shower. Wasn't that thing also always in the scum puddle in the shed? Maybe it had been digging, maybe a part of it had broken off and reproduced and grown and infected the water system, waiting for the right moment to strike. Maybe...

His next thought was interrupted by the agony of his bones snapping. The ooze had covered nearly his entire body except for his face and back – the entire area where he had been feeling the pain since he came inside from the shed.

He collapsed to the ground, unable to scream as the ooze entered his mouth. It seeped into his ears and it made every-thing seem like he was swimming underwater. It covered his eyes and the heat from it ruptured his eyeballs. Stanley wished it would just be over with, but his slow, terrible death seemed to be dragging on forever. The whole ordeal had taken under a minute but to Stanley, it had felt like an age. He didn't understand. He had done everything he was supposed to do. He had fed it, cared for it as much as he could care for some sort of horrific entity that seemed to exist beyond the understanding of man and forsaken everything in his own life to do so. It wasn't fair that he should die like this. The last thing Stanley felt was his back ripping open as the ooze crushed the life from his body. He felt no pain – his nerves had all been scorched – but he felt it tear from his body as his life was extinguished.

The creature that had been incubating inside of Stanley oozed and glorped its way from the mangled corpse that had been its womb. The ooze was quickly removing all trace of Stanley until only a few fillings remained in the tub. The ooze retreated back down the drain and disappeared. The creature, a greenish-brown thing that almost resembled the face of an infant human with its eyes on stalks and dozens of tentacles, made its way out of the tub and onto the floor, where it landed with a wet smack on the tiles. Innately, it knew where to go. It squelched and squeaked, making rudimentary sounds as it progressed through Stanley's home and out into the world.

The ground outside began to rumble and quake, and the shed exploded from within. In its place, a massive creature, hundreds of feet tall, regarded its offspring. It was humanoid only in the sense that it possessed what looked like a lumpish head on top of a many-armed body. Each arm was a tendril that ended in an insectile pincer. In the middle of what could only be called the creature's head was the monstrosity that Stanley had been taking care of for so many years.

The hideous thing reached a tentacle down and gently opened its pincer and grasped the newborn. The newborn wrapped its tentacles around the pincer and once it was secure, the massive creature placed the smaller thing on what could only be called its shoulder and the two slowly sludged their way towards the ocean to continue their plans. The newborn was so important, born of both worlds. Once it was taken back through The Rift, this world would become like so many others.

It would be *His.*

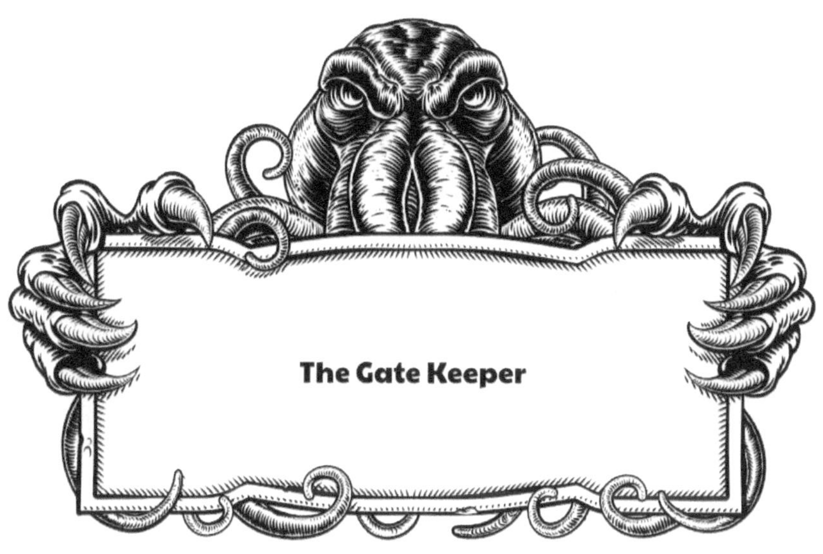

BY EV KNIGHT

I found the key, or rather it found me in an obscure little shop called The Reliquary. Tucked in between a laundromat and a health food store, it was the kind of place you drive by everyday but never really notice. What finally caught my attention was the fluorescent yellow "Going Out of Business" sign in the window. A bell rang as I entered. The gaunt old man behind the counter looked up from his record keeping and grinned. His smile gave me goosebumps; there was something wrong hiding behind it. I turned around to leave when I saw the key display.

I love skeleton keys; been buying them since I was a kid. I never really thought of it as a collection or even a hobby where you would say, "Oh, me? I collect skeleton keys," if someone were to ask. They hold so much possibility. I try to imagine what the door they open looks like. Once I have the door in my mind, I fantasize about the world on the other side. For me, it's a form of meditation, really, and a sense of power too, I suppose. All these places out there that no one can access because only I have the key.

The Reliquary had an entire wall devoted to keys. I must say I appreciated the presentation. Most shops just throw them into jars or jumbled up piles on a tray that you have to pick through. This man knew what he was doing. Examining each one by itself, I looked for unique or unusual markings; something that made it stand out from the rest.

I was deeply vested in my search when the old man whispered in my ear.

"I have others behind the counter if you don't find the one you're looking for." His voice was deep and gravely. It was the voice you would hear coming out of a crocodile, if one could talk and was tall enough to whisper in your ear. I hadn't realized he was there. I screamed and jumped, knocking three keys off their hooks.

"Oh! I, uh, I was just looking, I mean, I wasn't looking for anything in particular," I said handing him the keys I'd dropped to the floor. "Thanks anyways." I tried to step around him to leave. He slid into my path.

"Nonsense. I know an admirer when I see one. You are just the type of customer I save the special keys for. Come, please, let me show you and then, if you don't see any you like, you can be on your way." He smiled again. I swear the corners of his lips bumped into his ear lobes. God, there were so many teeth. Trance-like, I nodded and followed him to the counter. He pulled a tray out from underneath. On it, were some of the largest and most ornate skeleton keys I had ever seen. The one that immediately caught my eye looked like a twig with a labyrinth of copper and bronze vines wrapping around it. At the top, a tiny red enamel apple with a single green leaf sat in perfect condition. I stroked my thumb over the smooth, cool metal. The man put a gloved hand on top of mine and wrapped the rest of my fingers around the key.

"A gift to a fellow collector," he said. His cold skin was palpable even through the white leather.

"Oh, no! I couldn't. What are you asking for it?" The key warmed in my hand, contrasting the chill of the old man's. Whatever number he said next, I would pay.

"Take it, I insist," he said. "I'll just need you to sign this bill of sale."

He pushed a small document towards me. I picked up the pen and signed without reading. I just wanted to take my treasure and go. "…Formality really. They always have to have a piece of you." The man was still explaining away the paperwork.

I interrupted. "I don't need a bag. Thanks." I walked away. The bell sang me out.

That night, sleep did not come easy. I dreamt of the old man with his toothy smile. He was showing me the receipt I'd signed. My signature was written in blood. He started laughing and his mouth opened wide, showing rows of sharp, jagged teeth around a swirling, vacuous, black hole. I awoke panting. The key lay on my nightstand. I held it until I fell back asleep, this time dreaming that I was being chased. I ran through a thick grey fog that worked on my body like water slowing me. Saved by the alarm, I dragged myself out of bed and prepared for the day.

I decided to walk to work. The fresh air would help clear my head. The trip usually takes twenty minutes on foot but that day I left an hour early so I could take my time. As I strolled, I found myself fingering the enameled fruit on my key. I imagined a door to paradise. It, too, would be covered in vines. There would be carvings of exotic birds and flowers; each one painted by hand. Marring my fantasy, however, was the sensation that I was being followed. I nonchalantly glanced behind me.

A man in an ill-fitting suit followed about four feet back. He walked with his shoulders slumped and arms dangling limply at his sides. I thought he must be drunk even though it was only 7:30 in the morning. Why else would a man in a suit be weaving like that with his mouth hanging open like a dead fish? Plus it explained his lack of respect for my personal space. I quickened my steps and made it to work with plenty of time to spare.

I kept the key on my desk all day and every free moment I had, I touched it. I loved the feel of the lines and curves—so organic, so alive.

"Hello, and thank you for calling Fourth Circle Enterprises, how can I help you today?" I answered. As the supervisor, calls only came to me when the customer was unhappy. I fiddled with my key as Carol Winston from Wilmington prattled on about a lost order.

"Listen, if you put the wrong zip code on your address, you can hardly fault us for the extended time in shipping, you stupid bitch." It was out of my mouth before I knew I was going to say it. I disconnected and threw my headset down. Tired and irritable and not myself at all, I clocked out early.

Stepping out of the employee exit, I almost ran right into the drunk guy from earlier. Only now, he didn't look drunk, he looked sickly. His eyes were sunken; his jowls hung thin and loose. He didn't try to grab at me, he just stood there. I made an exaggerated maneuver to walk around him. In my peripheral vision, I could see him fall into step behind me. I stopped and turned around.

"Can I help you?" I asked. Although I was afraid to hear an answer, it would be even more terrifying if he said nothing. He said nothing. My heart pounded in my chest, I wanted to run but wasn't sure it could take any further strain. "Fuck off you sick bastard," I said trying to sound tough.

The moment the words left my mouth, another man came limping up behind the first one. He was younger and so much more frightening. His head caved in on one side. Blood and what I assumed to be gray matter had dried in crusty chunks on the side of his face. His left foot turned in at a strange angle forcing him to walk on his ankle.

I decided a jog home through a very public park would be good for the old metabolism. So I ran and my two stalkers straggled along behind me, keeping pace somehow. My mind was flashing with images of grisly violence; my emotions ran the gamut from fear to anger to rage. A duck waddled into my path. I kicked it. The soft thud as I made contact, coupled with the pained squawk, made me gag.

By the time I got home, I was so upset, I tried to put the skeleton key in the lock. My entourage was still advancing; I could feel the claustrophobia of two bodies closing in on mine. I swore and fumbled with my house key until I was able to open the door, squeeze inside and bolt it. I peeked out the window. They had retreated back to their typical distance which was good, but now there were three, which was not so good. The third was a woman. She had on a frumpy blue top and pencil skirt. I estimated her to be the oldest. Her hair was done up in what I like to call the church lady helmet. Her face was rotten, sinews of flesh stretched taught from cheekbone to jaw. She wore a deep-red shade of lipstick. It was all too hideous. I dug in my pocket for the skeleton key and upon grasping it, immediately felt better, calm even. As long as I had it in my hand, I was not afraid.

The following morning, the number of followers had doubled. Six now stood in attendance. As I took in their languid forms, I was reminded of the first horror movie my mother ever let me watch: *Night of the Living Dead*. These people looked like zombies! But based on my limited cinematic knowledge, zombies don't just politely follow their victims around and then wait patiently for them to come back outside. Something very strange was happening here and it started after I got that key. I decided maybe it was time to pay a follow up visit to The Reliquary.

But the shop was gone. I sat in my car staring dumbly at the empty building. There wasn't even a hint of recent activity. I called work to say I would be late and drove on into the next town. They had a small consignment shop where I'd purchased several keys before. The owner of that store was a little old lady who seemed very knowledgeable about her inventory. This place was called Some Things Old and thankfully, it was open. I took my key in, trying to ignore the morbid crowd gathering behind me.

"Welcome, first customer of the day. You're out and about early, aren't you? Well, you know what they say: The early bird catches the worm!" The plump, grandmotherly owner smiled brightly up at me from her perch behind the counter.

"Hi, I, um," I looked over my shoulder to make sure no one was coming in behind me. "Well I bought this key the other day." I pulled it out of my pocket, but before I could say anything more she interrupted me.

"You didn't buy that here." Some of the chipperness was gone

"No. I didn't, but I was hoping you might know something about it. Maybe where it was made?" I held it out to her but I really didn't want to let go of it. She didn't seem to want to take it either. She leaned across the counter and looked at it. Suddenly, I had an urge to grab her by her wrinkly old throat and squeeze the answer out of her. I shook the thought out of my head and stepped back away snatching my key from under her ogling eyes. I sneered at her.

She didn't seem to notice my irritation. "Well, the first thing that comes to my mind when I see that is the Garden of Eden: the apple, the leaves, the snake. Some kind of religious reference. You'd be better off asking Father Sheppard over at St. Michaels. He might know more about it." She started out around the counter as if she had more pressing matters to attend. "I can't help you any more than that. Go see Father Sheppard."

She walked over to open the door for me. The hoard of the half-dead waiting just outside obscured the beam of morning light that had illuminated the shop just minutes before.

The crowd allowed me to push through them without incident. They fell into step behind my car and by the time I got to the cathedral, there were more than I could count.

Father Sheppard, I was told by a lady sitting at the candles, was in the confessional.

"Forgive me Father, for I know not what to do. I'm not Catholic," I began.

"Then why are you here, my child?" the nice fatherly voice asked me not unkindly.

I took a deep breath; I didn't know where to start. "Because I bought this weird key and then these zombies started following me all the time and so I went to the store where I got it but he was gone and then I went to another store, and she looked at it and said it looked like the Garden of Eden because she saw a snake and an apple, but I never noticed the snake before. Anyway, she wouldn't even touch it, she said to leave and come here. The thing is, I love this key but I do not love the zombie people following me around. And I think the stress is getting to me too, because I yelled at a customer and I kicked a duck and I wanted to strangle the lady from the shop who told me to find you."

"This is not a matter for the confessional. I will meet you outside," Father Sheppard said.

"May I see your key?" he asked me. I was taken aback by him. He looked like a young Richard Gere and he smelled nice, not Fatherly at all. I am not sure you can say this about a priest but he was actually pretty hot. So, I handed him the key. He studied it for a moment and then looked back at me.

"Where are the zombies?"

I took his hand. It was warm and soft. I wanted to feel it caressing my naked body. I shook my head, clearing an image that would surely doom me to Hell. Instead, I pulled him to the front door where I'd come in. He opened it. There they were, the whole lot of them. He looked around.

"Where?" he asked again. I stared at him, completely astonished. How could he not see the mass of living cadavers?

"Look! They're all over the place! There has to be fifty to a hundred of them!" I said.

He shut the door. "Come with me. I think we should look at something."

This time, he took my hand. He was pushing his luck if he wanted to remain abstinent. We walked behind the alter to a room that I assumed was his office. Book shelves ran the length of the wall behind his desk. I noticed many of them had to do with the occult. I didn't think priests were into that sort of thing. Maybe that's why the lady at the shop sent me to him. He ran his finger along the books. I imagined him running that finger down my spine. It was getting very hot in that tight space.

"Ah, here we go."

He grabbed a book and flipped through it. Finding the page he was looking for, he tapped on the illustration with his finger. I leaned against him to look at a picture of a huge gate, all covered in vines. A large snake weaved through bars around the lock. On the tallest two posts of the gate sat apples that looked just like the one on my key.

"This is an illustration called *The Gates of Hell* by a relatively unknown artist named Dominick Tellegio. I suspect that your key was designed with this gate in mind," he said.

"So, my key opens the Gates of Hell?" I asked bending over as if to get a better look at the picture, resting my breasts on his arm.

"You understand that no one knows what Hell looks like —any picture you see is just a human's interpretation. It is likely that someone who saw this picture was inspired by it and created a key to go with it." He smiled and pivoted so that his arm slipped naturally away from my chest.

"Ok, so what do I do with all the zombie people then?" I asked him.

"Why do you call them that? Zombie People?"

'Because, that's what they look like. They look like they crawled out of their coffins just to follow me around. And whether you can see them or not, I can and they freak me out. It's like they're waiting for me to do something," I said irritated.

"And you say this started when you got the key?"

"Yes. The day I got the key."

"Then maybe they are waiting for you to open the gate," he said and shrugged.

"The Gates of Hell?" I asked, raising my eyebrow. "The one you just said was just a human's imagination? With a key somebody designed to go with it?" This guy needed to get his shit straight.

"I'm only trying to work this out with you. You can see people no one else can see, you say this started with a key. You think they want something from you. Many would write you off as crazy, you understand."

"I'm not crazy. Something is happening to me. I'm angry all the time, I yell and curse like a sailor. I can't sleep. Thoughts pop in my head that have no business there. The only thing that makes me feel better is that key, but every-thing bad started with the key."

"There is a quote by Sherlock Holmes," he said. "I try to live by it: 'When you have eliminated the impossible, what-ever remains, no matter how improbable, must be the truth'.

You say you aren't crazy, so that is the impossible in this equation. therefore, it comes down to faith, no matter how improbable."

"So all those people out there want to go to Hell? That makes no sense," I said.

"Souls must go somewhere. Heaven, Hell, or for those waiting to be judged: Purgatory. Personally, I believe in ghosts. I believe that a soul can get lost on its way to a final destination. I imagine that would be torture; like being on the cusp of death, the waiting is worse than the fate itself. Maybe your souls think you can lead them to the gate?"

"Well, I don't feel like going to Hell today. What did I do to deserve this? Why do I have to help them?" I asked.

"Because you have the key," he said. But I didn't. It was still laying on his desk.

"Well, you have it now. You let them in," I said curtly.

"I don't think I can do that. You chose the key, or perhaps it chose you. You are the gatekeeper." He handed the key back to me. "Only you can guide the souls to their journey's end."

"But I can't. I don't know how," I argued.

"I'm sorry," he said. "I think you have to do something before the key takes you with it. It's already having an effect on you. If you don't do this willingly, it's going to drag you there kicking and screaming."

I'd had enough. This was ridiculous. "Fuck this. I don't believe any of it, and fuck you and this church. Worthless bunch of nonsense." I was furious. There was a door on the other side of his office that led to the cemetery. I shoved him out of the way and walked out.

Behind the church, it was night. The only light was a fiery

orange glow emanating from a pit on the other side of a familiar wrought iron gate. The path on which I stood led straight to it. Echoes of pain and sorrow boiled up out of the hole. Inhuman roars and guttural growls pierced through the monotony of misery. I backed up intending to return and beg sanctuary, but when I turned around, the church was gone, swallowed by a thick grey fog.

Even in the darkness, the crowd of lost souls had managed to find me. They milled about nervously, as if they too could hear the cries of those who'd gone before them. The key grew hot in my hand. I gave in and let it guide me to the lock where it clicked into place. With a vacuous roar, the doors swung inward revealing monstrous tentacles, dripping with an acidic mucus that sizzled when it hit the ground. They rose up from the center of a swirling vortex that appeared when the gate opened. As they reached out for the damned, I saw a mouth appear, with thousands of teeth like daggers dripping blood.

I let go of the bars to cover my ears. The crunching of bones and the screams of pain and torment were too much. Like a child, I crouched to the ground and closed my eyes. The only sensation I couldn't block was the rumbling vibrations that came from the behemoth tearing through space to devour the dead.

A rubbery feeler wrapped itself around my arm, burning into my flesh. I gasped and opened my eyes. There were hundreds of fleshy tendrils whipping amongst the masses. Some had thick yellowed claws that punctured flesh, spilling necrotic bowels, others were covered in syringe-like thorns that bit into tissue, popping eyes like grapes. From the gaping mouth of the beast came a single black orb that surveyed the carnage before receding back inside. When it was gone, I pried the thing off; it wriggled around as I scrambled away.

Even after all the lost souls had been devoured, the creature continued to seek out bodies. I belly crawled along the doors and closed one at a time, trapping the beast behind the bars. The key was white hot and it scalded by hand when I grabbed it. When I jerked my hand away, the key dropped.

"Damn it!" I yelled. The beast's mouth opened again and the eyeball tongue came rolling out my direction. I turned and ran. Just beyond the blanket of night, the church appeared but I didn't want to go inside or see Father Sheppard again. Instead, I sprinted around the side and back into the light.

That was two weeks ago. I don't have the key anymore but I have a scar that matches it perfectly. Now, I just run my fingers along its smooth, shiny curves when I'm nervous. I'm doing it now, in fact, as I sit here thinking the same obsessive thought I've had every day since the incident at the church: did I leave the gate unlocked?

ACKNOWLEDGMENTS

A very special thank you to our amazing talented cover artist, Ivan Zanchetta. He not only created this amazing cover, but also created the cover for our first anthology, Seven Sins of The Apocalypse.

You can always find Ivan's amazing work at his website: https://www.bookcoversart.com

---

ABOUT THE AUTHORS

The contributing authors' bios for More Lore from The Mythos.

1. *Everything That Was Before* by Edward Morris

Edward Morris is a 2011 nominee for the Pushcart Prize in Literature, also nominated for the 2009 Rhysling and the 2005 BSFA. His short fiction has been published in over 150 markets worldwide since 2002; notably Interzone, Ross Lockhart's Tales of Jack The Ripper; the charity anthology Nightmares In Yellow, and Dark Regions' Press

Summer of Lovecraft. He finds it weird to write bios in the third person, and lives and works in Portland, Oregon as an author and bouncer.

facebook.com/edwardmorris5

2. *Little One* by Valerie Lioudis

While she mostly focuses on Horror, Valerie Lioudis is a multi-genre author who has been known to dabble in post apocalyptic, science fiction, and even metaphysical stories. The common thread with Valerie's work is her constant sarcasm, and love for bringing the unexpected to her readers.

https://www.instagram.com/valerielioudis/

3. *The Call* by Aaron White

Aaron White started drawing monsters when he was four years old. Throughout grade and middle school he drew various ghoulish creatures while pouring through books by authors such as John Bellairs, C. S. Lewis, and even Stephen King. Aaron went on to major in Illustration at Massachusetts College of Art, but still dabbled with creative writing here and there. Eventually he decided to focus his imagination on writing, and has since completed several short stories in the horror and sci-fi genres. Some of his stories can be found in the Horror Zine (as Editor's Choice) as well as at Limitless Publishing.
www.aaronmwhite.com.

4. *The Damned of Eldritch Creek* by Jon Tobey

When not pissing off his publisher...
Jon has been writing since the third grade. He says all of his stories are true, some of them just haven't happened yet. He writes across many genres, but is currently collecting his short stories and novellas, and working on some longer dark pulp pieces. You can follow his musings on writing, fishing, and photography at gointothelight.wordpress.com

5. *The Flood* by Oliver Lodge

Oliver Lodge, who also writes under the nom de plume of Solomon Fiore, is an author who lives in upstate New York. He has been published in a prolific number of magazines, quarterlies, and jouurnals. A selection of his work can be viewed at www.solomonfioreauthor.wordpress.com.

6. *The Mines of Innswich* by Ryan Colley

Although I have a love for horror in all forms, apocalypse and Lovecraftian fiction hold a special place in my heart. When writing characters, I remind myself that every hero is a villain in someone else's story. Plus a little dark humour thrown in for good measure.
www.amongthedead.co.uk

7. *The Time Guardian* by L.E. Harrison

L.E. Harrison is a lifelong avid reader and lover of genre fiction—from science fiction to paranormal romance, and everything in between. She is the author of the contemporary fantasy trilogy The Children of Corvus, as well as a collection of previously published poems and short stories. She lives in a one hundred and sixty year old farmhouse in rural Pennsylvania, where she is busy working on the next chapter in the universe of Soluna's children.
https://www.facebook.com/LEHarrisonAuthor/

8. *The Wyrd Voyage* by Kari Leigh Sanders

Kari Leigh Sanders is an author, editor, and avid reader. She prefers dark fiction, horror, fantasy, and sci-fi. When not living in her head inside of a story, she may be found petting the purrs out of her cats or watching horror movies.

fb.me/KariLeighSanders

9. *Last Orders* by Dale Drake

Dale Drake was born in Lancashire in 1975 and now resides in Cornwall with his wife and three children. After his career in the army, Dale moved to Hertfordshire to train to become a chef but his real love and passion has always been writing, something that he tried his hand at from an early age. Dale's first book, Blood Heritage, was written whilst he was still attending college and is a high fantasy book full of sword wielding heroes, dark magic and blood thirsty vampires. His second book, Dark Waters, was written some years later after he moved to Cornwall where he was heavily influenced by H.P. Lovecraft and his love of the sea. The majority of his stories are all set in his home village where he finally feels he belongs.

https://www.facebook.com/dale.drake.31

10. *The Maze* by Charles Reis

Charles Reis was born and raised in Coventry, Rhode Island, but currently lives in West Warwick. He graduated from the University of Rhode Island with a BA in English Literature in 2012, although he currently works as a museum tour guide. Additional works of his have appeared in "One Night in Salem", "Trembling with Fear: Year 1" and "Coffins & Dragons".

https://www.facebook.com/charles.reis.35

11. *Growing Just Beneath* by Steve Van Samson

Currently a content creator for Rough House Publishing, Steve Van Samson is the author of the "Predator World" series books and numerous short stories (published and otherwise). His writing tends to be on the pulpy side--intermingling genres like horror, dystopian with dark fantasy and adventure. He believes that character is king and there should always be little seeds planted between the lines, that the reader will only discover in subsequent readings. When not tapping the keys on his Chromebook, Steve co-hosts the Retro Ridoctopus podcast and watches entirely too many black and white monster films. Steve lives in Lancaster, Massachusetts with three amazing girls and one smallish dragon.

http://www.roughhousepublishing.com/

12. *The Shed* by Patrick Rahall

Patrick Rahall is a writer, podcaster, and actor. You can find links to his work and updates on all his current and upcoming projects at ThrowdownThursdayPodcast.com. He looks forward to the inevitable supernatural downfall of humanity as a good way to get out of his credit card debt.

13. *Sweet Oblivion* by Michael Clark

A storyteller of speculative fiction, sci-fi, and horror that comes from the home of the Brothers Grimm, Kassel Germany. As a consequence, he has always had a fascination for reading and writing darker stories. He's Worked behind the scenes in the publishing and print industry for years. From a graphic designer and press operator, to ghost writer and developmental editor.

Recently he opened a publishing company, Analog Softworks and writes full time.

Http://www.analogsoftworks.com/

14. *The Gate Keeper* by EV Knight

EV Knight writes horror and dark fiction. Her debut novel, The Fourth Whore, will be published in 2020 by Raw Dog Screaming Press. EV's short stories can be found in The Toilet Zone Anthology by Hellbound Books and Siren's Call magazine and the upcoming anthology Monstrous Feminine from Scary Dairy Press. She is also cohost of the podcast Brain Squalls with Knight and Daigh. She enjoys all things macabre; whether they be film, TV, podcast, novel, short story, or poetry. She lives in the cold northern woods of Michigan's Upper Peninsula with her family and two hairless cats.

She can be found on twitter @evknightauthor

ALSO BY FRACTURED MIND PUBLISHING

More Lore From The Mythos Vol 2

Christmas Kills